Nasu Rabi
(Old Bear)

D.L. Roley

Cover Art © Stephen Najarian/www.najarianart.com

Map Illustration by Veronika Wunderer/www.veronika-wunderer.com

DEDICATION

To my wife Jenny. Thank you for all the commas. I wouldn't have known what to do with them without you.

ACKNOWLEDGMENTS

Thank you to Linda, John, Dan L., Dan H., Corbrett, Ken, Sarah, and Morgan for all of your help and support on this project. Your feedback was invaluable. It truly does take a village.

Contents

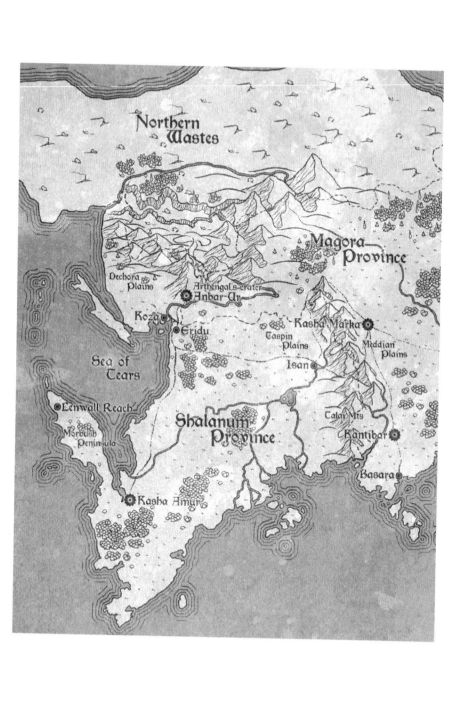

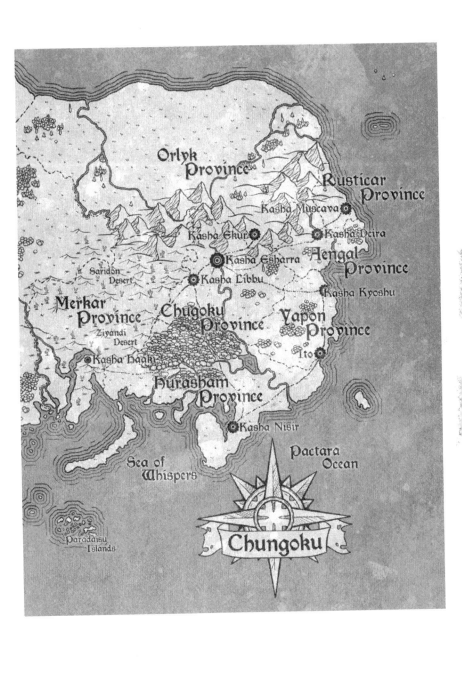

PART I

The Rise of Emperor Chung Oku Mai was one of humble beginnings, as is often the case with heroes of old. He was born the first son of a minor landowner into a world filled with chaos and strife. The lords of his time ruled the peasantry with iron fists. The people lived in constant fear of warlords, brigands, and starvation. Chung Oku Mai saw the injustice in the world and he wept.

The Rally cry for justice echoed across the land wherever Chung Oku Mai's banner flew. Support for his cause grew, and with it what would become the Great Imperial Army, first in his home of Esha Arra and then beyond. The unjust trembled at the sound of his trumpets, and one by one, the petty lords fell. The people cheered.

The Chungoku Empire, from the Sea of Tears in the west to the Pactara Ocean in the east, was completed when the final pact of fealty was signed on Chung Oku Mai's fortieth name day. He saw the people with food in their bellies and no fear of warlords, and he smiled.

The Dream of a unified land and a protected people lasted for nearly three thousand years as rule passed to the eldest son of each generation. Bliss was not eternal as some emperors were harder men than others, but the guidance of the imperial family maintained Chung Oku Mai's dream through the ages. The people were content.

The Fall of the great empire came at the hands of an emperor most foul. Chen Bai Jian ruled by greed, hubris, and corruption. His iron fist crushed the people and enforced his might. He refused the advice of the imperial family, and many were imprisoned or killed by the hateful tyrant. The people lived in fear.

The Rally cry rang again at the death of Lao Cang Yu. Vocal in his pleas for leniency and justice, Lao Cang Yu was marked a dissident and a traitor by his cousin the emperor. Against tradition, he was executed publicly in the traitor's square at Kasha Esharra. The people wailed in anguish, and the barons rose in anger.

The Great War shattered the empire but restored justice to the land. The nine provinces were founded, and the Barons rule the people with a fair hand. The dream of Chung Oku Mai is lost but not forgotten. The people are content again. Let it be our hope that the storm clouds shall not rise again and that injustice should be held at bay by the Barons of Magora, Shalanum, Merkar, Orlyk, Chugoku, Rusticar, Aengal, Yapon, and Hurasham. May the old gods and new guide their hands and bless their rule.

~Maharim Al Benost
Chief Historian to the honorable Baron Hurasham
Read in introduction to the Gathering of The Nine
Year 30 A.E.

Autumn - 30 A.E.

Chapter One
Raiders

The air was still, and Darius concentrated. The expanse of the wide meadow and the pine forest encroaching from the west faded from the edges of his vision. There was only the target: a flat, round piece of wood wedged against the trunk of one of the giant elms that added shade to the meadow. A yellow circle, the size of his palm, had been painted in the center of the disc.

The chattering of children from the village behind him and the incessant calling of gulls beyond the meadow faded to the recesses of his mind. The wisp of blond hair stuck to his forehead by sweat and dust no longer itched. The smell of venison roasting on a spit didn't cause his stomach to growl. His awareness was reduced to the soft, even sound of his breath and the feel of the bow.

"Draw back and take aim," Micah's soft whisper came.

His arm retracted, and he inhaled through his nostrils. His chest expanded. He felt the pressure of the bowstring against the pads of his fingers, sinew on flesh. His hold tightened on the bow, and his arm was straight, unwavering. The smooth, polished elm of the grip felt as one with his hand.

Darius was not a tall boy. Just two years older, his brother stood a full span taller. It was all he could do to reach full flexion, but once he did, he held the string and took careful aim. His elbow began to tremble as he waited for Micah's next command. The loose, beige linen shirt ruffled as a breeze gusted for an instant.

"Now release."

His fingers slipped from the string like an autumn leaf letting go of the branch. The bowstring let loose with a distinct twang, and the arrow covered the fifty paces with the hiss of parting air. It impacted the center of the target with a dull thump, and the fir shaft quivered.

He let his breath escape and gasped. The heavy musk of pine boughs baking in the mid-afternoon sun filled his sinuses. The scent from cooking fires wafted on the breeze.

"Huzzah!" Micah shouted. "Excellent job, Darius."

The clamor of the children returned with a rush and with it, other noises. Birds sang in the trees. A squirrel working a seed pod near the target chirped in protest at the disruption.

Darius smiled at the praise and looked up at his older brother. At sixteen, Micah was already one of the best shots in town and had done very well on his first few hunts. The praise was genuine, and Darius swelled with pride.

"Now again. On your own," Micah said. "Remember to breathe. If you hold your breath like that while you're waiting for a clean shot on a deer, you'll pass out before you get the chance to take it. Steady, even breaths, but you have to breathe. If you're going to hold it, do it at the last second before you fire."

Darius pulled a second arrow from the quiver at his hip and drew his fingers along the wooden shaft, feeling for blemishes. He repeated the methodical process of aiming. This time as he prepared to shoot, Micah shouted next to his ear. Darius's hand twitched as his fingers slid from the string and the arrow struck the outer ring on the target.

"Not bad, but you still need to work on that. Don't let distractions break your concentration. If you are going to join the hunters next season, you'll need to shoot true no matter what."

Darius was preparing for a third attempt when they heard a ruckus from the town. Shouts of dismay became more distinct. The drum of hundreds of hooves rose like thunder, and a cloud of dust was rising above the houses to the northeast. Then there was the distinct clang of steel striking iron and a shriek. Sharp cracks sounded like a whip, or many whips.

Darius swept his blond hair off of his forehead, unsure what to make of the sounds.

Riders cantered out of the southern edge of the hamlet and surveyed the pasture. There were four of them, dressed in black leathers. Their eyes had been outlined with charcoal, and greasy lines of azure and yellow were etched across their faces. Their bare arms were covered with an array of symbols applied with the same oily paint. Three of them wore thick beards and had long, unkempt hair. The fourth, in the lead, was clean shaven and wore his hair in a tight top knot.

The men sat astride tall, well-muscled stallions as dark as their armor. At first, the approaching horsemen piqued curiosity more than fear. That changed when the voice of Darius's and Micah's mother cried out. It was a piercing cry that drowned out everything else.

"Micah, run!" she screamed as she entered the far end of the glade.

Their mother's linen dress whipped like a banner in the wind as she ran. The light blue was smeared with dark streaks at the shoulder and the hem. The shoulder of the dress, where the white embroidered flowers began to trail down the sleeve, appeared to be torn. Panic strained her voice. Her flowing red hair was bedraggled and mussed.

The strangers spurred their horses to move in her direction.

Micah did not hesitate. He slung his bow across his back and prompted Darius to do the same. He cinched the bindings to keep the weapon from bouncing. His motions were rapid and trained. Within seconds, Micah was half running, half pushing Darius toward the trees. They glanced over their shoulders as they reached the edge of the woods.

The raiders were closing on their mother. Fierce cries echoed across the clearing as the horses angled toward the woman.

Their mother's long legs raced across the field in elongated strides, but her speed was no match for that of the horses. The earth churned beneath the hooves of the beasts. She continued to wave them onward as the front horsemen raised a net between them. The net engulfed her, and she tumbled to the ground in a tangle as the horsemen charged by, focused now on the boys.

"No!" Darius cried and turned around, ready to fight, but Micah held an arm out to stop him.

"Too many. Too late. Run, Darius." He spun Darius around and shoved him into the cover of the trees.

Darius ran like he never had before. He could hear Micah sprinting close on his heels.

Hoofbeats drew ever closer. The horses slowed to a trot as they entered the confines of the forest, and the boys extended their lead.

"Left! Jump! Right! Turn!" Micah's gasping commands came from behind.

Darius knew where his brother was directing him, but the commands helped him stay focused on the path ahead. He darted to the left around a deadfall then hurdled a bramble on the other side. He jerked to the right to avoid stumbling on a patch of rocks and cut into a dense thicket.

They dodged their way through the thick copse of spruce, but they could still hear the men circling around. Darius burst out of the trees and glanced around. His brother stopped short to avoid stumbling into him.

The terrain was a spider web of gullies and trenches as it approached the cliffs that overlooked the ocean beyond.

The barbarians rounded the far side of the grove and spotted them.

Darius leapt into a narrow gulch with Micah on his heels.

Two of the men tracked them from above while the others gingerly stepped their horses into the ravine. The walls steepened, and the floor of the trench sloped downward as they approached the precipice. Soon they were running through a canyon with walls twice their height.

The sea birds called ahead, a cacophony of squawks and shrieks. A strong, salty breeze assaulted them from side passages as they rushed past.

They veered right as the ravine forked and dove into a cave in the side of the rift. Darius crept forward as his eyes adjusted to the dim light.

Gruff, muffled shouts sounded from outside the cavern.

Darius scrambled ahead, clawing his way up a gravel incline. He was almost there.

Light flooded the passageway as the horsemen lit torches and thrust them into the darkness.

Darius and Micah had reached their destination, a gaping crevice in the floor. The smell of stale salt and dead fish drifted up from below. The blackness beneath them seemed impenetrable, but they knew where to go.

They shrugged off their gear, and Micah helped Darius maneuver into position.

"You two get in there with the torches. Drag them out if you need to." Darius heard a commanding voice giving instructions outside the entrance. The accent was thick and foreign.

The flickering torchlight drew closer, illuminating the back of the cave.

"Ulan, they're getting away. Take them out," the barking orders came again.

Then time slowed. Darius felt the familiar smooth groove against the small of his back. He released Micah's hand and slid downward with his hips pressed to the cold, wet stone.

Micah started to lower himself into position. He gave Darius a sly grin, and his eyes shone with victory. Darius watched, and hope changed to horror.

Torchlight flickered off of Micah's strawberry blond hair, then the look of triumph was replaced with shock and the grin transformed to a gape as he was struck squarely in the chest with a long, black arrow.

Chapter Two
Alone

Darius's scream was drowned out by the echo of crashing waves. Darius slipped free of the crack and was falling into darkness. The few seconds' descent lasted an eternity as he lost sight of his brother's face. Darius pointed his toes just before he reached the deep pool. He took a gulp of air, but the shock of the cold water made him expel it with a gasp. He plunged into the water and felt the familiar tug of the riptide. Tears mixed with seawater as he dove deeper toward the tunnel beneath the surface. The ever-present current pulled him along as he propelled himself forward with powerful sweeping strokes. His lungs burned. Then, like a sea monster of old, the underwater tunnel spit him out and the current was gone. Three more forceful kicks and his head broke the surface of the sea. He gasped and scanned the cliff tops above.

There was no sign of the attackers, but he didn't wait to see if they would appear. He paddled toward the several tall basalt spires offshore with long, practiced strokes. He had no idea if either of the riders from the cave had tried to follow him. However, unless they knew precisely where to drop, it was more likely that they would have been dashed on the rocks below the crevice than they would have found the tidal pool.

Darius scrambled ashore on the north end of the tallest spire. The white beach was hidden from view of the shore. The steep curving walls that surrounded the alcove protected the oyster farmers that frequented this beach from the winds that buffeted the rest of the steep coastline. The addition of a freshwater spring that bubbled from deep underground made this spire an oasis in the churning saltwater desert that surrounded it.

The airy linen fabric of his clothing clung to him, the light earth tones darkened by the sea. Darius climbed up the shore to the bubbling fountain and drank deeply. Then he collapsed to the rocky shore and began sobbing. Darius buried his head in his arms as shock and grief overcame him, and he slept.

The next morning, as the sun was rising over the shoreline to the east, Darius swam from the spire to the ancient steps carved into the cliff wall. The stone was rough but familiar to the touch. His hands and feet knew every hold and crack and loose rock. To a stranger he supposed that this ascent would look treacherous, but he had been climbing these rugged stairs for as long as he could remember. His mother joked that he and Micah had learned to walk on the steep, narrow staircase.

At the top Darius knelt in the grass beside a tall oak and listened, tuning out each sound in turn as his brother had taught him.

The crashing waves and howling wind faded to a whisper. The singing of birds and chirping of woodland creatures disappeared until there was nothing left. There should have been some noise from the hamlet, like wood being chopped for the morning fires or children playing. For that matter, where were the fisherman? Why weren't they here stretching out their nets in preparation for the day's work? He listened for anything that should not have been there as well, but he did not hear anything that could be attributed to the invaders.

He stood and trod home with feather-light steps. He approached the village with care, keeping to cover wherever possible. The silence was unnerving. No dogs barked. He couldn't hear the familiar cluck of chickens. As he entered the village, he froze in disbelief. The homes looked normal, untouched, as if the villagers had just left on an outing. The cooking fires smoldered, and thin tendrils of blue-gray smoke wafted skyward.

There was some evidence of fighting. Scattered patches of blood darkened the earth, but the only bodies littering the ground were those of the dogs and chickens. Mistress Nalla's sow had been slaughtered along with five piglets about half the size of their mother. The limp body of a calf lay in a nearby stable, but otherwise, the town was empty.

All the other animals were gone. A broken trail led north, earth churned by the passage of countless hooves and feet, leading away over a knoll in the distance. The shod prints of scores of horses flanked either side of the exodus.

Darius bent to inspect the disturbed soil. He could make out the markings of a soft leather boot among the cloven tracks of the animals. He glanced around and saw many others of all sizes. The people had also been *herded,* along with the cattle, much like human livestock. A tear rolled down his cheek as he thought of his mother's fate.

Not yet, he thought, and wiped at the tear with his shirt sleeve as he stood. He had cried enough last night. There was no time for that now. *This makes no sense. Someone else must have escaped. Why would the raiders kidnap everyone?*

Darius returned to the common house at the heart of the hamlet. Somebody must have locked themselves inside for safety.

"They have to be okay there," he mumbled.

Darius dropped to his knees on the hard-packed earth of the square and stared. The doors of the large two-story stone building were torn asunder. Debris littered the steps of the building. He examined one of the larger pieces that lay nearby. Long metal shafts pierced the heavy oak, hooked at the end to dig into the wood. Scraps of rope dangled from eyelets at the end of each shaft. He glanced around at the hoofprints of a dozen or more horses on the ground.

He surveyed the destruction, trying to grasp what had happened. His thoughts fragmented, and his mind felt like the scattered splinters of the door. He forced himself to his feet. *Get a hold of yourself, Darius. Someone else had to have made it. Keep looking.*

Darius walked up the wide steps toward the gaping entryway. Stooping, he picked up the remnant of an iron bracket. The thick wooden bar that had secured the door from the inside lay in the opening, split in two.

Had the wood been banded in iron it might have held. The local blacksmith had said as much more than once. He had said that wood alone was too weak to withstand a serious assault. The more polite members of the village council had dismissed his concerns with a condescending smile while the less tactful had ridiculed him.

"Barbarians never come this far south. We've never had no trouble discouraging any brigands before," Old Man Dagan had said in a scornful tone on one such occasion as he rapped his walking stick against the solid stone of the building. "Banded doors. Bah! Blacksmith trying to drum up business is what I say. As if iron grew on trees. You just worry about getting me a new head for my hoe so I can get some real work done."

Dagan had stomped off then, still muttering something about "fool-brained ideas" and "too much time with his head stuck in the forge."

Darius wandered through the smattering of houses that stretched away from the large building. The houses were all similar, more or less, squat, windowless buildings constructed of limestone blocks and topped with sod roofs. Most were single-room cottages, but a few, like his own, had an added bedroom. Master Amon had added a third room and had replaced his sod with thatch several years back when he had lucked upon three flawless pearls in a single oyster season. Very few of the buildings had doors. Most occupants would cover the opening with leather tarps or woolen blankets in the winter to keep the heat in, but the autumn nights were not cold enough for that yet.

Wash basins stood like sentinels in front yards and clothes hung flapping in the breeze next to most of the homes. Poles leaned against houses, and fishing nets lay abandoned near low wooden benches where their owners had been mending them. Wooden toys and an inflated sheep's bladder lay where children had abandoned them.

"Hello?" he called, hoping that someone could hear his voice. "Is anyone here?" he shouted louder.

Without realizing it, Darius had come to stand before his own home. He stared at the opening, taking long slow breaths before deciding to enter. The leather curtain hung askew, and flies buzzed around the cook pot overturned beside the fire pit, its contents leaking into the earth a few paces from the entrance.

With a heavy sigh he stepped inside. Their belongings had been thoroughly rummaged through. His mother's cooking utensils were scattered. Their clothing and toys were strewn about as though garbage. The larder was empty, and he failed to find any food in the house other than a few apples strewn across the floor.

Darius scooped one up and bit into it as he let himself drop onto his straw bed. Shock was setting in, and he was at a complete loss regarding what to do next. There really wasn't anyone left. His chest felt heavy, and his breaths were short and shallow.

The sun inched its way across the sky well past midday as Darius stared through mist-covered eyes at the floor. His mind churned. He was alone. His people were gone, and he didn't know where to go to find help. He fought the panic building inside him while he tried to consider his options.

Imbros was the closest settlement, a mining town about a week's hike to the northwest. The townsfolk might provide help, but he didn't know anyone there and wasn't sure exactly where it was. Besides, if he were honest with himself, the miners that had come to Koza to trade had always scared him a bit. They were rough, burly men and usually had thick beards and shaggy hair that made them look a bit like barbarians themselves. Eridu was farther south, along the coast, so it would be easier to find. He'd heard it was a bigger city and there would be soldiers there.

I would need a lot of supplies to get to Eridu, he thought to himself. *The raiders would have weeks to get away before I could get there. If I follow them, I'm sure I could catch them in a day or two. Maybe I can sneak in at night and at least rescue my mother.*

Finally, with a grunt of determination, he stood. He wandered, in a fog, returning to the cave where he had watched his brother die. The cave was empty except for the discarded weapons.

He retrieved his bow and quiver, loading it to capacity. His brother's body was gone but, in his shock, he barely noticed or wondered why.

In town, he scavenged the houses and managed to find a hunter's pack and filled it with an assortment of apples, cured meat, flint and steel for building fires, and waterskins that he found in forgotten corners throughout the village. He rounded out his supplies with a battered tin pot, an old hunting knife, and a lightweight blanket, rolled tightly and tied to the underside of the pack.

He shouldered the pack and surveyed the scene one last time. The low stone buildings, the empty gardens, a pig or sheep pen here or there, the desolation of it all. This was where he had been raised and had spent his whole life. Part of him could not bear to leave, but he knew that he had no choice. Alone he would surely die.

With a sniff, he turned north, following the broad path. His only option was to follow. He had no illusions that he could fight the barbarians. The idea of trying to rescue his mother gave him hope that at least then he wouldn't be alone. If he failed, he could surrender and join in whatever ill fate was to befall the rest of his people. He had no idea what to expect.

Campfire stories told of raiders farther to the north. At Imbros, the mining settlement, they would steal supplies and gold. Near Larissa, with its wealth of livestock, they would steal cattle and sheep. He had never heard stories of an entire town being taken. Not even the darker tales, meant to scare children, told of a horror like this.

Darius plodded wearily; his mind was in a world of its own. Sometimes a jumble of thoughts filled his head, racing, and impossible to process. If he could succeed in shutting them out, shock would take over, leaving him in a state of utter numbness as he marched in a fog.

He paid little notice as he crested a hill and descended into the heavily wooded southern boundary of their hunting grounds. The tall pines and firs blocked much of the late afternoon light, and dusk caught him by surprise.

His foot snagged an exposed root, and he stumbled. His palms scraped across the rocks and dirt as he tried to catch himself. As he stood and brushed off his hands on the legs of his pants, he noticed how dark it had become.

Darius examined his surroundings but could get no sense of where he was or how far he had come. He scrambled in the encroaching darkness and was able to gather enough dry wood to start a small fire. Huddling close to the fire, he munched on apples and jerky. This was not at all like his and Micah's overnight trips into the wilderness. Those had been all adventure and laughing around the fire well into the night.

He pulled his blanket closer and shut his eyes. The hum of insects, at least, was familiar. The comforting song of crickets was broken every now and then by the higher-pitched whine of mosquitoes.

A twig snapped just outside the light of the fire, and he

bolted upright.

A possum ambled to the edge of the light, raised its nose to sniff the fire, and then shuffled off in the opposite direction.

Darius lay back down. A bark in the distance made him shiver again. *It's just a fox*, he told himself. The hooting of an owl followed, and then the braying howls of several coyotes scattered throughout the night.

Yes, it had been much different camping with Micah.

His mind drifted to the very edge of sleep. That's when the moaning started. At least that's what it sounded like at first. It transformed into a low, mournful bay. The sound was answered by two or three others in the dark woods.

That's it, he thought.

Darius bundled up his gear and kicked dirt over the embers. He sought out the thickest fir tree he could find and scrambled up it to wedge himself in a crook between branches.

The calls continued from the gloom of the forest. Sometimes they sounded like low, ghostly moans, then they would change to a series of cackles or growls. Darius shivered in his tree.

Darius cried out when the night was broken by a high-pitched scream that sounded like a child being tortured. He recognized it for the death cries of a rabbit, but that didn't stop his heart from trying to beat its way out of his chest. The cackling and groans faded further into the trees after that, and he tried his best to find sleep. Instead, he spent most of the night sobbing into the gray wool of his blanket.

The second day was no better. Sleep deprived and frightened, he trudged northward at a pace driven by adrenaline and an intense need to find his mother. His muscles ached by midday, but he pressed on. Clouds moved in late in the day and threatened rain.

As dusk approached, the wailing howls returned. Were they closer than before? It must be his imagination. He found a stout stick, just in case, and made camp under a small outcropping. The rocks were sheltered by overhanging fir boughs. The first drops of rain started soon after he lay down.

The thick canopy and heavy clouds obscured any light from the moon. Dim shapes of trees loomed at the edge of his vision, but darkness obscured any details. He imagined that he saw sleek shapes loping between the large trunks. The pitter-patter of water striking branches drowned out most other forest sounds, but he could still hear the barks and moans. The steady beat of rain soon intensified to a dull roar, and even those faded as the creatures sought shelter. The memories of the past few days returned in a crash of emotion.

He looked up at the dark clouds and the faint shadows of limbs swaying in the wind above him and screamed. It was a scream born from frustration and anger and fear. It was a scream that cursed the gods, old and new. It was a scream that cursed their attackers and his mother for leaving him alone and his brother for getting killed. It was a scream that echoed in his ears and reverberated against the rocks around him but went no further. It was drowned out by the now intense drumming of the rain and the thunder that exploded across the sky above him. He yelled in rage again and was again drowned out by a barrage of thunder, as if Antu, the sky god, was mocking his pain and suffering.

A third time he announced his anger and a third time he was rebuffed. It reminded him distinctly of when Micah had first taken him fishing. Darius had struggled to tie the hook to the line. He had finally thrown the pole and hook to the ground in a howl of frustration. Rather than console him and help him, Micah had shouted at him.

"Pick that up. Tantrums are for children. You are here to learn to become a man. Men do not give up and cry when things are difficult. Men persevere and continue working until they get it right. If you want to be a child and throw a tantrum, then go back to mother's skirts and let me know when you are ready to learn."

Darius was shocked. Micah had never yelled at him before. But he did as he was told. It took a dozen more attempts, but he was eventually able to tie the hook as he had been shown.

"Excellent work," Micah praised. "I couldn't have done it better myself. Now, show me how to catch a fish."

Micah's praise had aroused a feeling of pride in Darius that he had never felt before. Not only was he proud that he had made Micah happy, but proud that he had completed the challenge. After that, he welcomed eagerly each new challenge that Micah presented, trying to recapture that feeling.

That same determination reawakened now. They would not get the better of him. They would not break him down. Not the raiders, not the gods, not whatever cursed banshee was wailing out there in the woods. He would persevere. He let out a resolute sigh as he ran his fingers through his matted blond hair and released his anger.

Darius pressed as tightly against the rock as he could, trying to find some refuge under the small ledge that jutted above him. He pulled his pack tightly to his chest and clutched his stick as streams of water ran by his inadequate shelter. He was still uncomfortable but refused to let it get the better of him. For Micah's sake and for his own.

The raiders were taking no measures to mask their passage, and even his untrained eye could follow easily. Spent supplies and cold campfires were spaced at regular intervals where the men had stopped to rest the horses or eat. The rain had made the trail muddy but did nothing to hide their passing. It was clear to all that a large troop marched north, but nothing illuminated the sinister nature of that party.

For the third night in a row, the cries and bays followed him. He sought shelter in the crook of an elm tree. He finally got a closer look at his pursuers, three thick-shouldered creatures roughly the size of a large dog. Their coats were covered with spots. They weren't wolves or wild dogs, but they had similar features. Darius had never seen animals like these and wasn't sure what to call them.

The chatter never stopped as they slunk around the base of the tree. One of them tried to claw its way up the trunk and snapped at Darius's feet. Darius was high enough that the animal couldn't reach him, but he pulled his knees a little closer to his chest despite knowing this. The large canines finally gave up and faded back into the woods in search of easier prey. Darius could hear them cackling to each other long after they left as if they knew a joke that Darius didn't.

Darius let out a breath he didn't know he was holding when the animals were out of sight. He glanced down at his cudgel and tossed it aside. It would be worthless against the creatures. If they caught him in the open, he would have to use his bow.

Chapter Three
Valley of Ravens

The next day, the forested coastal hills of his home gave way to rolling grasslands. Darius groaned as he scanned the waist-high grass. The wind played across the tufts making the plains ripple like a vast yellow sea. If those creatures tried to sneak up on him, they would be able to close on him before he was aware. He strung his bow and with a begrudged sigh plodded forward.

The sun beat down in the open, and Darius struggled to keep a steady pace. Blisters began to form on his feet, and his entire body ached. Despite this, he guessed that he had covered four or five leagues by midday. He checked his supplies when he stopped.

Darius was running low on food. He had not stopped to hunt where game had been more plentiful and now cursed himself for his stupidity. He had been so focused on trying to catch up to his people that he had not considered his basic needs. Gone too were the frequent woodland streams. He had to ration his water to make it between watering holes. Luckily, the barbarians faced the same problem and the broad swath of flattened grass picked its way across the plain from one oasis to the next.

The sun was low on the horizon when he heard the mournful howls in the distance behind him. His breath caught, and he scanned his surroundings for anything that could provide cover. There were few trees, mostly scrub pines, short and ragged looking. Atop a rise to his left, he spied a stand of ash, the red and orange of their autumn leaves marking a contrast to the yellowed grass.

The hunters had always warned against running from wolves or wild dogs. The animals loved to chase their prey. But Darius didn't see much choice. He took off at a sprint toward the trees. The distant howls immediately turned to that unnerving cackle.

He reached the hill, out of breath. He pulled an arrow free of his quiver and nocked it as he turned. The grass was shorter near the trees, and the knoll provided him a good view of the approaching landscape. He couldn't see the animals, but he saw the grass parting in three distinct paths several hundred paces away.

The branches of the trees were well above his head and were thin. He would have to shimmy the trunk to reach them, and he doubted they would hold his weight for long unless he clung to the tree. He wouldn't be able to hang there all night.

Last resort then, he thought.

He watched the snaking paths. They were moving fast. They would be within range any second. Darius drew the arrow. He watched the closest path hoping for a glimpse at the beast. He saw a flash of speckled brown and fired. The arrow struck well behind it.

He drew another arrow and fired. He overcorrected, and the shot fell short.

He saw the dusky shape and fired again. This time he found his mark. He heard a yelp and a growl. The animal slowed, but the other two charged on.

Darius fired a fourth time. This time he saw the arrow strike. It glanced off the second canine's shoulder. It didn't do much damage, but it caused the creature to pause and reconsider. The final animal was close and was running fast with long, loping strides. Darius barely had time to pull the arrow and fire before it was on him.

The arrow struck true, catching the beast at the base of the throat. Its momentum carried it forward, colliding with Darius as it stumbled and fell. Darius was knocked off his feet. He felt hot breath and heard a gurgling sound. Jaws tried to snap at Darius's face, but they had no strength left. In a panic, Darius pushed the animal off of him and scrambled to his feet.

The other two were circling him cautiously. Both were limping. One favored its foreleg and Darius could see the arrow sticking out of the hindquarters of the other. He didn't wait for them to decide whether or not to attack. As soon as he was stable, he released another arrow toward the closest. It struck the creature in the side. It yelped again and ran in the opposite direction, disappearing into the grass.

The remaining animal was the smallest of the three. Seeing

her companions dispatched, she decided against attacking further. She followed her pack mate down the hill, letting out a mournful howl as she fled.

Darius quickly checked himself for wounds. Other than a few scratches and scrapes, he was unharmed. As the adrenaline left him, his hands began to shake. He sank to his knees, trembling.

When he had recovered enough, he skinned the dead animal and cooked what meat he could over a pitiful fire of grass, dried leaves, and fallen branches. The meat was tough and gamey, but he choked it down anyway. Afterward, he huddled under his blanket next to one of the ash trees. The night was as cold as the day had been hot, and once again sleep eluded him most of the night.

He breakfasted on some of the remaining meat, but by lunchtime it tasted wrong and he left the rest for the scavengers. His pack hung slack on his shoulders, and his stomach growled. Despite his hunger, his determination did not wane. His resolve was unshaken.

As he crested the hill, that changed. He could see that a large campsite had occupied the shallow valley below. Three more dirty lines ended at the basin marking routes from the east and west. A much larger road continued north. The four raiding parties had joined here before continuing onward. That, however, was not the scene that had caused the bile in his stomach to rise into his throat. At the eastern edge of the valley, the grass was black with ravens.

He forced himself forward, reluctantly. The unkindness of ravens thundered into the air as he approached, and his worst fears were realized. The raiders had *culled* their herd. The ground was littered with bodies. The very old, the very young, the sick, and the lame. Anyone that would have added burden to the group had been murdered. Black arrow shafts jutted from the bodies like a sea of sickly reeds.

He retched.

Darius doubled over and heaved until his stomach was empty and then he heaved some more. Blindness overtook him and he hung limply, spittle trailing from his open mouth as he struggled to breathe. After an eternity his sight cleared. He tried to stand, but dizziness and nausea won out again and bent him low.

When he was finally able to move again, he drifted through the massacre in a daze. The faces were unrecognizable, thanks to the birds. He noticed, too, that many had survived the initial barrage of arrows and had been finished off by spear or sword. Gaping wounds in the backs of their heads made it more difficult to identify the victims. The smell and condition of the bodies threatened to overwhelm him several times, but he managed to keep from vomiting again as he completed his grisly search.

He looked for familiar clothing and signs. He recognized the batik patterns of Mother Shala's skirts. He saw Old Man Dagan's wooden leg jutting from beneath a pile of bodies. He recognized others from his village as he searched frantically for any sign of his mother.

She was a strong woman, in her prime, so it was unlikely she would be here. He scurried across piles, pulling one body off of another, expecting to see the powder-blue linen skirt that she had been wearing when he had last seen her.

He collapsed to his knees when he found Micah's corpse. The remains were bloated after a week and had been picked apart by scavengers, but Darius had little doubt that it was him. The shirt and pants looked the same, and a hole in his chest marked the place where an arrow had pierced it.

His mind grasped for understanding. Why would they bring Micah here and dump him in the midst of this slaughter? Why not let his loved ones give him a proper funeral? Not that they thought they had left anyone behind. They probably thought Darius had died in the plunge. But why here, so far from where they had killed him? Darius knelt beside what was left of his brother.

"Great god of the Underworld," he prayed. "Please take pity on my brother Micah and allow him some comfort. He was a good brother and a good son. It is not his fault that we could not lay him to rest properly."

He noticed more of the dead in a state similar to his brother, carried here from wherever they had been slain. Dozens more had been murdered here, and the yellowed grass was stained brown with their blood. He lost count of how many corpses he inspected. It had to be more than a hundred, more than the entire population of his village, but there was no sign of his mother. He half laughed, half cried as he finally accepted that she was not there.

He scanned the rest of the valley through a liquid haze looking for other signs of horror. The ravens circled thickly, waiting to return to their interrupted meal. He glanced furtively in their direction then continued his survey of the abandoned camp. The amount of debris showed that at least a portion of the army had been there for days. Perhaps they were waiting for the southern contingent to return before continuing north. He saw no other signs of death but his gaze fell on an overturned wagon at the opposite side of the camp.

A rush of wings and scolding caws erupted behind him as he moved in the direction of the wagon. The cart had a flat bed with warped wooden rails surrounding it. The front axle was twisted, and one of the rear wheels was shattered. It was unclear exactly what had happened, but the scene pointed to violence. Scuffs and gouges marked the earth, and a splintered club lay a few paces away. When he was close enough to see the details, he saw two bloody handprints pressed to the undercarriage. The left print was missing the two smallest fingers.

"Marku," Darius whispered under his breath.

The village blacksmith was large by any standards. He stood half again as tall as Micah, and his arms were the size of a normal man's thigh. Though imposing, he had always been kind and had held very stern views on justice. He had often served as the moral compass for the village. A calm word from Marku often carried more weight than the shouts of other men. Darius could not recall a time when he had ever heard Marku raise his voice or lose self-control. Even when his apprentice had smashed his fingers in a momentary act of carelessness, Marku had calmly wrapped his hand and instructed the boy to get Mother Belle. From the evidence, Darius could only suppose that the man had snapped when the raiders started killing the helpless. Darius had not seen Marku among the carnage, so apparently he had been subdued or had been killed elsewhere.

The wagon was empty except for a broken crate wedged under it. Darius examined the carton and saw why the soldiers had left it. The box was half full of turnips. It was no wonder that no one had bothered to liberate it. Darius hefted his pack, almost weightless now, and sighed. He stooped and began filling the empty space with the bitter root.

Darius stood once his task was complete and threw a defiant gaze toward the sky.

"You will not break me today."

A stray raven flew overhead at that moment and released its bowels. Darius turned a disgusted eye to the white smear on his right shoulder, calmly bent to pluck a handful of yellowed grass from the field and wiped his shirt clean. With a final unsmiling glance upward, he turned north.

"Not today," he grumbled.

Chapter Four
Marku

Marku spat a mouthful of blood onto the dark soil between his outstretched hands. His head was spinning, and he couldn't get his eyes to focus properly.

"Get up," the man standing over him shouted again.

It had been all Marku could do to raise himself to his hands and knees. He grunted as the man kicked him in the ribs.

"I said, get up." The command came again.

With a deep sigh, Marku slowly dragged one of his feet forward and then the other. His hands clutched the churned earth. He willed the world to hold still, and with a heave, pushed himself to standing. Marku couldn't bring himself to meet the man's eyes and instead focused on his chest. He studied the coarse woolen fibers of the man's heavy shirt. The raider wasn't wearing his black leather armor today. None of them were. The plains had been incredibly hot during the day, and most of their captors had shed the armor after that awful day in the valley.

"Pick it up," the man said, pointing to the sword which lay on the ground.

Today it was a sword. Yesterday it had been a heavy mace. The day before...Marku couldn't remember anymore.

Marku glanced at the sword and then at the other five men standing in a circle around him. They all held wrist-thick cudgels banded with leather straps.

"Please, no more," Marku begged. "I've learned my lesson."

The soldier laughed. "You've learned your lesson when I say you have. Pick it up."

Marku bent to reach for the sword's hilt. His hand trembled as he saw the men raise their clubs and take a step forward in anticipation.

"Pick it up." The sound buzzed in Marku's ears.

"Please, stop." Marku began to sob.

"Do we need to kill another one of your friends?"

Marku bit his lip and clenched his eyes shut as he reached forward the last few inches to close his hand around the hilt of the weapon. The rain of blows started before he could tighten his grip. He tasted dirt and spit out the dank earth that had filled his mouth. He didn't remember falling, but he must have, again.

His ears were ringing. There was a faint sound beyond the high-pitched tone. What was it? A voice? What was it saying?

"Get up." The words became more clear.

Marku couldn't move.

"No. I can't," he wailed. "I can't. I don't care anymore. Kill them if you have to. I can't...I can't..."

Marku curled up into a ball on the ground. Sobs wracked his body.

"Drag him back to the wagon," the leader commanded. "We'll go again tomorrow."

Chapter Five
Arthengal

When Darius first saw the line of trees in the distance, he thought he was seeing a mirage. The thick line of conifers seemed out of place in the sea of yellow grass. Overcome by thirst he had practically buried his face in the stream of water that flowed through the cool wood.

He stared now at the fat trout circling a deep pool beside a large flat rock. His mouth salivated. The turnips had staved off hunger, but each meal had been a fight between his mouth and his stomach. Water had been scarce on the plains, so he had not had any to spare to boil the roots. Instead, he had skewered them on his hunting knife and roasted them over the fire. More often than not, they ended up tasting like burnt resentment. It hadn't helped the flavor that the only thing, besides grass, that Darius could find to burn had been dried horse dung.

Darius considered the fish, wishing he had a net or a pole. He finally settled on crafting makeshift spears. There were plenty of suitable shafts in the surrounding wood. He sharpened them to points with his knife.

He tried several approaches, but lack of skill and the low quality of his weapons proved a deterrent. After several hours, he gave up and threw the javelins aside in frustration, Micah's words echoing in his ears despite himself.

"The water causes them to look closer than they really are. Try aiming down," a strong baritone voice called from behind him.

Darius jumped. He turned abruptly, reaching for one of the spears he had cast aside.

Leaning gracefully against a tree a few paces away was a tall, dark-skinned old man. He had to be at least as old as Dagan who had turned sixty at his last name day, ancient in Darius's eyes.

He had thick hair that fell to his shoulders and, while peppered with gray, was surprisingly dark despite his age. His neatly trimmed beard, on the other hand, was more silver than black. His face was weathered from a lifetime spent outdoors. He had a sharp nose and soft eyes that seemed to take everything in at once.

The stranger wore a lightweight green tunic that seemed to match the color of the nearby underbrush. The long sleeves extended to his wrists. His pants and boots both appeared to be handcrafted from cured leather.

"Easy, young sir," the man spoke again and smiled. It was a comforting smile, and Darius felt some of the tension in his shoulders release. "I only meant to help."

Darius glanced around, looking for others. "Where did you come from?"

"I'm camped nearby," the man chuckled. "I was merely fishing, the same as you. Although I like my method better than yours."

The stranger reached behind the tree and held up a fishing rod crafted from a type of wood Darius had never seen before. The wood appeared to be segmented yet unbroken at the same time. He cocked his head, peering at the rod.

"That is an unusual rod. What sort of wood is that?"

The visitor glanced down at the rod as if noticing it for the first time. "It's called *take* wood. I suppose it would look unusual. The wood doesn't grow anywhere near here. It was a gift from a friend a long time ago. It does make for an excellent rod, though."

The man nodded toward the water. "You have a nice hole there. Do you mind if I try my luck? I will share whatever I catch, of course."

Reason told Darius that he should be scared of this man, but the stranger projected an air of calm and quiet confidence that put Darius at ease. He stepped back and gestured toward the pool. "Be my guest."

Darius watched with curiosity as strong, wrinkled fingers expertly threaded a white grub on a bone hook and cast the line into the hole.

"The name's Arthengal, by the way," the man said, tugging gently on the line.

"I'm Darius," Darius said.

"A fine name," Arthengal replied. Then he jerked the rod and raised it above his head. He unfastened a small net bound with a wooden hoop from his belt and scooped the fat trout from the water. He tossed the fish up onto the bank and baited his hook again.

"You won't need that spear," Arthengal said. "I don't bite."

Only then did Darius realize he was still clutching the spear. He tossed it aside absently and continued to watch the man fish.

"Where are you from?" Arthengal asked.

"Koza," Darius answered. "It's a small fishing village to the south, along the cliffs of Whiting Bay."

"I know the bay, but I don't know the village. What brings you out here?" Arthengal asked. "You are a long way from...well, anywhere."

"My village was raided and my mother was captured. I am following them."

"To what end? Shall you fight them all to free your mother?" Arthengal flourished an imaginary sword.

Darius shrugged and looked down.

Arthengal studied the boy as he pulled in another fish.

"Darius, I am sorry for your loss. I truly am. However, the raiding party that you seek passed here more than two days ago. They raised quite a cloud of dust as they passed, and I went to investigate. I watched them as they passed. It was less of a party and more of an army. I know them, they are not to be trifled with."

Darius gasped. *Two days. How did I lose so much ground? I*

thought that I was catching up. He sank to the ground and buried his face in his hands.

Arthengal was quiet for a time, fishing, while Darius tried to reconcile the news. When Arthengal did speak, his tone was gentle. "They will reach the Northern Wastes soon, and once they do, they will be nearly impossible for you to track. The large band will disperse, and members will take their spoils back to their homes. I do not mean to be cruel, but it is not likely you will ever see your mother again."

Tears began to roll down Darius's face as he stared at Arthengal defiantly. "They killed my brother."

Arthengal stared grimly. "I am doubly sorry."

Darius wiped the tears from his face and looked up at Arthengal. "What should I do then? My mother is the only family that I have left."

"I don't know," Arthengal said. "But you look like you haven't had a good meal in a while. Why don't we go back to my camp and cook these up and we can talk about it?"

Darius rubbed his eyes again and noticed half a dozen fish flopping on the bank.

Arthengal ran a thin rope through the gills of the fish and hoisted his catch. "Come on, my camp is just this way a bit."

Darius rose, gathered his belongings, and followed a short distance downstream. He was surprised to see a small campsite nestled in a quiet copse beside the river. Darius had walked by this very spot the previous day and had seen no sign of it.

Darius crossed the stream and peered in the direction of the camp. Even though he knew it was there, he still could not make it out. The site was cleverly concealed using a combination of underbrush and what appeared to be lightweight nets dyed different colors to blend with the foliage.

Darius noticed a collection of trout and perch drying on spits over a bed of white coals. It was obvious that the fisherman had been here several days and had better luck than he.

Arthengal took the fish down to the stream to clean.

Darius continued his inspection of the camp and noticed yet another of the man's curious possessions. A bow leaned against a tree outside the carefully concealed tent. It was unlike anything Darius had ever seen. Unlike his own bow with a simple curving spine, it curved back on itself, creating a wavy line rather than a simple, elegant curve.

"Another gift," the woodsman said.

Darius jumped. He hadn't heard Arthengal walk back into camp.

"Much more powerful than a traditional bow, like yours." Arthengal feigned not to notice the startled reaction, but Darius thought he saw the hint of a smile play across the man's lips. "It can easily drop a stag with a single well-placed shot. It doesn't have the range that the Aengal longbows have, but then again, nothing does."

"You have a lot of unusual gifts," Darius said. *Who are the*

Aengals? What's a longbow?

"I travelled a lot in my youth and made many friends," Arthengal said with a shrug. "I keep their gifts to remind me that one man can make a difference in the face of tyranny."

What an odd thing to say, Darius thought.

Arthengal laid the trout out on a large, flat rock at the inside edge of the fire. He stoked the coals to flame, and soon the fish were sizzling nicely. He retrieved a small bag of herbs from a nearby pack and sprinkled them over the roasting fish.

Once he was done preparing the fish, Arthengal turned his attention to Darius. "If you don't mind me saying, I couldn't help but notice you were limping a bit. Are your feet okay?"

"Just some blisters," Darius said.

"Do you mind if I take a look?" Arthengal asked. "I may be able to help."

Darius pulled off his boots. His wool stockings were dark with dried blood. He peeled them off gingerly to reveal swollen feet, stained red on the bottoms and sides. New blisters had formed over the old ones. Darius winced as Arthengal gently probed his feet.

Arthengal frowned. "You are lucky to still be walking. We need to clean these. I have a poultice I can apply which will help them heal."

Arthengal set a pot of water over the fire. He produced a white linen shirt from his pack and tore it into strips. He mixed the contents of several small pouches, also from his pack, into a wooden bowl. He added a little water and mixed it into a thick paste.

"You said that the raiders were dangerous," Darius said as Arthengal worked. "Have you run across them before? Were you captured?"

"No, not captured, but I have tangled with them in the past," Arthengal said. He dipped one of the linen rags into the hot water and began washing Darius's feet. "And they are very dangerous. They are not what they once were, but they're still a thorn in everyone's side. Although I've never seen a group as large as the one that passed through."

"I think it was four groups that met up farther south," Darius said.

"Ah, that would make more sense, I guess. You said they captured your entire village?" Arthengal applied the paste to the sores. Darius felt a slight tingling in his feet.

Darius nodded. "Those they didn't kill, anyway. What do you mean they weren't what they once were, but then you said you hadn't seen a group that large?" Darius asked, confused.

"Oh, don't get me wrong, that was a large group, but they used to have vast armies all over. They were driven into the wilds when I was a much younger man. Since then they've contented themselves with the occasional summer raid into the settlements closest to The Wastes to gather supplies and slaves. The size of this group was...troubling." The old man finished by wrapping bandages around Darius's feet, and then sat back on his heels, stroking his beard with his thumb and forefinger as he considered.

Darius watched, not wanting to interrupt Arthengal's thoughts. A warm sensation seemed to cover his feet and inch up his legs.

After a time, Arthengal spoke again, his words slow and calculated. "I cannot make up for your loss, but I may be able to give you a purpose. I am not unskilled in the way of the wilds but, alas, I have no one to pass my legacy to. If you wish, you may return with me. You can apprentice with me and help me protect my little valley. I cannot promise you adventure, as my days of travel have ended. However, life in the valley is not without challenge, and the work I do is important, to me."

Darius shook his head resolutely. "I cannot give up on my mother. I could not live with myself if I abandoned her to a life of slavery. I must do something to try to rescue her." Desperation and anger added an edge to his voice.

Arthengal gave the boy an appraising look. "Is your mother strong?"

Darius nodded. "She has cared for my brother and me alone ever since my father died. She is the strongest woman I know."

Silence followed for several long moments. Darius watched the heat waves rise from the fire and listened to the musical bubbling of the brook.

Arthengal, too, stared into the dancing flames. His brow was knitted in careful contemplation as if weighing the fate of the world against his next thought.

"Okay," he finally spoke with a sigh. "I will help you."

Hope sprang in Darius's chest, and he ventured a glance at Arthengal.

"In a fashion," Arthengal continued.

Darius's shoulders slumped again.

"I will train you in the way of the sword and the bow and instruct you in the ways of the wilds. Then, when you are ready, we will go after your mother. I will not have time to pass on all of my knowledge before we go, but perhaps within a few years, you will learn enough that we might rescue her successfully."

"Years?" Darius cried in dismay.

"If you go now, your life is most certainly forfeit. Even if they just capture you as a slave, you will probably not ever see your mother again. My offer is the best chance for both of you. If your mother is strong, as you say, then she can survive a few years in captivity. Maybe she will be lucky and will be awarded to a married man with a wise wife. Slaves with a good mistress tend to suffer less abuse than the slaves of single warriors. A good mistress will protect a strong slave as a valuable asset to be treasured and nurtured for many years to come. Bachelors tend to burn through slave women rather quickly as they share her services with their fellows." He cleared his throat as if implying something but Darius clearly didn't understand, so he continued.

"In the meantime, we can build your skills to be adequate.

Once I am sure you won't get us both killed, we can go after her."

"Why can't we go sooner than that?" Darius asked. "We could sneak in and try to find her."

"They will have scouts placed to watch for intruders. No offense, boy, but I don't think you have the skills to sneak by trained scouts. That is one of the things I can teach you. Besides, even if we get in, we would probably have to fight our way out, and a twelve-year-old boy isn't who I would normally choose to guard my flank."

"I'm fourteen," Darius said indignantly.

"Apologies," Arthengal said. "But still."

"You would teach me to fight?" Darius asked.

"I will," Arthengal said. "If it helps your decision, I have trained men before. A lot of men. Give me a few years, and I will make a decent swordsman out of you. Better than most of the men that took your mother."

Darius stared at his feet for a long time. The man waited patiently for a response as both listened to the sizzling from the rocks nearby.

Finally, Darius nodded.

"Excellent. Then let us sup and enjoy the afternoon's peace. Tomorrow brings an end to my sojourn here, and I must return to my valley. You can stay with me. In trade for my training and help, you can aid me with my craft and help me care for the valley."

"Your craft?" Darius asked.

"I make nets and ropes. But more of that later. While we eat, tell me about your brother."

"He's dead," Darius replied glumly.

"I know. But it is important to talk about the dead. It keeps their memory alive, and it honors their life." Arthengal said simply, "Was he good with a bow? Your brother."

"He was the best," Darius said proudly. "Well, maybe not the best in our village but definitely better than any of the younger hunters. He could hit a target at a hundred paces even with the wind blowing. He brought home three deer this year alone, and he took third in the archery contest at *Emesh*, the summer equinox festival."

"Impressive. Did he teach you how to shoot?"

"He was teaching me. Next year I could have joined the hunters on my first hunt." A wave of despair washed over Darius, and his mood darkened again. "But that won't happen now."

"I promise to take you hunting in the spring. What was your brother's name?"

"Micah."

"We will make Micah proud of you and train you to be a better shot than even he was," the man promised. "Did you and Micah ever get into any trouble when you were younger?"

"Oh, no," Darius said seriously. "Micah didn't brook any foolishness, at least not after our father died. If I acted childishly, he would send me back to mother. Although there was this one time when we were very young, before father died, when we climbed out on the cliffs to steal razorbill eggs," Darius said with a laugh.

"Micah was so proud when we returned with three eggs. Mother was so mad she cried, but even when father strapped us, I could still see how proud Micah was of himself. Not for doing something stupid and dangerous, but for getting the eggs and helping bring food to the home. He told me later that was the first time he felt like a hunter even though he was only six or seven at the time. That was all he ever wanted was to be a hunter like our father."

"Your father, how did he die?" Arthengal asked.

"He was one of the hunters for our village," Darius explained. "His leg was gored by a boar, and he died from his wounds."

"He was a good man?"

"From what I remember." Darius furrowed his brow. "I was only five when he died. I don't remember much. But Micah adored him so he must have been."

"What was his name?"

"Jonas," Darius answered.

"And your mother's?"

"Cordelia."

Arthengal nodded his head, memorizing the names.

"What else did you and Micah do together?"

"Everything," Darius said with a smile, forgetting for a moment to be sad. "He taught me how to fish, and how to shoot. We would go camping in the woods together and swim in the ocean for hours." The last was garbled as Darius failed to hold back a wide yawn.

"We have an early morning tomorrow," Arthengal said. "Why don't you get some sleep? You can tell me more later."

Darius nodded and lay down close to the fire, resting his head on his arms.

Arthengal banked the fire and turned to the boy. "Sleep well, young friend," he said as he crept to his tent.

Chapter Six
Old Bear

Arthengal was up at dawn the next day. Darius had slept curled up by the fire and woke as he heard the man fussing around. Arthengal's long, dark hair was pulled back and tied with a leather thong. He kneeled on the ground, and in front of him were a ceramic bowl, a wooden spoon, a leather sack, and a waterskin.

Darius watched as Arthengal upended the sack and emptied a yellow powder into the bowl. He added water and stirred the mixture until it became a thick mash. Then he stoked the remaining coals and placed the bowl in the embers. Only then did he notice that Darius was awake.

"It is a beautiful morning, young sir. We shall depart for home within the hour. Your socks have been cleaned and should be dry by now." He pointed toward the fire where Darius's stockings lay on a flat rock. "You'll want to leave the bandages on for now. We can check them again tonight."

Darius flexed his feet. They felt better than they had in days. He reached for the socks and pulled them on over the bandages. He pulled his boots on before rising to gather his meager belongings. He watched with rapt attention as Arthengal broke camp with stunning efficiency. The netting and tent were stowed. The underbrush was rearranged. The dried fish were wrapped in treated skins and packed away.

By this time the yellow mixture had solidified in the bowl. Arthengal wrapped his fingers in a cloth and fished the bowl out of the coals. He knocked it against his leg, and a cake fell out of the bowl into his hand. He set the bowl down to cool before he broke the bread in two and gave half to Darius.

Darius sniffed the lump suspiciously.

"Corn bread, it's delicious. Try it."

Darius nibbled a corner and was surprised by the warm sweetness of the bread.

"Oh, wait," Arthengal exclaimed, and began rummaging through his pack.

Arthengal pulled out a cloth-wrapped package. Pulling back the layers of cloth, he revealed a very sticky honeycomb. He broke off a chuck and passed it to Darius.

"It's better with honey."

Darius alternated bites between the two delicacies. It was like a gift from the heavens on his tongue. Well, maybe not really, but after four days of turnips, it was close. Darius licked his fingers clean while Arthengal buried the fire pit and covered it with leaves.

Darius glanced around once Arthengal was done. Had he not just spent the night here, he would not have known the thicket had been occupied. There was no sign, that he could see, of human disturbance.

"Off we go then." Arthengal adjusted the pack on his shoulders and began heading southeast following the brook downstream.

Darius gave a final longing glance north toward his mother and then turned to follow. The morning was cool, and dew sparkled on the leaves.

"So, if I'm going to teach you what I know, there is no reason we can't start now. There's little else to do while we walk," Arthengal said. "Do you see those bushes there, along the bank? With the pink flowers and the red berries?"

"Uh huh, I know roses."

"Good," Arthengal continued, ignoring the tinge of sarcasm in Darius's voice. "And did you know that a tea brewed from the berries can help with a sour stomach and can help reduce inflammation in your joints?"

"No, I didn't know that. Is that helpful to know?"

"If you are going to learn how to use a sword, you will want to know all of the remedies you can for swollen joints."

That's right, Darius thought with wonder. *He's going to teach me how to use the sword. I wonder if it will be like being a knight from one of mother's stories.*

"That plant there, with the broad flat leaves..." Arthengal continued to point out various flora and fauna along the stream.

Old Man Dagan had a sword hanging over his fireplace. He used to talk about being a soldier in some war when he was younger when he was in his cups. I saw him bring it out once when he'd had too much ale. Mother Shala had rapped him on the head with her walking stick and told him to put the fool thing back where it belonged.

Darius laughed.

Arthengal looked at him curiously and then continued his lesson. "And the musk from a river ott--"

Without warning, Arthengal froze mid-sentence.

Darius almost crashed into him. Arthengal held up his arm, palm facing Darius, indicating that he stop. Without a word, he turned his hand parallel to the ground and pumped his arm up and down.

At first, Darius wasn't sure what he was doing until it occurred to him that Arthengal wanted him to kneel and hide. Arthengal settled on the balls of his feet, and his whole body seemed alert, ready to strike or run. He pointed to the opposite bank.

At first, Darius wasn't sure what he was supposed to notice, but the aura of danger was palpable.

Darius's eyes scanned the opposite bank, his heart racing. He saw the same poplar trees that decorated this side of the bank, more rose bushes, a patch of burdock. Burdock? How did he know that? And something about treating acne. He continued to search. His eyes passed over a rotted log and then jerked back. The log had been torn open. Stray grubs still wriggled on the ground next to the log, struggling to find a safe hiding place.

"Bear," Darius whispered.

He scanned for other signs and noticed a large tree several paces away from the log. Claw marks raked the bark. If Arthengal, who was a tall man, stood on his toes and reached as high as he could, the marks would still be a full arm's length higher than he could reach. Darius felt a chill go up his spine.

Arthengal moved with a quiet grace as he unsecured his bow and nocked an arrow.

Darius scanned the soft mud on the edge of the stream. There didn't seem to be any indication that the bear had crossed.

Arthengal stayed low, creeping alongside the stream. He stepped without making a sound, crossing one foot behind the next as his eyes darted along the opposite bank.

Darius followed Micah's concentration trick and began to tune out the sounds around them. First, the bubbling of the brook faded into the background. Then the chirping and whistles from insects and birds. The soft pad of Arthengal's leather boots. He could hear it then. The snorting breaths that sounded like a dragon stoking its inner furnace.

He touched Arthengal's sleeve and pointed across the stream to the left.

At first, the dark brown fur was indistinguishable from the underbrush, but then the motion was clear. The animal had torn open another log and had its snout buried in the rotting center, lapping up termites and grubs like they were candied fruit.

The gentle breeze was at their face, and the bear's muzzle was surrounded by decay, so it was no wonder he had not smelled them yet. Their luck could not last forever.

Darius freed his bow, too, and readied an arrow. He crept behind Arthengal, trying to imitate the woodsman's silent steps. And failed. A twig, hiding beneath a cover of needles, snapped. In his ears, it sounded like the crack of a whip. Man and boy froze.

The beast stopped scavenging and raised its head. It sniffed once then shook its head to clear its nose of debris. It turned and continued to test the air. They could now see it in its full grandeur. The creature was massive. It looked like it could rival a prize bull. Each paw looked to be the size of Darius's head. The dappled sunlight glistened off of its dark brown fur. With long, slow breaths that could be measured in heartbeats, the animal tested the air. Then it found their scent and it bellowed. Finger-long canines glistened like ivory daggers in its huge maw. The roar was deafening, and the wide jaws looked like they could snap Darius in half. At its full height, Arthengal would have been lucky to come up to its chest.

Arthengal drew back his arm. His weathered face bore a grim expression. The bear had not seen them yet, and he did not intend to give it the chance. He loosed the arrow, and before it reached its target, another was nocked and drawn. The first arrow struck the monster square in the chest and sunk a quarter of the way up the shaft. The second, striking nearly on top of it, lodged in a massive rib and stopped short. The behemoth roared with rage and brushed at the arrows like he was waving away flies. Both snapped off at the base like twigs.

Arthengal started to nock a third arrow when the animal dropped to all fours and charged. It saw them now. It moved with incredible speed. Darius was sure he could feel the earth shudder under its weight.

Without thinking, Darius drew the string back as he stood. He cleared his mind as his brother had taught him. He focused on his target. The beast rolled toward him like an avalanche of fur and claws and teeth.

"Now release," he heard his brother whisper in the back of his mind.

The arrow flew true and struck the center of the yellow target.

Darius blinked. His arrow had found its mark in the bear's eye.

The bear skidded to a stop at the water's edge. The sound that came from the creature was a mixture of pain and anger. It pawed at the shaft snapping it free but destroying the eye. Another bawl of rage and anguish echoed through the trees. The animal became very still. The undamaged eye glared with menace and rage.

Darius ignored the shivers that ran up his spine and drew back another arrow. His arm trembled under the intense stare.

The bear studied him and then inhaled deeply, like a child smelling the last apple pie of the season, not wanting to forget the scent. Then it spun, kicking up a flurry of leaves, and galloped into the bushes.

"The boy can shoot," Arthengal said, clearing his throat. "Now come on, before it changes its mind. We need to move. Now!"

Darius's heart was pounding, and his breath came in gasps now that the bear had run away. He whispered a quick thank you to the goddess of the hunt before Arthengal grabbed his elbow and dragged him onward.

They moved at a brisk pace the remainder of the day. Gone were Arthengal's lessons, replaced by urges to move. Arthengal allowed a few minutes at midday for a lunch of dried fish and nuts, but otherwise set a grueling pace. Arthengal seemed determined to put as much distance between them and the beast as possible.

Sweat was dripping down Darius's back, and thick strands of blond hair matted together where he had brushed them away from his eyes. His back ached, and his boots felt like they were made from stone.

"Can we take a break, please?" Darius pleaded a few hours after lunch.

Arthengal relented and allowed for a short rest while he kept a watchful eye.

Darius took the opportunity to look around. The brook had grown to the size of a small river, and the surrounding woods had thickened and spread. More pines and firs grew here and covered the rocky hills that sloped away from the stream.

"Why are you in such a hurry? The bear has to be far behind by now."

"Bears are crafty," Arthengal answered. "They can also be vindictive. I wouldn't trust that he has forgiven you that easily."

Darius gulped.

"Okay, rest is over. Let's go. I would like to put a few more miles between us and that bear before we set camp."

The remainder of the afternoon was more of the same brutal pace. Arthengal seemed to have a destination in mind, however, and was determined to reach it before dusk. The ground continued to get more rugged, but he refused to slow. Finally, after hours of hiking, he stopped.

"There," he said, pointing. "That is where we will make camp."

Darius followed Arthengal's arm. The ground rose sharply beside the river until it became nearly sheer. It reminded Darius very much of the oceanside cliffs near his home though not as tall. Midway up the face was a broad ledge that looked half overgrown with bushes. In the side of the cliff, back from the edge of the ledge, there appeared to be a hollow. It would definitely provide them shelter and protection if the animal was following them.

"Why here?" Darius asked.

"I use this area as a hunting camp from time to time,"

Arthengal responded. "It's safe and relatively close to home."

"How do we get up there?" Darius asked.

"We don't. We get down there."

"Huh?"

Arthengal led the boy back upstream a bit and then up the steep slope. The climb was challenging but not impossible. Darius pulled himself along using the trunks of smaller trees. Where handholds were sparse, he was able to scramble along thick granite shelves that overlapped like a broken staircase.

They circled widely until soon they found themselves on the top of a cliff staring down at the river. Below them was the ledge. It didn't look nearly as wide from this vantage.

"Can you climb?" Arthengal asked.

Darius peered over the edge and gulped. He could climb, but it had always been above the relative safety of the sea. If he or his brother fell, it was usually into the deep water at the base of the cliffs rather than the hard rocks that waited below now. He nodded slightly.

"Good." Arthengal produced a rope from his pack and secured it to a nearby tree. "Do you know how to use rope?"

Darius shook his head. It was true that he and his brother had climbed a lot along the cliff faces but never with rope.

"Don't worry, it will just be a safeguard." Arthengal tied a harness around Darius's hips and waist. "I will lower you. When you get a good hold give a shout, and I'll let the rope out as you climb down."

Darius nodded, uncertain, but not wanting to betray his fear.

"Okay," Arthengal instructed. "Just lie down on your belly there and push yourself over the edge of the cliff."

Darius's eyes widened, and his heart started to beat faster.

Is he crazy?

Chapter Seven
Escape

Darius inched feet first over the edge of the cliff until he was dangling just below the edge. He swayed toward the cliff face until he was able to grab a handhold. He pulled himself toward it and found two footholds. He tested his weight on the holds.

"Okay, I'm good."

Darius waited for the rope to slacken enough for him to move and then began descending the wall. The rock face turned out to be an easier climb than the seaside cliffs, and he soon found his feet on the broad landing. He shouted up again and freed himself from the harness.

Darius peered up to see Arthengal leaning back, feet planted firmly on the edge of the precipice. Arthengal had donned a pair of leather gloves. The rope was wrapped about him in a way that Darius couldn't quite see from this vantage. Arthengal's left hand grasped the upper portion of the rope and his right the lower.

What is he doing? Darius thought.

Arthengal tested the rope, and then with a mighty push, he leapt.

Darius gasped, but his fear was quickly allayed.

Arthengal was controlling his descent by applying pressure on the lower rope. With three great leaps, he landed with a soft thud on the ledge beside him.

Darius stretched his legs and back while he surveyed the rest of the ledge. His legs ached from the grueling pace and the rough terrain near the end of the hike. Flat slabs of granite formed a platform that sloped east to west. The higher end was closest to the river. Darius eased up to the edge.

The current roiled as it pressed into the steep canyon. The white froth of rapids was an unbroken tumult until the canyon made a bend and carried the torrent out of sight.

What had looked to be a tangle of bushes from below turned out to be a hedge of carefully cultivated berry bushes and one stunted orange tree. Soil had been packed into the natural cracks in the rocks enough for the roots to take hold.

He turned back to the wall and gave a start. What he had thought was a small recess from below was actually the mouth of a cave. In front of the cave, the ledge had been chipped away, and a channel had been formed in the rock.

"What's that?" he asked, pointing to the shallow trench.

Arthengal paused from securing the rope to a metal hook driven into the cliff face.

"It diverts the rain away from the cave and off the edge."

Just inside the cave, rough-hewn steps led away from the

ledge into the main cavern. The cave itself was dark, and Darius wasn't able to make out many details. He had expected an earthy or musty smell but instead caught the smells of hickory, leather, and something sweet. He could also hear a gentle dripping of water from somewhere inside.

Arthengal retrieved something from his pack and then walked into the darkness. A torch mounted on a wall bracket on the opposite wall sputtered to life.

Darius stared in wonder. The space was a rough square, a dozen or so paces to a side. A small bucket attached to a rope sat on the floor next to a deep-looking hole to the left. The dripping came from that direction. Rivulets traveled at a snail's pace down a dozen or more stalactites before ending their journey in tiny droplets that fell like a gentle rain into the well.

The rest of the left wall was dominated by a series of elaborate fire pits. A cooking kettle dangled from a spit over one, but the others were covered by a collection of metal racks. Each rack included several metal hooks. Darius examined the contraptions, trying to figure out what they were.

"What are these for?" he asked, giving up on the puzzle.

"For drying and smoking meat," Arthengal explained.

Near the pits was a neat stack of firewood and a small pile of wood chips. The walls behind the area were burned black from smoke and the heat of many fires. The large river rocks surrounding the fire beds looked similarly colored.

On the opposite side of the grotto, a long cot had been constructed using a sheet of leather stretched tight over a wooden frame and bound in place by a series of leather thongs. Several folded wool blankets were stacked behind the cot. It looked much more comfortable than the pile of straw that he had slept on most of his life.

Just beyond the cot was a tidy stack of tanned hides. They looked similar to a pile that Aunt Madra always had at her house. The men would bring her their hides, and she would make all manner of clothing and useful home items out of them.

Darius looked again at Arthengal's boots and pants. He saw, too, that a pile of hides hadn't been stripped of their fur but instead had been converted into thick fur blankets.

"Make yourself at home." Arthengal waved a hand, and then unstrung his bow and stashed it and the fishing pole on a narrow outcropping that formed a sort of shelf. The rest of his supplies he set on the floor near the cot.

Darius noticed several other "shelves" holding a variety of wooden and clay jars. A large, open sack of salt rested below one such shelf.

"I just have the one cot, but you should be able to make a comfortable bed out of the blankets there." He pointed to the pile of furs.

"When you said hunting camp I imagined something much different, like maybe a deer blind on the ledge out there. This place is nicer than most of the houses back in Koza," Darius said.

"Hmm..." Arthengal scratched his beard, considering. "Well then, maybe my winter hunting *lodge* would be more appropriate. I've spent quite a few years making it comfortable. There is a herd of elk that spends the winter in a valley just south of here. They make their way down from the high mountains to the east once the winter storms come."

Arthengal set about preparing a fire as Darius inspected the stack of hides. There were more than just elk in the pile. He chose a buffalo hide that felt almost as thick as the straw bed he had slept in most of his life. It was a deep brown color with an inch or more of fur that looked soft and warm.

He eased it out of the stack, careful not to disturb the others. He refolded it, fashioning it into a sleeping mat of sorts. He arranged it near the other cot and laid his belongings on the floor nearby. He collapsed with a sigh into the thick warm fur. He clasped his hands behind his head and stared up at the ceiling, happy that he would be sleeping somewhere warm and dry for the night.

He didn't realize he had fallen asleep until Arthengal was shaking him awake.

"Dinner's ready. You should eat. Today was a hard journey, and you need food and water or else you will surely feel it tomorrow."

Darius accepted the offered fish and nuts with a tired smile and gulped several cups from the basin. The water tasted fresh and clean, almost sweet. The wells back home hadn't been brackish, but there had always been sort of a briny taste to the water, or maybe it had just been the salt in the air. His mind had been too preoccupied to consider the taste of any of the streams or pools he had drunk from during his journey north. They had served to stave off dehydration, but little else.

He felt better after eating, but as soon as he finished, he collapsed once again into the soft comfort of his bulky hide bed. He reached over to the pile and pulled out another thick blanket. This one was tan with streaks of white. He didn't recognize what animal it may have come from.

He snuggled between the two blankets listening to the fire crackle on the other side of the cave. He was vaguely aware of Arthengal singing to himself as he tidied up. Arthengal's voice was deep and rich. The tune was somber, and Darius imagined he could almost hear drums beating a steady, rhythmic beat in the distance.

> *"The rain did drive a day or three*
> *When Aryn came to Shea Alie*
> *The men stood fast against the throng*
> *The battle lasted all night long*
> *The wind did drive and lances pressed*
> *For three nights more we got no rest*
> *Oh, I done lost my youth and more*
> *On the fens of Dun Magor*
> *On the fens of Dun Magor"*

The last word resonated through the cave. *Is that a battle hymn?* he wondered through the fog of half sleep. Darius drifted off to sleep as the second verse began.

Darius woke to a low whistle outside the cave. The whistle conveyed a sentiment of awe, and somehow, a sense of danger.

Roused, he scrambled up the steps to join Arthengal on the ledge. Arthengal had shed his tunic and wore only a light grey undershirt and trousers. Darius saw for the first time the thick muscles of the man's arms. His dark skin was etched with faded scars. He was peering over the edge, toying with the point of his beard.

"What is it?" Darius asked.

"I believe you have made an impression," Arthengal said and pointed downward.

Darius inched to the lip of the shelf and surveyed the lightly wooded riverbank below. It looked as if a savage battle had been fought below them. The ground was torn up. Several small aspen trees had been knocked flat, snapped off near the base. The underbrush was ravaged. There was no sign of the bear, but there was no doubt in either of their minds what had perpetrated the destruction.

"I guess he came to pay his respects and was upset that you were unavailable to receive him." Arthengal smirked, but his eyes held a hint of concern.

Darius blanched.

"So, should we wait him out or continue? If we travel at the same pace as yesterday, we should reach the valley by nightfall," Arthengal said.

"What happens when we get there?" Darius asked. "What if he follows us there?"

"Oh, I wouldn't worry about that too much. It's the getting there that worries me more. Once we are there, I have plenty of...defenses, shall we say, to dissuade unwelcome visitors."

Darius examined the destruction below, considering.

"I should warn you that once a bear like that sets about something, it is often difficult to change his mind. He could easily wait us out if he is determined," Arthengal said.

"Okay, let's go," Darius said.

"Good enough. I'll be ready shortly." Arthengal turned away from the ledge and disappeared into the cavern.

Darius returned to the cave and carefully replaced the blankets on the pile. They gathered their things and Darius shouldered his pack. His unstrung bow was strapped to the outside. Arthengal must have done that. He certainly didn't remember doing it.

"You will need a new string soon," Arthengal commented. "It looks as if you haven't unstrung it in a week."

"I haven't," Darius said meekly. Micah had scolded him about the same thing many times.

"The string loses its tension if it remains strung too long."

"I know," Darius said. "I forgot."

"You stay here," Arthengal said as they stepped outside onto the ledge.

The old man quickly scaled the rock face and leveraged himself slowly to the top. His head and shoulders were barely past the rim when Darius heard a snort and a scuffle followed by a growl.

Arthengal descended as quickly as he had climbed, and as Darius watched, a huge snout poked over the edge. One dark brown eye and one gaping hole stared fiercely down at Darius.

"Okay, maybe a different plan," Arthengal stated as he landed gently on the stone shelf. "Can you swim?"

"Huh? Yes, but..."

Arthengal had already disappeared inside the cave. He returned with a coiled rope and nothing else. The rest of his gear had been left behind. He brushed aside the berry bushes to expose another metal loop driven into the rock. He quickly secured the rope to the loop and tossed the rest of the rope to the shore below.

The bear watched with intense curiosity as Arthengal put on his gloves.

"Leave your things here. We'll come back for our things another day. They will be safe in the cave," Arthengal said.

Darius shrugged off his pack, quiver, and bow and ran inside the cave to toss them on the cot. When he returned to the ledge, Arthengal was kneeling. The rope was arranged in the same way as when he had descended the day before. He watched the bear observe them with menacing interest.

"Climb on my back and hold on tight."

Darius scrambled onto his back and looped his arms around Arthengal's neck and the outstretched shoulder. He grasped opposite wrists and held tightly. Arthengal stood, still watching the animal, and backed to the edge. With a mighty leap, they were falling. The bear howled, and its head disappeared from the outcropping above.

They descended smoothly with a few gentle leaps. When they reached the ground, Darius let go and dropped to the rocky bank.

"This way," Arthengal shouted.

Darius followed Arthengal as he sprinted toward the river. The water, rough when viewed from above, was a torrent up close. Without pausing, Arthengal dove into the tumult. He surfaced downstream and shouted at Darius to follow. The boy glanced backwards and could see flashes of brown fur through the trees up the hill barreling toward a point of descent.

Darius launched himself off the rocks near the shore and began swimming toward the man.

"Breathe in between the waves," was all Arthengal said before swimming toward the mouth of the canyon.

Darius had spent his entire life swimming in the ocean. He and his brother had even swum in somewhat stormy weather to test their skills and dare the sea god. Nothing he had done before prepared him for the unpredictable tumult that the river now provided.

He was tossed into the air only to be swallowed by a cresting wave a second later. He tried to remember Arthengal's advice, but the second time he was slapped in the face with an oncoming crest, he came out the other side coughing.

He tried to get control of his breath as they rounded the bend but a new surprise awaited. Large, half-submerged boulders were scattered throughout the narrow channel. His body quickly became bruised as he bounced from one to another.

"Feet downstream," he heard Arthengal shout.

Darius wrestled with the river god, Enki, until he managed to point his feet into the rushing froth. His feet bounced off a large rock with a force that shocked his spine. When he encountered the next slab, he bent his knees to absorb the impact and it was easier.

Enki let him get adjusted before playing with him again. Suddenly, the water was swirling around him. He was spun in a circle and found himself facing upstream. He thrashed to turn around but was too late as Enki tossed him into the cliff wall. His shoulder collapsed. He tried to scream through the river's smothering grasp.

"Exhale," Arthengal shouted. "Feet down."

What? Darius thought. The second delay was too long.

Suddenly, Darius was weightless. He fell in a flailing somersault, catching brief glimpses of the waterfall before he impacted the pool below. It felt like getting kicked in the chest by a horse. The air rushed out of his lungs. Instinct took over and he gasped. His lungs filled with water and darkness descended.

Darius awoke with a racking cough. He tried to breathe in and choked again. He had the vague impression of being rolled to his side before he vomited water. His lungs burned, and tears welled in his eyes as he struggled to expel the fluid and replace it with sweet autumn air. When he stopped coughing and could finally breathe, he glanced around.

He was lying on a small sandy beach next to a wide pool. The waterfall emptied thunderously into the opposite side. Nearby, the river, its energy spent, flowed gently out of the pond toward a broad crystalline lake. Beyond the lake was a picturesque valley.

Arthengal was on his knees beside him.

"Can you breathe?"

Darius nodded shakily. The throbbing in his shoulder battled to overwhelm the burning in his chest.

"Okay, this is going to hurt."

"What?" Darius barely had time to blurt as Arthengal stood and placed a foot against his ribs. Arthengal jerked his arm upward.

Darius felt pain, like a dagger being thrust into his shoulder. Fire radiated from the joint, spreading across his chest and back. His vision blurred. The pain lasted a thousand years and was over in a second. He hadn't even had time to scream. Darius heard a pop in his shoulder, and all that remained was a dull ache.

Arthengal helped him stand. "Welcome to my valley. We

took the shortcut. I do not recommend it in the future."

Darius peered around. The valley was broad and sloped away from the large lake in its center. The valley seemed to be surrounded on all sides by treacherous cliffs, similar to the one they had just so shockingly descended. He couldn't see much detail of the terrain inside the crater as tall cedars and firs blocked his view of everything but the lake and the far shore. There, Darius could just make out fields dark green with crops. Nearer to the pool and stream, on the long side of the lake, there was a small cabin.

The lake was a curious blue-green color that Darius had never seen before. Upon closer examination, Darius realized that it was the rocks below the water that were colored and the water itself was the clearest he had ever seen. In certain areas, steam seemed to rise from the surface of the water.

"What is this place?" Darius asked.

"My home," Arthengal answered simply but then took mercy on the curious boy. "The valley is formed in the belly of what used to be a great volcano. The walls, as you can see, are nearly impenetrable, although there are trails into the valley if you know the way. The lake is deep. I don't know how deep, I've never reached the bottom even with ropes and weights. The water from the river is fresh but don't ever drink the water from the lake. It's not fit for consumption. There aren't any fish in the lake nor any game in the valley. That's why I travel upstream when I have a hankering for trout and why I set up the cave as a hunting camp."

"What do you grow?" Darius nodded toward the fields.

"Hemp," Arthengal answered. "I use it to make my ropes and nets which I will trade for those supplies that the valley and surrounding area does not provide. I will teach you. But first, let's get to the cabin and find some dry clothes."

Darius looked down at his soaked and ragged clothing. "This is all I have."

"We'll figure something out." Arthengal frowned as he rubbed his graying beard.

As they set off toward the cabin, Darius turned back to the river. "Thank you for not killing me today."

The water seemed to bubble in amusement as it trickled from the pool toward the lake.

An hour later, Darius was wrapped in a soft elk-hide blanket sipping tea on the floor of the cabin while his clothes dried by a steel barrel stove nearby. The cabin was simple and sparse. It was constructed from whole logs crisscrossed to form a single rectangular room inside. Mud and straw had been used to seal the gaps between logs. A single open doorway and a single window let air and light into the room. The roof was made from smaller logs, covered on the outside by cedar shingles. The floor was bare earth but pounded hard and flat.

In addition to the stove, there was a simple wooden table in the center of the room and a single wooden chair. Though inelegant, the craftsmanship on both was flawless. There was also an open fireplace, currently cold, with a spit and a kettle. A clay basin and pitcher rested on a narrow counter near the stove, and a collection of herbs and small masonry jars decorated several shelves mounted on the wall behind it.

The sleeping area was equally simple. A simple hemp hammock hung from wall to wall. A large wooden footlocker rested near the bed. Above the hammock, another shelf had been built into the wall. Darius counted eight books on the shelf, all thick volumes.

"Feeling better?" Arthengal asked. He had changed into dry clothes, blue woolen pants and a red tunic this time.

Darius nodded.

Arthengal noticed Darius eyeing the books. "Do you read?"

Darius shook his head. "Mother told us stories when we were younger. She taught us our numbers and most of our letters but Mother Shala had the only book in town, something to do with herbs and such, but she never let anyone borrow it. Books are expensive, and we didn't have anything of value to trade, especially after father died."

"Well, I shall teach you then. Books are amazing things. A source of knowledge beyond what many men can learn in a lifetime. We can start with this one." He pulled a thick, red leather-bound tome off the shelf. "It is probably more to your liking for the time being."

"What is it?" he asked as Arthengal handed the volume to him.

"The completed works of Han Yu Pin. He was a court bard in the eighth dynasty. He tells of adventurous heroes and ill-fated romances. Of dragons and warriors and of the battles between nations. It is best to learn to read using something that will hold your attention." He winked.

"What's a dynasty? What's a dragon?" Darius asked in awe as he fingered the glossy leather of the binding.

"Later. I don't want to ruin the surprise," Arthengal smiled. "For now, just get warm and settle in. I think I have an old straw mat somewhere that should make a more suitable bed."

Arthengal exited from the open doorway and returned carrying a rolled bundle. He cut the string that held it with his belt knife and unrolled the woven mat out on the floor near the hammock. It was about a finger's width thick. It wouldn't provide much padding, but it would be better than the hard-packed earth of the floor.

Arthengal rummaged through the footlocker and pulled out a green tunic similar to the one he had been wearing on the first day they had met. He tossed the garment to Darius.

"That should be good enough for sleeping. You can change when you're ready. I'll start working on something to eat. Today we can rest and recover. Tomorrow we have work to do."

Chapter Eight
Cordelia

Cordelia kept her head down but her ears open. She ventured furtive glances at the proceedings. This was not at all what she had expected. The men that had captured them were a rough lot and looked every bit the barbarian raiders that they purported to be. However, as soon as they had crossed through the pass, the whole affair took on a military precision.

Soldiers had waited for them at the end of the pass. They were adorned in armor made from overlapping bands of hardened leather. Unlike the black armor of their captors, the soldiers' gear was a more natural brown. The leader of this group wore a thick, padded jerkin over his armor with a decorative patch sewn onto the left breast.

As soon as they arrived, the commander began shouting orders. The captives were sorted into pens, and a series of long tables were assembled nearby. Several scribes sat at each long table. One at a time, a prisoner was brought before each of the scribes who asked a series of questions.

The first few captives hadn't been quick enough to answer

and had been *encouraged* by the butt of a spear to the back from one of the soldiers.

"Name?"

"Raoul."

The scribe dipped a quill in a bottle of ink and made a note on a long scroll.

"City of origin?"

"Imbros."

"Trade?"

"Miner."

"Send him to the iron mines."

The man was shuffled off to another pen.

"Next."

Cordelia watched the leader of the raiders conversing with the guard captain behind the tables. The two men laughed and looked congenial. Had she not just spent almost two weeks under the cruel control of the bandit, she would have thought him an average man.

She watched as they dragged Marku forward.

Poor Marku, she thought.

He had lost control when he had seen the fiends butchering the children and the aged and they had broken him for it. His body was a patchwork of bruises. His head bowed forward, chin nearly resting on his chest. He shuffled forward, barely aware of his surroundings.

"Name?"

"Marku." His voice was a whisper.

"Speak up." One of the soldiers jabbed the butt of his spear into Marku's ribs.

"Marku," he said louder.

"City of origin?"

"Koza."

"Trade?"

"Blacksmith."

At that, the leader of the raiders interrupted his conversation and burst out laughing. "You've got to be kidding me."

The scribe turned to look at him.

"He's not going to be much use at the weapon forges. Not anymore." The devil of a man continued to laugh. "Send him to one of the farms. Maybe he can help maintain the equipment there."

The scribe shrugged and made a note, then nodded to one of the soldiers. Marku was dragged off to another staging area.

A soldier grabbed Cordelia's arm and began leading her toward the tables.

"Name?"

"Cordelia."

"City of origin?"

"Koza."

The bandit leader gave a low whistle. "Now she's a pretty one, isn't she? Should we send her to the swine farms? Ivan's men could make good use of her." He shot a wicked grin to the captain, who just rolled his eyes in response.

"I'm a farmer's wife," Cordelia blurted.

"Very well," the scribe said and waved a hand. He also didn't seem amused by the crude comment.

She gave a sigh of relief when she was tossed in the pen with Marku.

She gazed longingly to the south.

Darius, I hope you're okay. My sweet boy, I hope you escaped and can find a life.

She already knew Micah's fate, but she hadn't seen Darius at all during the trek north and hoped that he had survived. Somewhere.

Chapter Nine
Training Begins

"I have been gone for more than a week," Arthengal said as he set a plate of dried fruits and nuts on the simple wooden table. "Will you help me inspect my other buildings for damage and intruders?"

"Intruders?" Darius mumbled through a mouthful of dried apples. He sat in the single chair wearing the baggy tunic that Arthengal had loaned him. It hung nearly to his knees and felt more like a nightdress than a shirt.

Arthengal smirked.

"Yes, there is a particularly troublesome squirrel that likes to raid my stores when I am away and a family of otters that thinks I split wood specifically for them to use for home repairs."

Darius laughed and coughed apple chunks across the table.

"I don't suppose you have any pants I could borrow?" Darius asked. "My clothes are still damp from yesterday."

Arthengal rummaged through his clothes and found a pair of black wool pants. They were baggy, but Arthengal gave Darius a length of rope to cinch them at the waist. He had to roll up the cuffs to keep from tripping on them, but they were comfortable enough.

After their meal, Arthengal grabbed a burlap sack and two waterskins and led Darius to the cellar. The room was dug into the side of a hill near the main cabin. From the outside, only a firm wooden door was visible.

Arthengal lit an oil lamp that hung in the center of the room. The light illuminated a massive crypt. Squared-off timbers supported log rafters. The beams were notched to fit snugly atop each pillar. A dark green, fibrous goo had been caked and dried in between the logs.

"What's that?" Darius wrinkled his nose as he pointed at the ceiling.

"It's a mixture of shredded hemp and pine tar. I heard somewhere that sailors use something similar to seal the gaps on boats and thought I would try it out. So far, it works pretty well to keep the rain out, but it needs to be reapplied every so often as it flakes off," Arthengal answered as he hung the fish near several other strings of dried meat.

The walls were reinforced with stone to keep the vermin out. Long wooden shelves extended along each and between each of the three rows of support beams. Barrels were carefully arranged at the end of each shelf.

Darius inspected the shelves. Each was meticulously organized. One held a collection of masonry jars filled with dried flowers and roots. A symbol decorated the outside of each jar, presumably to identify its contents. Another held ground spices and herbs in small, clear glass bottles sealed with beeswax. Darius recognized many of them as cooking seasonings. Large clay pots decorated a third shelf.

He lifted the lid on one and was assaulted by the smell of fermented cabbage.

"Ah-ha!" Arthengal exclaimed.

Darius bobbled the jar as he was replacing the lid. He breathed a sigh of relief as he stabilized the jar with both hands. If the jar had broken, the pleasant bouquet of herbs, spices, and meats would have been shockingly disrupted.

Darius put down the jar and hurried to Arthengal's side. Arthengal was poised in a guard stance with a spare axe handle extended before him.

The enemy stared down at him from the top shelf near an overturned bag of acorns. Unconcerned brown eyes considered the old man as sharp teeth busied themselves on a carefully grasped nut.

"Thief." Arthengal raged and rattled the shelves with his makeshift sword.

The squirrel scolded in return, almost as loudly, and threw the acorn with a remarkable aim.

As the acorn bounced off his forehead, Arthengal swept the axe handle along the shelf, scattering the bag of acorns and knocking several more tightly packed bags off the shelf.

The squirrel bounded down the shelf and then slipped to the

floor. It perched on the edge of a hole near the base of the rock wall, turned to unleash a final torrent of insults at the man, and then disappeared into the burrow beyond.

"And stay out." Arthengal rattled the wood loudly against the rocks near the hole.

He cast his eyes about looking for more intruders. Seeing none, he retrieved a palm-sized stone from a pile at the front of the cellar. He wedged it into the squirrel's escape tunnel and then pounded it firmly with the axe handle to secure it in place.

Arthengal finally glanced at Darius who held a hand over his mouth trying not to laugh.

"That will keep the little pirate away for a time," Arthengal said with wink.

Darius burst out laughing and the old man chuckled.

Arthengal opened his sack and loaded it with several apples from an open barrel and several handfuls of nuts from another barrel. He added some lengths of jerked venison, lifted the lantern from its hook, and moved toward the door.

"Okay, now we have to set the trap lines."

"Trap lines?" Darius asked, confused. "I thought you said you only hunt outside the valley."

Arthengal only smiled and led the way toward the freshwater stream and pool. He paused briefly at the stream to fill the waterskins and then pointed to the brook.

"The easiest way to cross to the other side is across this

stream. It is half a day's hike to circumnavigate the lake. I would advise against trying to swim across. For the most part, the water is safe and warm, but there are places that are super heated by the belly of the volcano. Some are predictable, but others are not as the fires below shift. Also, there are occasional waterspouts in the center of the lake let loose from deep below."

They crossed a narrow part in the stream and turned away from the lake. The slope steepened the farther they got away from the lake, and Darius soon found himself breathing hard.

"Where are we going?" he panted.

Arthengal looked back and smiled. "To the front door."

The forest stopped short of the sheer cliff walls where the ground was at its steepest and covered mostly with crumbling granite and volcanic glass rather than the lush soil that filled the rest of the valley.

A wide rift appeared ahead of them. Darius followed Arthengal into the crack. It was wide enough to drive a small wagon through. A few paces in, the rift opened into a wider expanse, and Darius could see a carefully designed trail winding upward.

"We start at the top," Arthengal said.

Darius was astounded at the craftsmanship and precision of the carefully carved ramps and shaped expanses of the trail. It had been carved out of the natural lines of the cliff but shaped and designed in such a way that the running water of storms would not wear away the stone. All along the path, long metal rails had been mounted into the cliff wall.

"How long have you lived here?" Darius wondered aloud.

Arthengal laughed. "Sadly, I cannot take credit for this feat of engineering. Emperor Tizqar had this trail cut several hundred years ago, during the ninth dynasty. The volcano was once home to a very productive gold and sapphire mine. Once Tizqar had extracted all he could from the valley, they abandoned the mines and the volcano reclaimed them. The valley was allowed to flourish and became what you see below. The only thing that remains of that era is this trail and a few mine shafts that haven't fully collapsed yet."

"Emperor Tizqar?" Darius asked.

Arthengal glanced back. His brow was furrowed in question. "You don't know the old emperors?"

"I don't know any emperors."

Arthengal laughed. "Thirty years then."

"Huh? Thirty years for what?"

He stopped and turned to look at the boy. "Thirty years for a legacy to fade and for the people to forget about the emperors."

"I guess so," Darius shrugged. "Old Man Dagan would sometimes talk about the war from when he was younger. When he'd had too much to drink, anyway. I think that's where he lost his leg. Mother Shala would always shush him, though, and chastise him about raising bad spirits and what-not. But he never talked about emperors. He would ramble on about some '...bloody tyrant who thought he was a god. Weren't no god in the end though when three feet of steel opened his belly.'" Darius mimicked a gruff deep voice that sounded a bit drunk.

Arthengal chuckled.

Darius brightened, remembering something. "I don't know anything about any emperors, but Baron Shalanum's tax collector came once a few summers ago. We didn't have any coins though so we paid them in fish." Darius laughed. "You should have seen the look on his face. Magistrate Engar finally gave them a few pearls, which seemed to satisfy the tax collector. He never came back after that."

Arthengal nodded and continued the climb. "Baron Shalanum is a good man. He wouldn't harass the small folk if they had nothing to pay. We are also far from the capitals here in disputed lands between Shalanum Province and Magora Province. The land is disputed, not for its value, but lack thereof. Neither wants the responsibility of protecting the *wilderness,* and neither probably invests much in the taxation or preservation of these lands. That's probably why the *Daku Rabi* prey on these people and raid them for slaves and supplies."

"The *Dapu whatsi?*" Darius asked.

"*Daku Rabi,*" Arthengal corrected. "It means Old Guard in the ancient tongue. They are all that remains of the imperial guard. They fled to the north when the last emperor was killed at the end of the Great War. The land barons that rule the empire now leave them alone for the most part. The north is rugged, and the Old Guard are scattered. They only band together for raids. A force as large as the one I saw returning north is a rare event. It may be a portent of events to come, or it may just be an isolated incident.

"When we go to Eridu in the spring, I'll send word to Baron Shalanum. He can send scouts to keep a closer eye on things. The larger picture is for the barons and their armies to worry about. You and I will focus on your training so we can rescue your mother and leave the politics to other men."

"Tizqar was the emperor in the ninth dynasty and the book you showed me last night was from the eighth dynasty," Darius commented. "How many emperors were there?"

"Emperors, I don't know exactly," Arthengal considered, scratching his beard. "But there were twelve dynasties over the empire's three thousand years."

"And what's a dynasty?" Darius asked.

"Rule generally passed from father to eldest surviving son. If there were no sons, it might have passed to the emperor's brother or nephew. As long as the empire was ruled by the same family, it was all part of the same dynasty," Arthengal explained. "If there were no heirs, then another member of the larger royal family would be chosen to succeed. When that happened, a new dynasty was usually formed."

"Who is the royal family?" Darius asked.

"Anyone who can trace their lineage directly to the original emperor, Chung Oku Mai. He had twelve sons and fourteen daughters."

"Twenty-six children!" Darius exclaimed. "His poor wife."

Arthengal laughed uproariously.

"Wives," he corrected after he caught his breath. "He had ten wives over his lifetime. It is rumored that he lived to be over one hundred years old."

"Still, that's a lot of kids."

"Most of his early descendants had very large families as well," Arthengal continued his explanation. "Over three thousand years, all of the noble houses and many commoners married into the royal family. Some theorize that over half the population can trace ancestry to Chung Oku Mai in one way or another. Succession was usually determined by the most direct lineage."

They walked in silence for a time.

"What are the bars?" Darius changed the subject and pointed to the railing attached to the rocks.

"I don't know exactly what they were used for, but my guess is that they helped transport the heavy gold out of the basin. I have repurposed them as you will soon see," he said with a wink.

They reached the top of the trail and the ground leveled out. Canyon walls extended upward on both sides. Darius turned his back to the canyon and was startled as he saw the valley in all of its grandeur for the first time.

High, jagged peaks surrounded the broad bowl, snow-capped even now, in late autumn. The cliffs to the east dropped nearly to the edge of the blue-green lake, leaving only a narrow trail along the water's edge. The valley was broader and sloped more gently elsewhere. The water sparkled in the sun, reflecting the peaks that were closest.

Darius could just glimpse Arthengal's tiny cabin on the western side of the lake. In the distance to the north, he could make out the lush green fields. He could not see the waterfall that he knew was there, hidden by the outcroppings to his side, but he could clearly make out the stream that flowed from it into the lake. Aside from the areas where Arthengal had cleared for growing, the valley was heavily forested with hemlock, fir, and cedar. Here and there through the trees, Darius saw caves cut into the mountain wall from the mining operation that Arthengal had mentioned.

Darius trotted to catch up with Arthengal who had moved up the canyon. The ravine blocked out most of the sunlight, casting dark shadows along the trail. Up ahead, the gorge ended abruptly at a mass of dense foliage. When they reached the thick plant growth, Darius saw that it wasn't exactly natural. Arthengal had pulled and shaped brush, ferns, and vines to hide the mouth of the canyon. They checked the integrity of the screen, and then Arthengal led Darius to the first trap.

Just past the mouth of the canyon ran a series of carefully covered pits. Arthengal removed the wooden covers and stowed them in concealed niches. Darius peered into the exposed holes. Each was about hip deep, and rather vicious-looking spikes had been driven into the porous rock at the bottom.

Arthengal staked tarps over the top of each pit and scattered dirt over the top. Once he was done, Darius could no longer see the pits even though he knew they were there.

"Mantraps," Arthengal explained. "There is only one type of animal that I set a trap line for."

Darius cocked his head. "Why? Are you that opposed to visitors?"

"Suffice it to say that there are some among the Daku Rabi that would consider it a great honor to take my life. It's been more than a decade since any have tried, but that doesn't mean I plan to make it easy for them if they try again."

At the other end of the canyon, Arthengal demonstrated how to set the second series of traps. Large nets were obscured in the dirt. They had passed right over them earlier and Darius hadn't noticed. Arthengal connected the ropes to a series of weights and pulleys hidden along the walls. He pulled heavily on the ropes to raise the weights and then tied them off with tripwires.

"The weights are enough to lift even a couple large men." He pointed to the pinnacle of the trap halfway up the canyon wall. "A fall from that height would be...damaging."

Shock and wonder filled Darius's eyes as he appraised the elaborate snare.

Who is this man? he wondered.

The final set of devices were set all along the winding entry trail. Hidden plates and tripwires were armed as they backed down the path. Each trigger was slightly different than the last but the result was the same. Each of the traps pulled one of the metal railings across the trail. At waist height, the bars would be enough to sweep a man off the precipice to the next switchback far below.

It was well past midday when they finished their work. They rested at the edge of the forest to eat the lunch that Arthengal had packed. Darius gnawed on a piece of jerky as he stared out across the turquoise-blue waters of the lake. It was very peaceful. He could see why Arthengal had decided to make this his refuge.

"How long *have* you been here, Arthengal?" the boy asked.

"Since the end of the Great War." Arthengal, too, stared out across the serene mountain lake. "I had had enough of people for a while after that war. At first, I just came to get away from the chaos of the city and the trappings of politics, but after a few years I found a peace here that I had never experienced in my previous life and decided to stay."

"Politics? What did you do before you came here?"

"I was in the army. I was an officer in service to Baroness Magora."

Darius waited for further explanation, but that was all that was provided. The man seemed deep in thought, his brow furrowed, and he stroked his beard absently. After several moments of silence, Arthengal stood and started trudging toward the stream they had crossed earlier.

"We have one more stop before we head back," he called over his shoulder to Darius.

Darius scrambled to his feet and followed after him. When they reached the waterfall, Arthengal circled the pool and disappeared behind the cascading curtain. Darius inched his way along the slippery rocks behind the waterfall. He found Arthengal in a large cave behind the waterfall. Darius gaped at what was inside.

Crates and boxes of all different shapes and sizes were stacked all over the room. To his left were three stacks of long oak crates stacked six high. Beyond that a dozen or so square boxes with bits of straw poking out between the slats. Opposite the oak caskets were several massive trunks as tall as a man and nearly as wide.

"What is this place?" Darius said in awe, thinking of the treasure rooms described in his mother's stories.

"My armory, I guess you'd say." Arthengal was leaning over a great chest in the center of the cavern. "It was a different time after the war, and I tucked away a few things just in case. As it turns out, I haven't had much use for most of it, but there's not much else to do with it now."

Arthengal shrugged and continued his search.

"Here." He thrust a small parcel toward Darius without answering. "Everyone should have a good belt knife. That one you have has seen better days."

Darius unwrapped the package. Inside was a simple hunting knife. The grip felt comfortable in his hand. The blade was surrounded by a black leather sheath. A belt could be threaded through the two slits cut into the back. He pulled out the blade and checked the edge with his thumb. It was sharp.

Arthengal pulled out two long objects covered in oiled cloth out of the chest. He reverently unwrapped the two objects.

Darius gasped as he saw two long swords.

Arthengal returned the wrappings to the chest, and retrieved two scabbards. He slammed the lid of the chest shut. Then he inserted a sword in each scabbard.

A mixture of emotions played across the old man's face as he handed one of the blades to Darius.

"I promised to teach you. This evening your lessons will start." Arthengal strode out of the cave, leaving Darius behind looking in shock down at the ornate scabbard.

The sword itself was utilitarian. A fine steel blade with a simple cross guard. The pommel balanced the sword nicely. The weapon wasn't as heavy as Darius thought it would be, and it felt comfortable in his hands. The leather grip was still slick with oil, so Darius fingered it lightly. The scabbard is what held his attention. It was dark brown leather with a matching belt. Each end was decorated with silver, and a web of silver and gold threads etched its way down the length. In the center of each diamond, formed by the crisscrossing filaments, was embossed the head of a roaring bear. He laced the knife onto the belt and carried the bundle toward the hidden exit.

Arthengal was already well on his way back to the cabin by the time Darius emerged from the cave. He hurried after, catching up as they reached the cabin.

"Here." Arthengal tossed Darius a linen rag. "Wipe off the rest of the oil and then strap the belt around your waist."

Arthengal did the same with the other weapon. Then he retreated just out of reach and stood facing Darius. Arthengal took a position turned perpendicular to him. Darius fumbled with the belt trying to mimic what Arthengal had done. The grip was low on his left hip, within easy reach of his right hand.

"Before we start, we need to be clear about a few things, my boy," Arthengal said in a firm voice that carried. His smile had faded, and his face was all seriousness.

"Okay," Darius said tentatively.

"First, understand that I like you. But liking has nothing to do with weapons training. My goal is to keep you from getting yourself, or me, killed should you ever need to use these skills. You must agree to listen and do exactly as I say at all times."

Darius nodded eagerly.

"It may seem, at times, that I am being unkind, but what I do is to get results and develop skill and good habits. Every order I give will have a purpose, even if you don't see it. Feel free to ask questions if you don't understand what I am asking, but never question a command once understood. I expect you to give everything you have to this training and more. Strength is not built on half measures. If you decide the sword is not your forte, you can quit whenever you want. But know that if you choose to, done is done. I will not train you another day. There are other weapons we might try, but once you abandon a course, there is no going back." The last was said in a firm, no-nonsense tone.

"Got it," Darius said. Then he added, "But I won't give up. Micah taught me better than that. Men don't give up, they keep trying until they get it right."

A slight grin returned to Arthengal's face.

"Okay, then. Let's begin," he said as he unsheathed his blade.

He raised the weapon and extended it toward Darius. His hand was held just above his hip, a little more than a span away from his body. The blade angled up, guarding chest and head.

"Always present your enemy with the smallest possible target," he instructed. He motioned with his hands, indicating the narrow profile presented to Darius.

"Create a solid base and keep your knees loose and flexible." He separated his feet slightly more than shoulder width with his knees bent slightly. His back was straight, and his torso was centered over his hips. "Elbow bent when in a defensive position, wrist loose, and grip the hilt like you are shaking a man's hand firmly. Now you try."

Darius tried to draw the blade, but it jerked at the belt.

Arthengal smirked. "You have to unfasten the straps first."

Darius glanced down, and for the first time, noticed two

leather bands that wrapped from one side of the scabbard to the other, holding the cross guard securely in place. He blushed and flipped his thumb to release the catches. He tried to free the blade again, but the bindings still got in the way.

"You can secure them on the underside of the casing when you are using the weapon. They are only meant to keep the blade secure during transport or storage," Arthengal explained patiently.

Blushing, Darius did as he was told and finally managed to free the blade from its scabbard. He studied the man's positioning closely and tried to copy it.

"Straighten your back," Arthengal suggested. "You are leaning too far forward. Never sacrifice balance for position."

Darius adjusted, and Arthengal nodded approvingly.

"Now attack. Try to hit me."

Darius stepped forward, gripping the hilt with both hands and swung down like he was swinging an axe at a piece of wood.

Arthengal stepped aside smoothly, and the point of the sword struck the ground, vibrating up Darius's arm.

"You aren't chopping wood, boy. Always strike for the body. It is the largest target and will be the easiest to hit. Try again."

Darius repositioned himself and then swung sideways, aiming for Arthengal's chest.

Arthengal's wrist barely twitched as he shifted to the left to block the blow. The clang of steel rang out, and the shock of the blow nearly caused Darius to drop his weapon.

"Again."

Darius swept from the opposite direction.

Another twitch of the wrist and Arthengal blocked right.

They continued for several minutes, Darius putting more force behind each subsequent swing. Arthengal barely seemed to notice, and his sword didn't budge as he blocked each blow.

"Good. Let's try a lunge." He demonstrated the maneuver. He extended the point of the blade toward Darius and stepped forward. His back foot didn't shift, and his front knee bent deeply as the point surged toward the boy.

Darius yelped and jumped out of the way. The point extended well beyond where he had been standing.

"You try."

Darius found the starting position and then tried to replicate the lunge.

Arthengal swept downward in an arcing circle and knocked Darius's blade away. They repeated the technique several more times. Arthengal blocked each attack with a different movement. His body never moved. Arm and weapon seemed an entity separated from the rest of him, and his motions were always slight, never wasting energy.

Darius was beginning to breathe heavily already, but Arthengal just grinned at him.

Next, he demonstrated several types of sweeping attacks. First, the sword tip traced a line from shoulder to hip coming downward at an angle. Darius practiced this motion. Then Arthengal demonstrated the reverse of the technique and made Darius practice sweeping from hip to shoulder. They practiced each technique on each side a dozen times. By the end, sweat was trickling down the sides of Darius's face, and his shoulder, elbow, and back ached.

Arthengal finally called for a break and instructed him to get water.

"Next, you learn your first form."

Forms? Darius thought. *Why not just keep practicing like we have been?*

Arthengal read the confusion on Darius's face. "Mastering the sword isn't just about hacking and slashing at your opponent. That would actually be the quickest way to get yourself killed against a skilled swordsman. Forms help train your mind to anticipate and respond to different attack styles, and they train your body to react more quickly. As I said before, I will not help you rescue your mother if I think you are going to get us both killed. I have to be able to trust and depend on you. Do you understand?"

Darius nodded.

"We'll begin with Lazy Viper. In battle, the method is meant to be used with a buckler, but even without a shield, it's a good novice style to build balance and leg strength. Sit while I demonstrate. Then you can follow along with me the first couple of attempts," Arthengal instructed.

Arthengal started from the defensive position that he had

demonstrated earlier. He moved slowly through an intricate pattern. The blade danced from block to sweep to feint to a deep lunge. Arthengal executed a final sweep and ended in the same position that he had started.

"I'll show you again. Watch my feet as well as the blade."

Arthengal stepped through the movements again and then turned to Darius.

"Now, stand next to me and we'll do it together."

Darius stood next to Arthengal and mimicked each of the slow, exaggerated movements. After several iterations, they were moving together as one. Arthengal stepped away to observe as Darius continued. Darius ran through the form three more times while the man watched.

"Raise the tip on the thrust."

Darius tried again.

"A bit more."

The difference seemed insignificant to Darius, but he kept repeating the maneuver, making minor adjustments to the thrust until Arthengal nodded with satisfaction.

"Firm up your grip on the sweeps. Imagine that you are striking a solid target."

Arthengal pointed out several more minor corrections as he repeated the form over and over again. Darius's shoulders were beginning to ache and his hand was cramping, but the drill went on. Determination forced him to push his limits. If this would help him rescue his mother, it would be worth a little pain.

"Now faster," Arthengal said.

His legs screamed as he moved through the motions more quickly. Darius gritted his teeth and forced himself to move faster.

"Faster."

A dozen or was it two dozen more times he ran through the moves, each repetition faster than the last. His legs started to wobble, and his sword arm was dipping again on the thrusts.

Finally, Arthengal called a halt to the practice.

"Form is most important. If you find you are too tired to maintain proper form, then you must stop. There is nothing more dangerous than practicing the styles incorrectly. Your body must learn to move without thought."

Darius nodded, gasping for breath. His legs felt like jelly.

"You did very well for your first day," Arthengal commented.

Darius felt a surge of pride.

They sheathed the blades and removed the belts. Arthengal took them back inside the cabin while Darius downed a few gulps of water.

"Now we run. You mustn't allow your muscles to stiffen or your flexibility will suffer. Come on." Arthengal set off at an easy, loping pace. He didn't seem tired in the least from the practice.

Run? I can barely walk. Darius started in a staggering run behind him, gasping for breath as they trotted along the edge of the lake.

The tree line stopped a few paces from the lake's edge, and the shore was heavily carpeted with rounded rocks. There were the typical granite and basalt rocks that Darius was familiar with, but others were strange and new. Some appeared to be glass and shimmered green and black and purple in the early afternoon sun. Others were rough and porous, covering a range of more muted colors from white to dark gray.

Darius tripped several times on the uneven terrain and almost went down once as he struggled to keep up with the man's steady jog. When they finally reached the far end of the lake, Arthengal called a stop and Darius collapsed to the ground.

"Stand. Keep moving," Arthengal urged and passed Darius a waterskin.

He drank greedily and walked slowly as he glanced around.

The ground sloped gently away from the lake here and Darius saw rows and rows of tall plants. The plants had broad leaves with seven petals fanning out like a large hand. He had seen the fields from afar when they had first entered the valley, but up close, the fields seemed to stretch endlessly. Each plant was taller than Arthengal, and the rows extended away from them, obscuring the walls of the valley.

"You said this is hemp?" Darius asked, still trying to catch his breath.

Arthengal nodded and turned to the fields at the question.

"Yes. I make ropes and cables to trade with ships' captains at Eridu and nets to trade with the fishermen there. Do you know the city?"

Darius nodded slightly. "It is south, a little more than a week, walking, from my village. Traders would come north to trade cloth and spices for our wool and some of Marku's work. Marku had a good reputation as a blacksmith and was said to do better work than anyone in Eridu. Sometimes they would also bring nets to trade; our fishermen always needed good nets. I guess I never thought of where the nets came from. Maybe some of them were yours?"

Arthengal shrugged. "Quite possible. This is the only thing I use for trade, and it allows me to get supplies that the valley doesn't provide. It grows very well in the volcanic soil of the valley." He laughed and swept his arm out at the endless fields. "Once we harvest, we will spend the winter making rope and nets. You will help me, of course, and I'll pay you a fair apprentice's wage. It is always good to know a craft. Then, in the spring, you can go with me to Eridu."

Arthengal examined the tall stalks of the plants. "They are ready. We should start harvesting tomorrow after your training. I will cut. You can bundle," he said with a smile. "The work will keep your muscles loose."

"Come on." Arthengal clapped Darius on the shoulder. "You've worked hard today. Let me introduce you to one of my favorite things about the valley."

He led Darius down a well-used trail to the lake. There was a pool dug into the bank. It was four or five paces wide and twice that in length. Smoothed stones decorated the edge of the pool, secured with some sort of mortar. The pool was dark green and, unlike most of the lake, was very opaque. Darius could see that the stones extended below the surface but could not tell how deep the pool was.

Thirty paces out in the lake, Darius could see the water bubbling furiously. Steam rose from the surface of the lake, and every so often, a spout would gush from the turbulent surface to nearly the height of a man.

"That," Arthengal pointed, "is one of the volcanic jets that I told you about. Don't stray too far into the lake here. The temperature near the geyser would boil you alive. But here," he waved his hand proudly across the pool, "the temperature is perfect. Just hot enough for bathing and the minerals in the water ease sore muscles like nothing else."

Arthengal began stripping off his clothes and folding them neatly on the bank. He stepped into the pool, Darius saw now that it was chest deep, and walked across to the center.

Arthengal reached the far edge and settled with a deep sigh on some sort of abutment, invisible below the murky surface. Ripples lapped just below his shoulders as he settled his head on the stoned bank.

Darius removed his clothes and dipped a toe in the pool. It was hot but not too hot. He stepped in gingerly and found that the stones lined the bottom of the bath as well as the walls. The blisters on his feet had healed from Arthengal's medicines, but the water in the pool made the old sores tingle again. It was a warm, soothing sensation.

"There is another bench there." Arthengal pointed to the side opposite the lake then settled his head back and closed his eyes.

Darius felt along the wall until he felt a broad flat stone jutting out from its surface. He sat down and let the hot water wash over him. He had to sit tall to prevent his mouth and nose from slipping below the surface. Fatigue left his muscles, as if by magic, the longer he relaxed in the pool.

"Nice, isn't it?" Arthengal said, looking at Darius through a cracked eye.

"Very," the boy said.

"Best bath in the nine realms," Arthengal said with a sigh and closed the eye.

Chapter Ten
Unwelcome Visitor

Arthengal's hands rested atop a long wooden staff as he watched Darius practice. His long, black hair had been pulled back and tied with a leather thong. The grey streaking his temples contrasted with his dark skin. He wore a leather jerkin without sleeves, and his biceps bulged as he leaned against the quarterstaff.

The steel weapons had been replaced with practice swords after the first day. They were made from solid oak and had lead bands secured at key points to make the weight feel similar to the real thing. Sweat glistened on Darius's bare chest as he completed a thrust.

"Elbow up," Arthengal admonished.

The quarterstaff flicked up and caught Darius on the underside of the arm. Darius winced at the bruise forming there and then raised his arm a little higher.

Since the first day, Arthengal had used the staff to help *remind* Darius of proper placement in the forms. After two weeks of the same, his body was a patchwork of bruises. It was effective, though. He rarely made the same mistake more than once or twice.

Each morning, he had used Lazy Viper as his first exercise to stretch out tight joints and sore muscles. He could flow through the form a dozen times without any comment from the old man. Following the warm-up, Arthengal would always show him a new form. So far, he had learned Wary Badger, Mongoose Staring, Willows in Wind, and Rose at Sunset.

The stick came down on Darius's foot, hard, catching him by surprise.

"It's called *Dancing* Lights. That implies quick and light movements. My ninety-year-old mother's steps would be more spry than that, and she's been dead for twenty years."

Darius repeated the form, staying on his toes and moving his feet in short, quick bursts.

"Better." Arthengal nodded with approval. "No one's going to invite you to a ball, but you might not embarrass yourself at the tavern in Eridu. Keep at it."

"All of these forms seem similar," Darius commented as he jumped to the right, blocked left, and dropped into a low crouch before springing back to guard stance, raising the blade parallel to his body until it was higher than his head.

"In what way?" Arthengal asked with a hint of a smirk.

"They all seem to be comprised of blocks, dodges, and lunges that would drive the opponent away; unless he was stupid enough to take the blade in the belly."

"Very good observation. They are all defensive forms. I want to teach you how to keep yourself from getting killed before I show you any attack forms. Why don't we call it for today? Your endurance is getting better, and I think after today we can have more focused one- or two-hour sessions instead of pushing your body to the point of collapse."

Darius leaned the oak sword against the cabin and wiped his face and chest dry with a linen cloth and glanced up at the sky. The sun was at its peak.

"Are we going to eat first or head to the field?"

"We'll eat when we get there. It's never fun running on a full stomach."

Darius pulled an old work shirt over his head. Arthengal had found it in the bottom of his footlocker. It was yellowed and torn in a couple of places and hung on Darius like a tent, but it was better than ruining his only shirt working every day. He rolled the sleeves up to the elbow and tied a thin rope around the waist. It looked more like a dress on him than a shirt. Thankfully, the other boys from home weren't here to make fun of him. He cringed at the thought. Actually, it would have been better if they were here, for them. He shuddered to think of their actual fate.

Darius scooped up a couple bundles of rope and trotted to catch up with Arthengal who was already a good way up the trail moving at a steady jog.

When he arrived at the field, Arthengal was swinging a scythe to chop the tall plants off at the base. Darius inspected the field. They had made good progress, a dozen or more bundles a day since they had started, but the field seemed to stretch on forever. It would be a month or more before they finished.

Arthengal stacked six hemp stalks together in a pile and then returned to chopping. Darius loosened the bunch of ropes and shook three lengths free from the rest. He reached underneath the heap and pulled the cord through from the other side. He wound it around the plants several times, pulling the stack tighter with each loop before finally tying it off. He repeated the process with the other two ropes and by the time he was done, Arthengal had another bunch ready to go.

"That's it. I'm so hungry I could eat the backside of a skunk and come back for seconds," Arthengal called after four bales were ready.

Darius sank to the ground and laid flat. The muscles in his shoulders and back sang with relief as he stretched his arms as far as he could over his head. Arthengal tossed a small package beside him. He attacked the contents of the package with a vengeance. The lunch of apples, dried meat, and corn bread made him warm and a little sleepy. He stretched out again while he waited for Arthengal to finish his meal.

"Up and at 'em, these bales won't haul themselves." The man was hefting one of the bundles onto each shoulder.

Darius climbed to his feet and followed. They hiked to the house to deposit their loads on the ever-growing mass piled behind the cabin. By their fourth trip, the sun was settling low over the mountain peaks casting a pink glow over the brilliant snowcaps.

"That should do it for today, I think," Arthengal announced as he pressed his palms to the small of his back and extended his chest. "If it weren't so far back to the bath, I could do for a nice soak. I guess a warm fire and some potato soup will have to do."

The next morning, Darius woke and went outside to splash water in his face from the lake. He glanced up and paused. The day before only the permanent glaciers at the peaks of the mountain had shown white. This morning the snow came halfway down the tall cliffs that surrounded the crater. While a bit cooler, the air where he stood still felt comfortably warm. He shook his head, trying to reconcile what his eyes saw with what his body felt.

"The valley remains temperate throughout the winter," Arthengal commented from behind Darius. "In the surrounding mountains, snow will get deep, but we will see very little here. The lake and the heated sulfur pools keep the air inside the valley too warm for snow most of the time. I don't understand it myself, I only know it is so."

"That's pretty amazing," Darius said.

"That's the upside," Arthengal said. "The downside is once the snow gets heavy, we're pretty much stuck here. Not much chance in surviving a hike out of these mountains in the winter. Anyway, breakfast is ready."

Arthengal was dragging two large plants toward Darius when suddenly he stopped in mid-stride. He was staring across the lake toward the hidden entrance to the valley. Darius followed his gaze and saw a red flag flapping in the wind high above where the trail wound into the crater. The brilliant color of the flag stood out in stark contrast against the white peaks and deep gray sky.

Suddenly a second flag went up. Arthengal dropped his load and started running toward the cabin. Darius followed, not understanding the urgency but not having time to ask questions. They paused at the cabin only long enough to retrieve their swords. Two more flags had raised by then but nothing more.

"What is it?" Darius asked in a gasp during the quick break.

"The traps are sprung," was the only explanation the man provided before hurrying off in the direction of the trail.

With alarm, Darius hurried after him, struggling to keep up. He caught up to the man when he finally stopped to crouch at the entrance of the chasm that led to the foot of the trail. He was listening. The air was still, and a gentle wind whistled low out of the mouth of the chasm.

A sudden mighty roar broke the silence. It sounded to Darius like the bellow of a dragon or some other mythical beast. He felt his stomach tighten and bile rise slowly in his throat.

Arthengal crept forward slowly, entering the breach. His eyes scanned stretches of the trail as it came into view. Nothing moved on the winding path.

The bellow came again, echoing through the canyon. They were able to pinpoint the sound this time. It came from the mouth of the canyon at the top of the trail.

The two started the climb slowly, stepping carefully over tripwires that would trigger the traps along the path. As they reached the top, Arthengal stopped and let out a low whistle.

Darius stared in disbelief. A mass of fur and a tangle of ropes strained against the binds of the final man trap. The weighted nets hovered only slightly above the trail as the massive creature clawed at the ground trying to gain purchase to tear away. The remnants of the three previous traps trailed behind and added to the tangle. Darius continued to stare as the dark snout turned to him. One fierce brown eye and one ruined eye socket stared at him defiantly.

The bear sniffed the air and, catching Darius's scent, roared again and strained heavily against the cables, his energy renewed at the sight of his quarry. Darius saw the ropes stretch taut.

Arthengal's body relaxed slightly now that he knew the nature of the danger.

"It would seem that he is seriously upset at you," he quipped at Darius. "I mean, I would be upset if you took my eye, but I can't say that I would spend as much time as he has tracking you down to even the score."

Darius trembled as the animal continued to lunge in vain. Arthengal fingered the pommel of his weapon.

"I would have to say this is your problem to resolve." He tapped the hilt of his own sword and gave Darius a meaningful glance.

It took him a minute to understand the man's meaning.

"You want me to kill it?"

"Finish what you started, I always say," Arthengal said seriously.

Darius gulped and looked at the bear. He drew his sword shakily. He advanced slowly on the creature, holding the blade in front of him. His arm quivered, but his grip remained sure. The dark brown eye watched him as he approached, and the beast snorted in defiance.

Darius extended the tip of the sword through the tangled ropes and held it inches from the bear's thick neck. A low, deep growl rumbled in the creature's chest, and it leaned forward with a look of pure insolence as if daring him to do his worst.

The point of the blade dimpled the thick flesh at the base of the monster's throat. Darius cocked his head to one side, studying the beast. The eye showed intelligence and anger. Frothy spittle seeped out from the edges of tightly clenched lips. It snarled and curled back fat lips to reveal vicious teeth.

Darius lowered the weapon. Something like curiosity crossed the bear's eye, replacing, only for an instant, the hateful gaze. They stared at each other for several long moments before Darius made a decision.

"I am probably going to regret this."

He raised the sword high above his head and swept the blade down evenly. The bear braced for the blow, and then definite surprise crossed its face when the tension slackened.

Darius heard the soft sound of Arthengal's sword clearing its scabbard. He continued to hold the bear's gaze as he raised the sword again and severed the second thick rope.

The tangle of ropes still covered the behemoth, but his front paws dropped heavily to the ground, no longer held by the trap.

Darius lowered the point of the blade, holding it in a low defensive position. He didn't break eye contact with the creature as it shook its body mightily. Strands of rope fell away as it lifted each paw, shaking it free from the tangle.

The massive creature leaned forward slowly, its chest leaning over the extended sword arm. His muzzle hovered inches from Darius's face. Darius resisted the urge to blink as the bear snorted again and a blast of warm air and mucus showered his face. The bear studied him for a second in doubt. Anger seethed in the one good eye as it opened its mighty jaws and roared.

The sound was deafening, and Darius was sure the creature could have engulfed his entire head in the gaping jaws. He stood his ground even though his insides churned. Saliva dripped from Darius's ear as the animal settled back again.

With a final snort, the creature spun on its haunches and loped toward the entrance of the canyon, deftly avoiding the hidden pits. Darius didn't move until the creature was gone and then his knees buckled. He dropped heavily. His knuckles, still clenching the blade, dug painfully into the dirt path.

Another low whistle sounded behind him.

"Well, I never," Arthengal said under his breath as he came forward to help Darius to his feet.

Darius stood but then stumbled toward the canyon wall and doubled over. He emptied the contents of his stomach.

"So, I guess you're even," the man said a few minutes later, looking after the bear, as Darius stood and wiped the back of his hand across his mouth.

"We'll have to fix the traps, of course." His eyes examined the tattered mess of ropes.

Darius just looked at the man in amazement. How could he be so casual? This caused the man to laugh out loud. He clapped the boy on the shoulder.

"Come on. I think you just earned yourself the rest of the day off," he chuckled as he led the boy back down the trail.

Winter - 30 A.E.

Chapter Eleven
Story of the Fishing Pole

Darius finished wrapping some cornbread cakes left over from dinner in a white linen cloth and stacked it neatly on the counter. He put the stopper in the jug of apple cider and stored it next to the bread. Life here in the valley had grown comfortable in the preceding months and lessened his sense of loss. Still, he focused on his goal.

Darius practiced hard every day. The more quickly he learned, the sooner they would be able to rescue his mother. He would have practiced all the time, if that were possible, but he knew it wasn't. His heart ached when he thought about his mother and how slowly his training was progressing.

The work in the fields and other responsibilities around the valley had helped. It allowed him to focus on tasks and kept him from dwelling on what he couldn't change. The constant labor was also changing his body. His once skinny arms and legs were filling out. His borrowed clothing, while still too long, fit better as his shoulders and hips broadened.

Arthengal leaned his head in the doorway. "When you're done there come on out. Tonight we need to begin stripping these stalks down for yarn."

Darius wiped his hands and walked outside. Arthengal had placed two large rounds of pine on their ends to act as stools. A round wooden pole about waist high had been driven into the ground in front of each, and a large pile of hemp stalks was set between the two seats. He peered behind Arthengal and winced as he saw the extent of the task before them. They had spent the past week spreading out the bundles of hemp to dry. The carpet of hemp stretched as far as he could see, disappearing into the trees.

Arthengal sat on one of the makeshift chairs and picked up one of the dried hemp plants.

Darius sat down and watched.

"Okay, first strip off the smaller branches and leaves until you have the main stalk," Arthengal said as he demonstrated. "You can pile the refuse over to the side. We'll strip the leaves off later to make compost to fertilize the fields and the garden behind the cabin.

"Once you have a clean stalk, bend it back and forth like so to break the wood beneath." Darius watched as Arthengal worked his way down the stalk, flexing it with his hands. Darius could hear the crunch of the fibers as they broke. "Then, starting at the base, peel the fibers up. Be careful not to let it break."

Arthengal demonstrated half a dozen more times until he had a thumb-thick pile of fibers.

"Now, take your bundle all together and loop it around your rod. Pull tightly and twist the threads together until they start to kink, then weave the two cords together until it's tight and tie the end off. Pull the other end off the stake, tie it, and presto! You have made a length of yarn. Do you think you can do that?"

Darius nodded.

"I'll go grab some baskets to store the yarn. Once we've converted all of the plants, I'll show you how to make ropes and cables. It's pretty much the same process, although we may need to use tools for the thicker cables to get them tight enough."

He returned with two baskets and a long metal rod. A bar of metal bent into a half-circle was mounted on each end of the pole. Each curved bar was about as long as Darius's forearm.

"You know how long a span is, right?" Arthengal asked, demonstrating the length between his extended thumb and little finger.

"Of course," Darius said. "We measured most things in spans and paces at home."

"Good," Arthengal nodded.

"Well this," he held out the iron shaft, "is a *rod*. It measures a little more than twenty spans. We will use this to measure the cables once we are done. Each coil will be *cable length,* which is forty-four rods. The rails here will keep the rope contained while we wind it. I'll show you once we get to that stage."

The days that followed were much the same as they had been during the harvest. Instead of stopping at the fields after their run, however, they would turn back to the cabin and spend the afternoon making twine. Darius's hands became hard and developed thick calluses both from practice and the work of making rope.

Sometime around mid-winter, Darius had mastered four of the defensive sword forms, and Arthengal began including offensive techniques in the new lessons. He learned Searching the Sea, Striking Adder, The Dragon Whips His Tail, and a style that Arthengal said he had developed called Fashionably Late. He chuckled at the name, but Darius clearly didn't understand the hidden joke.

"Spend many days at court and you will understand," was all the explanation that he gave.

The movements were elegant and smooth with all the appearances of a defensive posture until the end when, without warning, it delivered two quick ripostes, a low driving slash to the inner thigh, a dancing series of diversionary sweeps, and a deep lunge to the heart.

Arthengal returned to the cave with his weapons cache and retrieved an elm bow and several wax-covered strings. Arthengal further switched up Darius's training regimen to include bow work so his skills would not diminish. The bow was not as finely crafted as Arthengal's oddly curved bow, but it was still better than the one he had brought from home. They began with stationary targets but soon moved on to practice with moving targets. Arthengal crafted several plate-sized targets from spare leather bound with green branches. He would toss the discs into the air and Darius would practice shooting them down.

The work and training were hard but invigorating, and Arthengal would keep Darius entertained with stories of his many adventures from his youth.

"So, there I was, surrounded by seven Mortikai warriors. All of us were drenched with rice wine from the ruptured cask. The leader of the band scowled at me. Not only was he angry at his ruined dinner and that I had drenched his crew, but he was furious that I had shamed him in his home tavern and that the proprietor had ordered us out into the street and forbade us from ever returning." Arthengal stood in a defensive stance as if facing his foes anew.

Darius tied off the length of rope he had been winding and trimmed off the excess yarn. He grabbed three more lengths of yarn out of the nearby basket while Arthengal continued with the story.

"His long, curved saber gleamed in the moonlight. I held my blade, ready to defend. Now, mind you, it wasn't like the nice blades I have now. This was my first sword. It was a plain, unadorned blade crafted by the local smith back home. It was a fine blade and it held an edge well, but it wasn't the same quality of steel as a Mortikai saber. I was sure he could have broken it with a few strong, direct blows. I was going to have to be crafty and stay on the defensive.

"The others formed a ring around us. We circled each other,

him looking for an opportunity to attack, me waiting to defend. Each time he would slash or lunge, I managed to block the attack or dance away. We were creating quite a spectacle. Little by little, a crowd gathered as word spread of the illegal duel.

"I could see the young man with the queerly embroidered robes watching us intently from near the alehouse door. A bruise was darkening on his cheek from where the Mortikai leader had backhanded him. Had I not come to his defense, he surely would have been beaten senseless. His companions huddled close behind him, also watching the fight with unveiled curiosity.

"The warrior lunged again. I blocked and countered with a quick upward slash. I had only meant to drive him back, but his momentum carried him too close to my blade and a long gash opened on his cheek. It was pure luck, but I had scored first blood, a serious honor amongst the Mortikai. Or rather dishonor, in his case. Enraged, he charged me, trying to tackle me to the ground. I danced away and brought my pommel down between his shoulder blades. He was already off balance, and this caused him to fall, sprawling in the dirt."

Arthengal danced as he replayed the scene.

Darius's hands worked from memory as he listened, entranced by the story.

"He stood, his bright red tunic now streaked with mud from the combination of rice wine and dirt. His anger grew, and he became more reckless. He came at me with a series of violent, hacking swings. I blocked and dodged. Then as one swing passed, barely missing my nose, I circled left and got inside his guard. I thrust quickly up and then danced away. I felt the pressure from the strike, so I knew I had hit him but didn't know where yet.

"I remained on guard as he turned. His arm hung limply and his grip on the hilt was loose. He struggled to lift the blade, but it only quivered. Then I saw the stain of blood expanding across his right side below his shoulder. I had severed something, and his sword arm was useless. He switched the blade to his left hand and tried to recover.

"He was just getting ready to come at me again when a booming shout disrupted the whole affair. 'That is quite enough!'" Arthengal mimicked a gruff voice.

"The magistrate shouldered his way into the circle with eight city guards clad in banded armor. While the Mortikai were fierce warriors to be sure and were a well-respected sect in the army, they were still subject to local law when inside the city walls, same as the rest of us. They all bowed their heads respectfully, and the leader dropped his weapon and took a knee. I followed in kind and quickly returned my sword to its scabbard and stood quietly, my eyes inspecting a scuff on my leather boots."

"Oh, no," Darius blurted. "Did you get arrested?"

"I'll get there," Arthengal smiled. "Anyway, the magistrate was furious. I glanced up out of the corner of my eye and saw that his face was all puffy and red. A cloth napkin was still tucked into the front of his shirt. 'Someone explain the meaning of this,' he blustered. Only then did he notice the napkin and snatched it away from his shirt. His face grew redder with embarrassment.

"But, by the command, I could tell he expected an answer. I stole a glance at the others, and when it seemed that none of them were going to respond, I opened my mouth to speak. Before I could utter a word, the young man in the embroidered robes entered the circle and, with the thick accent of the eastern islanders, said, 'Sir, if I may. This is an unfortunate misunderstanding which has gotten out of hand. I am a visitor, here on a mission of diplomacy and trade. My companions and I only stopped here for a brief meal before continuing to the capital. In my clumsiness, I shamed this most honored warrior.'" Arthengal's voice was lighter and lilting in what Darius assumed was the accent he had described.

"The little diplomat pointed to the injured leader of the Mortikai. And by shamed, you will remember, that he bumped the table and overturned a near boiling bowl of noodle soup on the soldier's lap." Arthengal laughed again at the memory.

"Anyway, he continued to explain how the dishonored warrior had stricken him, not knowing his station, and that the 'westerner', that was me, came to his aid, obviously recognizing his garments as belonging to the house of the emperor."

Arthengal paused and looked at Darius meaningfully. "I had no idea who the little guy was. I just didn't want to see him brutalized. I also still think it hilarious that he referred to me as a westerner as if I had come across the ocean from some mysterious other land. We were all part of the same empire, but the provinces of the east always treated those of us from the western provinces as bumpkins or foreigners."

"Wait, did you say the house of the emperor?" Darius asked.

"Yes, I'll get to that in a minute," Arthengal responded, waving away the question.

"So anyway, the magistrate did recognize the embroidered symbols on the emissary's robes and immediately took on a different tone. He said, 'I apologize sincerely for the actions of these men. They will be dealt with assuredly. Please carry on with your business and convey our best wishes to the palace.' With that, the guards gathered up the Mortikai warriors and began escorting them toward the stockades. A nod from the diplomat caused the guards and magistrate to leave me be. After the crowd cleared, the emissary approached me.

"He introduced himself. 'I am Prince Lao Cang Yu--'"

"What!" Darius exclaimed, incredulous. "A prince? What was a prince doing in a common tavern?"

"Believe me, I was as shocked as you are," Arthengal said. "So he says, 'I am Prince Lao Cang Yu. I am here on my father's behalf to visit my cousin, the Holy Emperor Chen Bao Mu, to lobby for his good grace on the peoples of my province to lower taxes and increase trade with the capital. I severely underestimated the incivility of the locals and was overconfident in recognition of my station.'"

Darius laughed. "So, he just thought that people would recognize him as a prince just because he was wearing fancy clothes?"

"They were nice robes," Arthengal admitted. "And they were clearly decorated with the symbols of royalty. We should have probably recognized them, but like you asked, why would a prince be in a public house? The Mortikai probably thought him an over-pompous minor lord that needed to be taught a lesson.

"Anyway, he tells me, 'I would greatly appreciate it if you would accompany me on the rest of my journey to act as escort.' I was dumbfounded. Here I was, just a kid really, off to explore the country for a year before joining military service, all of a sudden being asked to escort a prince to the capital. Of course I agreed.

"The rest of the journey was without incident, but over the course of the next six weeks, Cang and I formed a deep friendship. He was kind and respectful with the best interests of his people in mind. Quite the opposite of his cousin, Chen Bai Jian, who would rise to power a few years later.

"We had a lot more in common than I would have thought of the imperial family. He loved the outdoors, which was one of the reasons he had decided to travel as he did, and he loved to fish. He said that 'There is no greater joy than to stand beneath the clear blue heavens surrounded by the music of the river god and to be blessed with his bounty.' And I completely agree with him.

"When we finished the journey, he thanked me for my service and awarded me with his personal fishing pole. And that is the story of how I got my fishing pole. I should also give credit that even from the farthest eastern province, Lao Cang Yu's favor and influence helped to shape my future and my career. I was awarded a commission rather than serving in the infantry and rose quickly through the ranks. He helped me later, too, when I fell out of grace with the Emperor Chen Bai Jian.

"I was very sorry, indeed, when I heard that his cousin had had him executed for treason for speaking out publicly against the emperor's treatment of his people." Arthengal said this last with a clear tone of bitterness in his voice.

"But then many good people died in that war for little less. Those were dark days that ended the rule of a cruel tyrant. I like to think the life of the people has improved since then and that Prince Lao did not die in vain. But I guess I really wouldn't know. I've been here most of the past twenty years and have little contact outside of Eridu. My friends there always seem to be content, but Shalanum is far from the center of the old empire. Not much news reaches us 'westerners'," he chuckled.

Darius shook his head in awe. "I can't imagine meeting a real prince," he said. "My mother told us stories of the grand cities, like Kasha Marka and Kasha Esharra."

"Kasha Marka is a remarkable sight," Arthengal agreed. "The Imperial City was once, but Kasha Esharra is abandoned now and has fallen to ruin as far as I know."

"And she told us stories of the heroes of old like Jasmarana, Orlin Malamay, Sadko Novgordov, and Nasu Rabi."

Arthengal burst out laughing and then recovered when he saw the hurt look on Darius's face.

"I'm sorry, I'm not laughing at you." He changed the subject. "You know I met Orlin Malamay once."

"You met him?" Darius's angst was replaced by wonder.

"Yes, he had a brilliant mind and was a skilled tactician." He glanced up at the darkening sky. "But that is a tale for another day. Let's clean up here. There might still be time for a bath before it's full dark."

Darius smirked. The man did love his baths.

Chapter Twelve
Winter's Bitter Chill

Cordelia set the cloth down and blew on her hands. Her fingers grew numb so quickly it was hard to sew for more than a few minutes at a time. The small adobe structure protected her from the winds that buffeted the valley, but the small fire in the center of the shelter barely kept the temperature inside tolerable.

They had finished planting the beans and peas that would keep the fields covered through the winter more than a month ago. Since then, most of the men had been mixing mud and grass to patch the hovels that they all lived in while the women sewed clothing more suitable for the colder months.

A blast of cold air made Cordelia shiver as Dacia pulled aside the leather tarp and entered the one-room building. She dropped a bundle of rabbit and fox hides on the floor next to Cordelia and then pulled a makeshift stool closer to the fire.

"They brought in a group from one of the other farms, about fifty by the look of it," Dacia said as she selected one of the cloth jackets Cordelia had sewn and began stitching the fur into the lining.

"Really? Why? We have more than these huts will hold as it

is."

Dacia shrugged. "Apparently there was a fire. Took out most of the farm and half the workers. They're settling them here rather than trying to rebuild. It's mostly women. I guess all but a few of the men died fighting the fire. That's what chivalry will get you."

"They can put some of them in Alena's cabin," Cordelia said. "They let the fire die last night, and the whole lot of them froze to death."

"Stupid girl. I always said she shouldn't have been a lodge leader," Dacia scoffed. "I don't know why Minah picked her. Even with the open hut we'll still need to take in another lodger. Do you want me to pick or do you want to do the honors?"

"I'll go," Cordelia said. "I need to stretch my legs anyway."

She pulled on one of the completed coats and ducked out into the cold. The wind took her breath away, and she clutched the hood of the jacket more tightly around her face.

Across the snow-covered fields, she could see the mass of women huddling under the guard of half a dozen reluctant soldiers. Several other lodge leaders were already plodding through the snow in their direction.

Cordelia surveyed the group as she approached. They didn't look much different than the rest of them, haggard, hungry, and cold. She saw a flash of movement in the center of the group as a small woman repositioned herself to block the wind. No, not a woman, a child! Cordelia glanced frantically at the guards but they hadn't noticed. How had a child survived this long? How had a child even gotten past the selection process?

Cordelia pushed her way through the group of women and kneeled in front of the girl.

The small face looked up at her, and fear was evident in her eyes. The girl looked like she was eight or nine years old.

"Oh, sweetie. What are you doing here?"

The girl didn't answer.

"What's your name?" Cordelia asked.

The girl still didn't answer.

"They call her Lianna," one of the other women whispered in response. "We do our best to keep her out of trouble. The foreman at the last farm didn't care as long as she worked."

Cordelia glanced at the guards again, but they were engaged in their own conversations, paying little attention to the captives.

"You," Cordelia pointed to the woman who had spoken. "Select five others and come with me. There is a vacant cabin that you can use."

Cordelia spotted the matriarch of their farm surveying a group of women nearby.

"Minah," she called. "I'm giving Alena's lodge to..." She looked at the woman, the obvious question hanging in the cold air.

"Frayda," the woman answered.

"...to Frayda here."

Minah nodded and continued her inspection.

"Come on." Cordelia wrapped her arm around Lianna. "Let's get you out of here."

She shuffled the girl out of the circle in the direction of the huts, hiding her from view between the other women.

Chapter Thirteen
Hunting Trip

Darius hugged one of Arthengal's thick wool cloaks around him. The morning chill had lingered well beyond breakfast. A hard winter wore on outside, but here in the valley, they had escaped the worst. An occasional morning saw a dusting of snow in the trees, but more often than not, the snow had melted by midday. Nighttime frosts were frequent, however, which did prevent them from planting any fresh vegetables.

Arthengal scratched his silver beard and mumbled again as he examined what remained of their dried meat and fish. He had already checked the barrels in the cellar twice, and every pot on the shelves was empty and had been cleaned to be refilled once spring arrived.

"If I had known you were going to eat so much, I would have packed in more stores," Arthengal chided with a wink.

Darius stammered and blushed. The truth was they had eaten well over the winter. Darius felt a pang of guilt at his good fortune and wondered how his mother was surviving the harsh conditions to the north.

"Come on. There's still too much snow in the mountains to make it to Eridu." He slapped the boy's shoulder as he turned. "We will have to go on a hunt."

"It's the middle of winter. There can't be any game in the mountains," Darius protested.

"I know of a valley nearby where a herd of elk winter. We should be able to find something there, with a bit of luck."

"You had mentioned that when we stayed the night at your cave," Darius replied.

"Ah, right. It's much closer to the cave so we can dress the game there. We shouldn't be gone for much more than a week or so."

They left the cellar and returned to the cabin. Darius brushed aside the thick hide curtain that had been hung over the doorway to keep the chill out. The window had been similarly covered, which made the interior of the cabin dim. The only light was from a pair of oil lamps that sputtered and filled the air with an acrid scent most of the day.

Darius wrinkled his nose as he entered and his eyes began to itch. He couldn't wait until the day warmed enough that they could tie up the blinds to air out the room.

Arthengal stuffed two packs with provisions and tied a tightly rolled wool blanket atop each. "Hold on," he said.

The gust of air as he left the cabin was refreshing and relieved some of the irritation in Darius's eyes.

When Arthengal returned, he held two thick fur coats and

four very odd-looking contraptions. Each one was formed from a length of wood as thick as a man's thumb, bent in the shape of an egg. It was as wide as Darius's forearm was long at the top and half that width on the bottom. Flat leather straps crisscrossed throughout the interior of the thing, and a flat leather patch the size of a man's foot had been affixed to the center. Buckled straps hung from each end of the leather pad.

Arthengal tied a pair of the devices to each pack.

"What are those things?" Darius asked.

"They will help us walk on the snow if it becomes too deep. Come on. If we leave now we can camp at the top of the canyon. From there, it will be at least a day's hike to the cave. We can retrieve our other bows there before we hunt."

Darius had all but forgotten about his bow, left behind in their frantic escape from the cave.

"To be honest, I like the one I've been practicing with better," he said.

"Suit yourself. I prefer my horse bow. Here, put this on."

Darius shrugged out of the cloak to don the proffered coat. It extended to his knees, and his shoulders sank under its weight. He had to roll up the sleeves, no easy task, to free his hands.

Arthengal tossed him a pair of fur-lined gloves which he stuffed into the pockets of the coat. The bulk of the coat made it awkward to pull the pack onto his shoulders.

Darius sweated as they hiked across the valley floor but was grateful for the thick coat when they reached the top of the trail. He gasped at the bitterness of the wind that howled through the canyon. It kicked up flurries of snow the length of the narrow passage. Billowing gray clouds shrouded the sky in darkness and threatened more snow.

Well back from the mouth of the canyon, Arthengal discharged his pack and began preparing a fire. The blaze caught with some difficulty, and even once it was burning, its warmth was devoured by the chill a few steps from the stone circle.

"This is quite a change from below, isn't it?" Arthengal asked, struggling to keep his teeth from chattering.

Darius shivered in response and nodded his head as he inched closer to the crackling fire.

"This winter seems worse than most, but the valley does tend to spoil one from the hardships of the season," Arthengal grinned.

Darius untied the wool blanket from his pack with fingers growing more numb by the minute. He draped it around him and held his hands close to the fire. Soon, feeling returned to his fingers, and his body stopped shivering.

That night, they slept close together and as close to the fire as they dared. Darius buried himself in the warmth of the fleece. He was warm enough but would wake every few hours when Arthengal roused to feed additional fuel to the fire.

"It seems the gods are to favor the hunt," Arthengal exclaimed as he stood and stretched the next morning.

The wind had died down and the clouds had rolled away. The sky was a brilliant blue strip above them. The snow at the mouth of the canyon had drifted as high as Arthengal's shoulder.

"We're to have a bit of a scramble to get out of the canyon though, it seems," he said. "Here, let me show you how to put on the snowshoes."

Darius placed his feet as instructed and watched as Arthengal bound the straps and tightened the buckles. His heel was tight against a band to the rear of the pad, and a belt wrapped over the middle of his foot to secure the rest. He lifted each foot in turn to make sure the shoes weren't loose. Pulling on his gloves, he followed Arthengal up the powdery drift in a scramble.

As soon as he was up and out of the canyon, Darius surveyed a landscape covered in white. Stark, oblique ridges webbed away from the mountain toward the foothills in the distance. Thin pine trees, mere shots of green and brown in the sea of white, grew in irregular patches on the steep slopes. An ancient road, wide enough for two wagons to pass abreast, was carved into the side of the mountain and wound west.

Arthengal took a few minutes to show Darius how to walk with the snowshoes without falling before marching west. The instructions did little good. For the first hour, Darius plodded behind Arthengal inelegantly. Several times he tripped himself as he tangled the broad contraptions strapped to his feet. Each time he would pitch face first into the snow, Arthengal would help him right himself and then continue on.

After an hour, Darius was starting to get the hang of it and even when he stumbled was able to stop from toppling over. The travel was hard, even on the road, and their pace was slow. With each step, it seemed to Darius that the sun inched across the sky. By mid-afternoon, the road came to an abrupt end at a landslide.

"A tunnel used to be carved through the mountain, but it collapsed ages ago. We'll have to climb to the top of that ridge there and pick it up on the other side," Arthengal explained. "We'll have to take the shoes off to climb."

They pulled themselves up the slope using rocks and the trunks of stunted pines for leverage. Darius sank up to his knees with every step. Each stride made his legs ache as much as an hour of practicing sword forms.

When they crested the ridge, Darius was surprised by a wholly different landscape. The rough ridges had been smoothed and flattened. A large city, desolate and abandoned, stretched out before them. Most of the buildings had been ravaged by time, and for many, nothing remained but the remnants of stone foundations.

The road was wider beyond the ridge and branched out in several directions forming thoroughfares crisscrossing the once great city. Towering walls remained, guarding the entrance to the city from the south and west. The wooden gates had long since rotted and disappeared, but the road stretched out into the distance beyond them. On a flattened hill to the north, Darius saw a large stone fortress. The timbered roof had collapsed years before, as had one of the walls, but it still looked like it would provide good shelter.

The only building that seemed fully intact was a mill on the western edge of town. The great wheel was still and the stream that fed it looked frozen solid.

In the distance, beyond the city to the south, Darius could see a broad patch of green. The snow cut a jagged white line along the surrounding foothills marking a border between winter and spring. The millstream widened its banks, meandered toward the lowlands and joined with other mountain tributaries. A narrow ribbon of blue cut an irregular line across the green before disappearing between a pair of low hills to the south. It was too distant to see the herds of elk that Arthengal had promised would be there, but the sight of the valley offered him hope.

"The cave isn't far from here," Arthengal said, "but I'm afraid it would still be past dark by the time we reached it. We can camp here for the evening and make the final push in the morning."

"What was this place?" Darius asked.

"It was the city of Anbar Ur. It was a thriving mining city until a century ago. The gold and sapphires were processed here before being distributed south and east. It was abandoned soon after the mines were. The roads from here are well made and serviceable even after all this time. I keep my wagon in the fort there to shelter it from the worst of the winter weather."

"Wagon?"

"Of course. Did you think I hauled my nets and ropes sixty leagues to Eridu on my back?" Arthengal laughed.

"How do you pull the wagon?"

"Donkeys. They winter in the valley there." Arthengal pointed to the swath of green. "With the elk. They make their way up here when spring arrives. I keep them well fed and they are loyal. You can't see it now but after the snows are gone there is good grazing land just beyond the southern wall. We'll also plant oats and corn in a couple of fields there and use the mill to grind it to flour for us and feed for the donkeys."

The ridge below them was terraced for farming, and well-worn paths wound between them. Crumbling stone foundations marked what were once homes near each garden plot. Stone stairs had been cut into the slope at intervals adding to the maze of streets winding into the city proper. Arthengal moved through the warren with ease, taking the shortest path to the decrepit fortress.

The wagon was covered by a leather tarp in the corner of two of the solid walls and further protected from the elements by a stout lean-to. They set up camp near the wagon. The walls of the keep blocked the winter breeze, and as soon as Arthengal had started a fire, the space warmed tolerably despite the lack of a roof.

Darius felt much more rested when Arthengal woke him at first light. By mid-morning, they had reached the top of the cliff. Arthengal produced a climbing rope and they rappelled down, Darius clinging to his back. Inside the cave, Darius stored their supplies while Arthengal inspected his bow and replaced the string.

"Why do you use this for a hunting camp rather than the fort?" Darius asked.

"It's better protected. There are several packs of wolves in the surrounding hills drawn by the elk herds. Even though they have no problem hunting on their own, they also are not likely to pass up an easy meal after we've done the hard work. It will take us several days to dress out and dry the meat if we do kill something, and I'd rather not be fighting off wolves while we do. And, it's more comfortable. When I get the fires going to dry the meat, it will be like a sauna in here."

"What's a sauna?" Darius asked.

Arthengal laughed and shook his head. Darius thought he heard him mutter the word "bumpkin," but he wasn't sure.

"Sort out some supplies for tomorrow," Arthengal instructed. "You should find belt pouches in the corner over there. We'll set out each morning a few hours before dawn and try to be back here before dark. That should give us at least eight hours of hunting each day."

"How long does it take to get down there?" Darius asked.

"The first trip will take the longest, but as long as it doesn't snow anymore it shouldn't take more than a couple hours once we get a good trail packed. Keep the quivers light, too. Half a dozen arrows each, at most. If we need more than that, then we have no right calling ourselves hunters." Arthengal smiled.

The sun's full breadth hovered above the horizon as they entered the basin the next day. The temperature had risen steadily as they descended, and they had shed their coats and gloves more than an hour before. Beyond the green of the ankle-deep grasses, the vale was alive with early signs of spring. Vast orchards of apple trees covered the expanse, their stark branches starting to come alive with the pink and white of early blossoms. Fields of crocus and daffodils erupted all around them.

Arthengal knelt beside the river where they had stopped to refill their water bags. He ran his fingers over the soil and pointed out several split-hoofed prints in the mud.

"They are nearby. Many of these prints are from just this morning. This way, I think," Arthengal said, pointing south.

They moved on cats' paws through the trees and settled into a crouching walk as they approached a nearby rise. Arthengal motioned him even lower, and they crept on elbows and knees to the crest of the hill. From their vantage they could see a wide field. The pasture, encircled by the orchards, was at least a thousand paces across. A light fog shrouded the grass, hiding daisies and dandelions from view. On the far side, well out of bowshot, Darius could make out a dozen or more dark brown forms.

"We will need to circle around," Arthengal whispered.

They would edge over to the field every so often to check on the status of the herd. The elk seemed unconcerned by anything other than constant grazing. The trees around them, by contrast, had come alive with sound. Birds sang in the branches and squirrels skittered about on their quest for food. Darius even heard the braying of a donkey in the distance. They were close enough now to see the herd in detail: six to eight cows, half a dozen yearlings, and a truly magnificent bull. The beast's rack of antlers extended behind him past his shoulders.

It took about an hour to find a secluded spot within range. Birds fluttered around the glade gathering debris for nests. The ankle-deep haze that had covered the field had burned off and the green carpet was dappled in white and yellow.

Darius noticed none of it. He could not take his eyes off of the bull. His mouth all but watered at the thought of fresh venison for dinner. With a careful grace, he eased an arrow from his quiver and nocked it. He drew the string back, visualizing his target. He let his breath out slowly.

Too late, Arthengal recognized Darius's target.

"No!" he shouted as Darius released the arrow.

As one, the herd jerked their heads up and turned to run, but it was too late for the bull. As it turned, the arrow sank up to the fletching in its side just behind the shoulder. It took a faltering leap then tripped and fell, turning up furrows of deep brown earth as its massive antlers plowed into the ground.

Arthengal sighed in frustration.

Darius was surprised by his dismay. "What did I do wrong? I

got him."

"Yes, you did." Arthengal sighed again.

"What's wrong, then?"

Arthengal looked at the boy. Then in a patient voice he explained. "I'm sorry, I forgot that this was your first hunt. I should have explained things better before we left. Never take the leader of a herd. That is where the herd's strength lies. He provides strong bloodlines and is the guardian of the herd. Always take a cow or a yearling. This herd will be vulnerable now to predators and will no longer produce strong offspring. Also, he is much too large for us to transport. We will need to section the carcass and carry each section to the cave. We might get two sections before the scavengers move in, and after that the rest of the meat will be lost."

"I'm sorry, I didn't know." Darius's voice was sullen.

"I know," Arthengal said gently, and rustled his hair. "Now you do. You won't make the same mistake again."

Darius shook his head, looking at the ground. He could not bring himself to meet Arthengal's eyes. He was crestfallen, and his heart ached with having disappointed Arthengal. He had so wanted to make the man proud.

"Come on. Our work is just beginning." Arthengal gave him a charitable smile and clapped him on the back. He shouldered his bow and strode into the field toward the elk.

"It was an excellent shot, by the way," Arthengal called over his shoulder.

Darius followed after him, revived a little by the praise. Arthengal removed a long knife, a bone saw, and a small hatchet from his pack and they spent the next hour dividing the carcass into sections that they could carry.

Arthengal hefted a large haunch onto his shoulders and showed Darius how to carry a smaller section. The first trip to the cave went slowly as the path through the snow was still uneven, if not deep. Arthengal had to rig ropes to allow them to lower the meat to the ledge. They left their bows and packs on the cave ledge as well so they would be able to carry more in the second trip.

They were surprised when they returned that the only scavengers were a handful of crows that scattered with a ruckus of cries to the branches when they approached. The second trip was easier as the path became more solid. The sun hung more than midway between its peak and the horizon by the time they finished dropping off the second load.

Arthengal peered warily at the sun. "We have maybe two more hours before sunset and a couple hours of decent light after that. Should we try for a third trip?"

Over half of the great beast remained.

Darius nodded vigorously. His blond hair shook and stuck to his sweaty forehead. He swept his fingers through his hair, brushing it back. His muscles throbbed, but he wanted to claim as much of the meat as he could to lessen his guilt.

When they arrived at the site of the kill for their third trip,

Arthengal paused.

"It's too quiet," he said.

Darius noticed then, too, that the woods around them had taken on an eerie hush.

"Come on, let's work quickly," Arthengal prodded.

They had just finished preparing the third load when Arthengal froze. "Don't run."

Darius glanced up. At the edge of the trees, five lupine forms crouched low and were slinking toward them. Crystal blue eyes stared at them as they inched ever closer. Darius turned his head at the glimpse of motion and saw two more wolves creeping up on them to their left. Arthengal eased a small hatchet out of his belt and took a step toward the elk's head.

With a mighty swing, he broke off one of the great antlers. He scooped it up and tossed it to Darius as the wolves charged.

The wolves covered the space between them in a blur of gray and brown fur.

Arthengal barely had time to chop off the second antler and raise it in defense as a gray wolf, with jets of white at its muzzle, pounced. He knocked it aside in mid-air. It fell to the ground with a yelp, rolled, then turned to face them again.

Darius and Arthengal stood back to back. A brown wolf lunged at Darius, and he brought the antler down with a sharp crack. The weight of it bruised the animal's flank, and one of the sharp points punctured its shoulder. It yelped and growled and then scurried away.

The pack was circling them now, looking for an opening. At practiced intervals, they would dart in pairs to test their defenses and then dance away.

A beast with a glossy black coat bounded off the remnants of the elk carcass toward Darius's chest.

Darius stepped out of the way and Arthengal brought his weapon down on the animal's spine, but in doing so he exposed his right side.

One of the other wolves took advantage of the opening and darted in to nip Arthengal's calf before he could swing the antler around. The leather pants tore and blood began to trickle down his leg.

Several more coordinated attacks left similar wounds on both of them as they spun valiantly to defend themselves. Both were limping now, and their defensive strikes were getting slower. Soon, one of them wouldn't be able to block a pouncing attack in time, and it would be over for both of them.

Chapter Fourteen
Antu

The wolves were circling for another attack when the black wolf stopped and sniffed the air. It growled low in its throat and sniffed again. The silence of the valley was broken by a mighty roar and a massive brown shape charged from the trees. The bear stopped and surveyed the scene before it rose onto its hind legs and roared again.

The wind from the roar seemed to shake Darius's body, or maybe he was just trembling with fear. His feet were rooted to the ground, and he couldn't move. He was starting to regret setting the monster free. The bear looked leaner than he had the past fall. Darius was sure he could almost see wrist-thick ribs showing through the thick brown coat. Almost. It was probably just the shadows playing tricks with his eyes. Thin or not, the creature was terrifying.

The wolves turned from the humans to face this new threat. Two of the wolves charged the massive beast while the others circled it. The bear swiped with a massive clawed paw, tossing the first wolf through the air. It whined as it crashed into the ground and began limping slowly into the wood.

The second wolf was not so lucky. Jaws filled with teeth the size of Darius's fingers clamped on the animal's neck. The giant muzzle shook from side to side until the wolf's body went limp.

The behemoth turned to face the black wolf and let out another mighty roar. The other wolves gave a final growl of their own and then faded into the orchard.

Arthengal and Darius were both frozen in place as the form of the mighty bear turned toward them. A glaring brown eye and a ruined socket stared at them disapprovingly.

"Help yourself," Arthengal said, waving a hand toward the elk carcass as he retreated. "The rest is yours."

The bear grunted with a huff and lumbered to the side of the elk to sniff it.

The antler hung limp in Darius's hand as he watched the beast in awe. Arthengal grabbed Darius by the collar and started pulling him backward, away from the beast.

The bear bit a massive chunk from the meat and began chewing slowly.

"Thank you," Darius stammered to the bear as he stepped away.

The bear lifted his head to stare at Darius for a long time. Its mighty jaws continued to grind the meat as he watched the boy. Finally, the bear swallowed, grunted again, expelled a sniff, and then returned his attention to the carcass to take another large bite.

"I think it's time we were going," Arthengal whispered.

They did not rest easy until they were safe in the cave. They collapsed in exhaustion as soon as they were secure in their shelter. Darius's heart hammered in his chest for a long time.

Arthengal mixed some salves out of the assortment of herbs that he always carried. He cleaned their wounds and applied the ointment. He wrapped the more vicious bites with strips of cloth.

Afterward, Darius huddled in the warmth of the hide blankets next to a crackling fire, still shivering occasionally as his mind replayed the encounter with the wolves and the bear. His eyes grew heavy, but something toyed at the back of his mind the more he thought about the bear. The creature had seemed less feral than the wolves. There was an intelligence there that Darius hadn't expected from a wild beast. There was something...*different* about him.

"He must be Antu," Darius said the next morning, with sudden inspiration.

"Who?" Arthengal asked, looking up from the venison roast that he was slicing into strips.

"Antu, the Sky Father. When I was following the raiders, I defied him. He must have come down from his sky palace in the form of a bear to challenge me. Maybe he is testing me to see if I am worthy."

The look of skepticism was clear on Arthengal's face.

"Or it could just be a bear," he said in a tone of gentle sarcasm.

"Or maybe Antu just sent the bear." Darius ignored Arthengal's comment. "It must be a test of some kind. Why else would the bear not have attacked us?"

"I think it more likely that he has had a hard winter without much game and he was hungry. He was drawn by the scent of blood. He chased off the wolves, and when he saw that we offered no threat, he attended to his hunger. I would not expect a similarly indifferent response if we meet again."

Darius was unconvinced. "No, the bear must *be* Antu. This is just the sort of thing that he would do, in the old tales. Antu would visit mortals in the form of a stag or a boar. Why not a bear?"

Arthengal laughed and then saw the look of hurt on Darius's face.

"Maybe so," he said in a consoling tone. "I know very little of the old gods. The world was a very different place when I was young. I was raised as a soldier, and back then we were not allowed to recognize any gods other than the emperor. We were taught that the emperor was the embodiment of all divine power and that his will was sacrosanct. The God Emperor certainly would have *tested* anyone who challenged him."

Darius scooped up a pile of raw venison and hung the strips on drying racks over the smoky fire. Arthengal had added dried wood from an assortment of fruit trees to add flavor to the smoke. Darius watched the smoke curl upward to the ceiling of the cave before flowing out the mouth of the cave, the natural drafts and currents in the cave ushering smoke outside.

"Maybe Antu could help us," Darius said, suddenly bright. "Maybe that's what he's here to do. We could leave and rescue my mother sooner. With Antu on our side we would surely win."

Arthengal laughed uproariously.

"Boy, I will make you a deal," he said, wiping tears from his eyes. "When you can knock the blade from my hand, when you find us two good horses for the journey, and when you can make that bear do what you say, I will pack our bags myself and leave that day."

"Done," Darius said.

Arthengal was shocked at the firmness.

"But until then," Arthengal said, "you agree to listen and learn and be patient. If I think we are ready before that day, I will let you know."

Darius nodded firmly. "Agreed."

"Are you sure it's not too tight?" Arthengal cinched up the straps of the pack on Darius's back and studied the fit as he fingered his beard.

Darius rocked his shoulders and hooked his thumbs under the straps that angled across his chest. He could feel his body leaning to the right under the weight.

"It's heavy but not too tight."

Arthengal fiddled with one of the buckles and the load

became more balanced. Now it only pressed his shoulders down and drove into the base of his spine rather than making him feel like he was about to topple over.

"Aye, even cut and dried it's nearly more than we can carry. I don't know what we would have done with the rest if that bear of yours hadn't staked claim to it."

Darius was surprised at how much jerky even half an elk made. It had taken them more than a week to cure it all. The pack was stuffed almost to bursting. Additional packets of meat had been bundled together tightly with leather thongs and secured to the outside with strips of leather.

Arthengal shouldered his own pack and carried his unstrung bow in his hands. His quiver was strapped at his waist for easy access if they encountered the wolves again. Or the bear, Darius supposed. Darius hoped that Arthengal didn't react too hastily if they did run into Antu.

They plodded along the trail toward the ruins of Anbar Ur. Their multiple trips to the valley had packed the snow to a solid, if slippery, path. The sun was warm today and rivulets of water trickled across the trail forcing Darius to step with more care.

"Psst."

Darius stopped at the hissing sound from Arthengal. He raised his head and looked back.

Arthengal nodded silently toward the trees down slope.

Several hundred paces down the hill, lumbering heedlessly,

searching for food, was the giant bear. He waddled to a rotted stump and sniffed it before tearing it open with a massive paw. The animal lapped greedily at the grubs and ants that spilled into the snow with the shattered wood.

"Antu!" Darius shouted excitedly.

"What are you doing?" Arthengal shushed him.

"Look at him," Darius whined. "He's practically starving."

The bear raised its head and peered up at them. Its single dark eye considered the two. The beast raised its snout into the air and sniffed as if savoring the aroma of a baking pie. He glanced back down at the skittering bugs and snorted with dissatisfaction before turning uphill, in the direction of the hunters. A long, pink tongue circled its muzzle and scooped up a stray grub dangling from his chin.

"It smells the meat," Arthengal whispered.

"The meat, of course," Darius exclaimed, not bothering to quiet his voice.

"Antu, are you hungry?" He shouted to the bear as he fumbled behind him for one of the packets of meat strapped to the pack.

Darius's fingers worked the leather knots as the animal climbed the hill toward the road. The beast looked unperturbed as Arthengal strung his bow and nocked an arrow.

Darius looked sidelong at Arthengal as the binding finally came loose and two packets of meat fell into the snow.

"Don't shoot him," Darius pleaded. "Antu is just hungry. Here, you'll see."

Darius picked up one of the bundles and heaved it down the hill. It landed with a muted thump in the snow. The bear approached the bundle and sniffed it, salivating. The packet tore open easily under the thumb-thick canines. His jaw worked steadily grinding jerky and leather alike.

Darius heaved the second packet, and the animal jumped slightly as it hit the snow near his head.

"See, he is just hungry," Darius said to Arthengal. "You don't need to shoot him."

"Boy, you are playing with fire feeding a bear like that," Arthengal grumbled under his breath. "You had better toss down some more, and we best put some distance between us and him."

Darius glanced down at Antu. Arthengal still didn't understand. Antu hadn't been sent to hurt him, just to test him. Although, he considered, some lessons could be harsh and might result in injury. He began working on the ties on the other side. He had been starting to lean to the right again.

The first bunch of meat was gone and the beast was halfway through the second by the time Darius loosened two more packages and tossed them down the hill. The bear jumped again when the first landed but then deftly snatched the second out of the air. A growl of contentment rumbled deep in its chest. Antu's fervor had slowed with the third bundle as his hunger ebbed.

"Come on, let's go," Arthengal hissed as he passed Darius. He still held his bow and an arrow in one hand.

Smiling with satisfaction, Darius readjusted his load. At least the pack was lighter now. He considered dropping the remaining four packets strapped to the outside, but he would have had to take off the backpack to undo the knots. Instead, he turned to follow Arthengal, who was well down the trail and moving at a much quicker pace than before.

When they reached the city, Arthengal didn't slow. Instead, he headed directly toward the winding paths through terraced gardens on the far side of the city. When they reached the crest of the hill, he turned back and pointed.

Darius saw Antu shambling casually along their path in the distance. A shiver went down Darius's spine, and he wondered if he had made a mistake. No, he shook his head. He was sure that he was right. His confidence was renewed as he watched Antu turn onto the broad boulevard that exited the city from the south. He was returning to the valley.

"Let's go," Arthengal urged and began picking his way down the uneven slope to the mining road. They paused only briefly to reattach their snowshoes. Their progress was painfully slow, and Arthengal remained on edge until they were safely in the cabin where he could shrug off his pack and collapse in the chair.

"Boy," he said with an exasperated sigh. "You and that bear of yours are going to be the death of me."

"But Antu....," Darius began but stopped at a sharp look in Arthengal's eyes. Now was not the time, he decided. He would see though, eventually. Antu was here to help him. He was sure of it.

"Go store the meat in the cellar, please," Arthengal said as he pulled off his boots.

By the end of his third trip to the storeroom, Arthengal had a fire crackling in the hearth and was stirring wild onions and bits of dried meat into a broth that bubbled in the large kettle.

"Another month," Arthengal said, "and the snows will have cleared enough for the trip south."

It was obvious to Darius that Arthengal was done talking about the bear. Just as well, he thought. *Some fish take longer to skin than others, Mother Shala used to say. But they all end up in the pot.* Arthengal would come around.

Spring - 31 A.E.

Chapter Fifteen
The Story of the Bow

"How many more..." Darius panted as he struggled up the hill after Arthengal, "...trips do you think?"

Darius felt a trickle of sweat run down his back and reached behind him to scratch the resulting itch. The sun was creeping toward its zenith and it promised to be another hot day. Spring had come with a vengeance once it had decided to arrive. He clutched at his stomach when it rumbled for the third time this trip.

"We've been at this since dawn and I'm starving," he complained.

"Not more than a dozen or so," Arthengal called over his shoulder. Darius had never seen someone so cheerful following a near week of downpours.

Darius stared in despair as they reached the blocked tunnel. The hill was a mess. The earth that had been wet from the spring rains when they started was now churned to mud. He glanced at his pants and boots which were caked with the stuff.

"Now that spring is here, we have to be on our way. Hurry

up. Winter would not have affected the southern merchants as much. I will be lucky if there is a boat left in Eridu that hasn't already restocked its supply," Arthengal said with excitement.

"A dozen more? We've already filled the bed to the top of the box. Don't we need to still pack supplies for the trip?"

"Top of the box," Arthengal sniffed dismissively. "We'll pile the ropes to the tops of our heads and then strap the mess down with a couple of firm nets. Supplies we'll strap to the side of the wagon."

Arthengal paused to look back at Darius. He wiped his hand across his glistening brow, oblivious to the dark smear he trailed across his forehead.

"With you helping me all winter, we've doubled my usual haul. Most years I'm forced to take a few barrels of yarn with what I couldn't wind. This winter we converted the entire crop, and I mean to sell it all."

He started walking again. "We won't be running low on supplies again this winter, I tell you. Cornmeal, turnips, pota--"

Darius mimicked gagging at the mention of turnips. "If I never eat another turnip in my life, it will be too soon."

"That's because you've never had my turnips. Baked by the hearth with a little garlic. Garlic! We will be able to afford garlic, bundles of it. And onions."

Darius's stomach growled again.

"But we have fresh vegetables already. Why buy more?"

"Boy, that garden we planted behind the cabin will be great

through the summer. We will have plenty of lettuce, tomatoes, and squash, but without preserving them, none of it will keep very long. A couple of barrels of potatoes in the cellar will last the whole winter. Same with carrots and turnips. We won't have to survive on pickled cabbage this winter. We can dine on venison stew." As he crested the hill, Arthengal picked up speed with the more even footing of the terraced pathways.

Darius sighed at Arthengal's exaggeration and followed him into the ancient city. They had eaten a fair amount of fermented cabbage, but they had also had plenty of venison, fish, and apples. There would be no shortage of apples with the orchard just in the next valley over. Arthengal had already mentioned a dozen times that with Darius there to help, they would double their stores of apples. He cringed at the thought of spending the entire summer carrying crates of apples down the trail.

"You should think about building a staircase or at least a better trail on this side of the hill," he complained as he reached the ridge and stumbled after Arthengal along the rock-lined path.

"That's a great idea," Arthengal replied. "We can buy some tools in Eridu and use the bricks from some of the fallen buildings. With you to help, it shouldn't take more than a month or so."

Darius groaned. Why couldn't he have kept his mouth shut? Every time he made a suggestion, it amounted to more work for him. Although it would make this easier. And hauling apples to the cabin. And any other supplies. Okay, maybe it would be worth the effort of carving a trail into the hillside and paving it with stones.

Darius heaped the coils of rope onto the wagon with a grunt and a sigh.

"Maybe I should go put some more grain out for the donkeys to lure them in closer while you do the next trip?" he suggested as he worked a knot out of his shoulder.

Arthengal laughed and hopped into the back to rearrange the ropes for a tighter fit.

"Come on, boy. Hard work builds character. Besides, you need to put on more weight. You're skinny as a reed."

Darius laughed at the mock. Between sword practice every day and the hard work of harvesting hemp and turning rope, Darius had put on almost two stone over the winter. His lean frame of a year ago had filled out and tight muscles strained at the confines of his shirts and trousers.

Arthengal appraised the boy. "As soon as we sell our goods and get some coin, we need to get you some better-fitting clothes, too. Those rags you're wearing are about to fall off of you."

"It's either that or the tent of a tunic and pants you loaned me to practice and work in. It would never do for hauling rope up hills. I'd spend half my time cinching the rope that barely holds them around my waist."

"Come on." Arthengal hopped out of the wagon, a broad smile on his face. "I promise you a midday meal when we get back to the cabin."

The meal helped his stomach, at least, if not his aching back and screaming thigh muscles. Arthengal had been wrong in his estimate. It took fifteen more trips to empty the storehouse of rope and netting and another four to load all their supplies. Darius tightened the straps that secured the final leather bag of supplies to the side of the wagon and glanced west. The sun was but a gentle orange glow at the edge of the hills.

One thing Arthengal had not underestimated was the size of the load. The mound of ropes and nets towered above the riding bench. Everything was secured with three nets, and the mass wouldn't budge when Darius shoved it.

"How many donkeys came in?" Arthengal asked.

"Six, the last time I counted," Darius replied. "I haven't seen any more since we picketed those."

"That should be enough. We'll have to move slow, though. I'd plan on an extra day or two for the trip. The road is good but gets a bit uneven in places once we enter the forest. It wouldn't take much for this thing to tip," Arthengal said as he inspected the wagon and its load.

"Okay, I think that should do it." He slapped the heap with a smile. "We'll sleep here tonight and leave at first light."

A long, low, unmistakable grunt echoed in the valley below them. The donkeys danced in their hobbles and Arthengal shivered.

"That bear of yours better stay away from our camp tonight.

Maybe we should sleep in the mill just to be safe."

"Antu is not *my* bear. He is his own...well, bear. I don't think he will bother us, though. It wouldn't serve as a very good test to sneak up on us in the middle of the night."

Arthengal raised an eyebrow.

"Unless he means to see how well we keep watch," Darius considered, itching the nape of his neck.

Another frustrated grunt sounded from the valley below.

"So you say, but I still think I'll sleep in the mill. You stay out here and cuddle with him if you like."

The bear did not stray any closer to their camp that night, but their sleep was disrupted several times by both the territorial howls of wolves in the hills and the challenging roar that Antu gave in response. They each took turns standing watch over the donkeys and the wagon, but no animals entered the boundaries of the broken city.

As they dressed the next morning, Darius insisted on belting his sword around his waist.

"You won't need that, boy, and it will just make travel less comfortable."

Darius eyed the solid oak plank that made up the bench doubtfully.

"*Less* comfortable?" he said with a smirk.

"Aye," Arthengal smiled.

"Whatever you say," Darius said smugly as he climbed into his spot on the right side of the bench.

"Maybe this is one of those lessons you need to learn for yourself," Arthengal said with a wink.

"If you want to keep the sword handy, it's better to place it at your feet. But as I said, you won't need it. If you want to stand guard, your bow would be more useful." As if in response to his own suggestion, Arthengal strung his bow and hung it and the quiver across two low pegs which extended from the left side of the wagon bench and secured them in place with a leather strap.

Darius blinked. He had not noticed the pegs and thought the arrangement genius. With a momentary excitement, he glanced down to look for similar pegs on his side and was disappointed to find the oak board sanded smooth.

"But no self-respecting brigand is going to try to rob us on our way *to* market," Arthengal continued. "What would they do with a load of rope and nets? It's far more likely they would rob us on the return trip when they think our pockets are full of silver."

Darius wasn't sure whether he was excited or wary. He also couldn't tell if Arthengal was joking or not.

He tried to adjust the sword belt again. The bench forced the scabbard up at an awkward angle and caused the belt to crimp at his waist. He settled on the least uncomfortable position with the sword resting flat against his thigh, half its length jutting out past his knee.

"Looks comfy," Arthengal quipped.

Darius grunted in response and his cheeks colored. "Do you really think someone might try to rob us?" he asked, changing the subject.

"One never knows," Arthengal said in answer to Darius's question. "Most brigands stay closer to Kasha Amur and the larger cities to the south, but it is a long, lonely road between here and Eridu and anything can happen."

"How far is it to Eridu?" Darius asked

"About sixty leagues."

"So, it should take about a week?" Darius asked.

"More like ten days, if the road is in good shape. The cart won't move as quickly as a man on foot, and we'll have to rest the donkeys more often."

Arthengal slapped the reins and the donkeys jerked. The axles groaned and the wheels began to inch forward. Another slap and the wagon was rolling. The hard-packed ground of the road had grown over in places with grass, but it was still discernible, and the cart moved with ease, if slowly.

The valley was alive with color. The apple trees were in full bloom and a delicate floral scent filled the air. Surrounding the trees were waves of wildflowers. Pale lavender saffron battled with pink and orange rhododendron to carpet the pastures between groves while the brilliant white of yarrow and chamomile decorated the ground beneath the trees.

Darius glanced behind him toward Anbar Ur and the snowcapped peaks that surrounded the hidden valley. The sun was just starting to light the eastern peaks and the snow glimmered white. After three days of rain and heavy clouds, the sky was beginning to clear, and the mere sight of pale blue breaking through the dark gray warmed him even though the sun wasn't fully up yet.

Out of the corner of his eye, Darius thought he saw a flash of brown. He craned his neck to see around the apple trees but whatever it had been was gone.

Near midday, the road began to turn upward out of the valley. Darius sighed with disappointment as the apple orchards gave way to the fir and pine of the rolling hills beyond the valley. Arthengal pulled the leather strap to release his bow and began to limber the string. He scanned the trees looking for pheasant or turkey.

"Did I ever tell you the story about how I got this bow?" Darius shook his head.

"I was a colonel in the emperor's third army at the time. They called us the Hala Atu, the Peace Keepers. My regiment was called The Fist. Our job was to enforce the emperor's peace on the denizens of the land. Mostly that meant we quashed rebellions before they had the chance to grow, and arrested outspoken dissidents before they had the chance to foster rebellion.

"The emperor had an odd definition of the word *peace*," Arthengal added dryly. "For an army devoted to peace, we rarely saw any. We were in near constant motion moving from one battle to another killing and killing and killing." His voice was taking an edge, and he paused to take a breath.

"Anyway. The summer that I turned thirty, my regiment was in the northern steppes. The area that is now Orlyk province."

"Where's the Orlyk province?" Darius asked.

"We really need to get you a map," Arthengal gave an exasperated sigh. "It's the northernmost province of the empire. The closest border is over seven hundred leagues to the east.

"Anyway, the people of the steppes were the Sisuma, horsemen. They were nomadic and by and large peaceful. They lived for their horses and *the journey*, as they called it. Their mustangs were lean and fast, and their riders could shoot a bow from horseback at a full gallop. Which they often did when hunting the antelope of that area."

"That's incredible," Darius said. "If we had had horses that could chase down a deer, our hunters would have never had trouble bringing in enough food for the village."

"Emperor Chen Bai Jian agreed with you, although not necessarily about the deer. The previous summer, he had decided to add several companies of light cavalry to his armies to round out their ability. Emperor Chen cared nothing for the Sisuma themselves. He saw them as undisciplined rabble, but he did envy their mustangs. He had ordered the seizure of one thousand mounts.

"To the Sisuma, their horses were as important as their children, more important to some. The emperor's order was tantamount to stealing away not only their livelihood but their family. The peaceful people were enraged and cried for justice.

"Justice was answered in the form of Orlin Malamay."

"Oh!" Darius said excitedly, now paying attention with even more interest. "This is your story about meeting Orlin Malamay."

"Yes. He was able to organize the Sisuma with incredible efficiency. In less than a year, those who could not fight had disappeared west into the Northern Wastes. Anyone of fighting age, men and women alike, were organized into groups of forty or fifty riders. They would strike with the ferocity of a lioness guarding her cubs. They raided supply depots, army outposts, and patrols. He vowed to take back the steppes and free the Sisuma from the grip of the 'tyrant king.' Orlin refused to recognize the title of emperor."

The wagon hit a bump and Darius nearly toppled out of his seat. His sword jabbed him in the side uncomfortably as he righted himself. Arthengal waited for him to get adjusted before continuing.

"Throughout the winter and spring, the raids went unchecked, and in early summer, the emperor sent in The Fist. We were to crush the rebellion without compassion. No quarter was to be given and the land was to be '...scrubbed clean of this ungrateful filth....' Those were the orders, written in Chen's own hand."

"Wouldn't it have been easier for the emperor to just pay them for the horses he had stolen?" Darius asked. "Couldn't he have ended the rebellion without all the bloodshed?"

"The emperor didn't think that way," Arthengal explained. "He saw everything in the empire, people included, as a resource to be used however he chose. In his mind, the horses were his to begin with, and if he chose to take them without compensation, that was his right. The fact that the Sisuma questioned that and defied his will was an affront worthy of death."

"That's crazy."

Arthengal chuckled. "A shared sentiment at the time."

"So, I had my orders. I led two thousand infantry and a thousand heavy cavalry north to the steppes. At first, the Sisuma didn't stand a chance. They were unorganized and used to striking small groups with hit-and-run tactics. They had never faced an opponent of our size or level of organization. We extended our perimeter, positioning troops well outside our main camp. My scouts would warn those units when the Sisuma approached, and they would hide, and let the raiding parties pass unprovoked. Once the Sisuma were far enough inside our perimeter, they would close from behind and catch them like a hammer striking them against the anvil of the main army. The first few raids were crushed in this way with very little damage to our forces.

"But Orlin learned from his failures and changed his tactics. He knew that we were after them and would hunt them, so he let us come to him. We were lured into several traps, and the next few encounters were much more balanced. They were fierce in battle when allowed the chance. Their steeds raced circles around ours, and one of their men could fire three arrows from horseback at full charge in the time it took our archers to fire a single volley. I had lost several hundred good soldiers by mid-summer when Orlin sued for parley."

"If he was starting to win, why would he try to make peace?" Darius asked.

"A fair question," Arthengal said. "If you know ultimately that you are likely to lose an extended war, sometimes the best time to sue for peace is when you have a perceived advantage. It gives you a stronger bargaining position. Unfortunately for him, the emperor's orders were very clear. Still, I wanted to hear what the man had to say.

"Against the recommendation of my command staff, I agreed to meet Orlin accompanied by a guard of a dozen men. My first captain, Sengiin Sharav, was furious. Sharav was from Rusticar Province. The *Rus,* as his people were called, were unmatched in their loyalty to the emperor. They also had a personal grudge against the Sisuma. Generations of territorial disputes and blood feud between the Sisuma and the Rus fueled his hatred.

"Captain Sharav vowed, on the edge of insubordination, that, 'His Holy Emperor will hear of your disobedience,' and 'You will regret this decision, *Colonel* Alamay.'" Arthengal mimicked a thick accent. "He wasn't wrong, but I'll get to that later," Arthengal added with a note of disgust.

"Is Alamay your family name?" Darius asked.

"Yes," Arthengal said. "I guess I've never mentioned that, have I? Come to think of it, I've never asked your family name either."

"Uh, Kabir, I guess. We didn't really use family names other than for the elders of the village, like Mother Shala. I do remember that Mother Shala would call mother *Mistress Kabir* sarcastically when mother was acting above herself."

Arthengal laughed. "I really wish I could have met this Mother Shala that you always talk about. She sounds like a profound woman."

"She was." Darius's brow furrowed. "She was always ready with a kind word of advice when you needed help or a stern hand when you needed *guidance*. She "guided" my backside more than once when I was a child." Darius laughed.

"What happened next?" Darius asked.

"We rode to the agreed meeting place and were met by twenty of the plains warriors who would lead us to Orlin's encampment. We followed our escort to a tall, long mesa and up a treacherous, twisting trail to the top. Twenty men could have defended the trail against my entire regiment as long as they didn't run out of arrows. The mesa stretched half a league north to south and was almost as wide. It provided a commanding view of the steppes beyond, and one could see for leagues in any direction.

"Orlin's army was camped in the center of the mesa and would have been invisible from below. At least five hundred fighting men and women occupied the site and twice that number of horses. My eyes took in everything. He had stockpiles of supplies that could last this group well through the winter. Assuming he had additional forces in the steppes that could harass our supply lines, a siege of the mesa would have been as damaging to us as it would be to them. Ultimately, such a tactic would have worked in our favor, but it would have cost the emperor dearly in troops, mounts, and supplies.

"We dismounted and gave our horses over to a dozen grooms who appeared out of nowhere. I surveyed the people around me. I had met the Sisuma in battle when they wore breastplates atop loose-fitting robes and riding pants in muted colors that blended with the grasses of the plains. I had never seen them in their own element.

"The camp was alive with color. The men wore shirts that were black or red or white with broad bands of colorful embroidery at the cuffs, collars, and in a wide stripe that covered buttons along the left side. The elaborate stitch work shocked the eyes with vibrant blues, yellows, and greens. Each man wore a thick sash tied around his waist in the same color as the stitching of his shirt. The dress of the women made that of the men look tame. Lightweight blouses stitched with flowers and wide skirts banded with every color of the rainbow.

"Across the field, I saw a man approaching. He had a broad chest and wore red riding britches and a loose white shirt open half-way down his hairy chest. A long red and green robe trailed off his shoulders. His thick mustache was waxed to points that extended beyond his cheeks. His eyes were bright and clever."

"Was it Orlin Malamay?" Darius asked.

"It was," Arthengal said. "And he was a sight. I couldn't help but be impressed with the man. He moved with the grace of a warrior, but his demeanor was that of a long lost friend finally reunited. As he approached me, he extended his arms and said, 'My dear Colonel Alamay, you are most welcome.'

"My guard shifted uneasily as he embraced me and kissed me on both cheeks. 'Come, come,' Orlin said. 'Your men and horses will be fed while we talk. Tonight we shall celebrate our meeting regardless of the outcome. For today, we are at peace. Let us behave as friends and as brothers. Come, come.'

"I nodded to my sergeant, and they were led toward the cook fires. I followed Orlin to a large, colorful tent in the center of the camp. I was surprised to find that, inside, the tent was cool despite the heat of the day. Oil lamps hung from hooks mounted to the tent beams and provided more than enough light to illuminate the surroundings. Large piles of pillows were arrayed in a half-circle in the center of the tent. A low table rested in the center of the circle and a pot of steaming tea awaited.

"Orlin poured the tea into two porcelain cups and handed one to me. 'Sit, sit.' Orlin gestured to the pillows on the opposite side. Without waiting for me, he lowered himself to the pillows on the other side. I set the teacup on the table, unstrapped both of my swords, and laid them on the ground where they would be at hand if things went south. I settled into the pillows and retrieved my tea. I took a sip. I can still remember the delicate aroma of jasmine and honey. I've tried time and again and have been unable to replicate that perfect cup of tea that Orlin brewed.

"I was surprised by how at ease the man was. He settled into a comfortable conversational tone as if we had known each other for years. 'Arthengal. Can I call you Arthengal, Colonel? Or would you prefer Old Bear?' Orlin laughed."

"Old Bear? Why would he call you that?" Darius asked.

"It was a nickname that my men had given me," Arthengal answered and then continued.

"'Arthengal is fine,' I responded.

"Orlin's smile was warm and gracious. He took a sip of his tea before continuing. 'Thank you for joining me here. It is a great day. The sun is shining on the Sisuma, and you do us great honor.' Orlin's grin was infectious, and I found my own tension fading. 'I am not of the court, and I have no tongue for speeches of deception and games. Might we speak plainly as brothers would speak?'

"I nodded and let him continue.

"'The Tyrant King has committed a great sin against the Sisuma. He stole away that which means most to our people in the world and didn't even bother to compensate us for the loss. We were heartbroken, we were angry, and we were bitter. We acted out of spite and out of hate, and we blacked our enemy's eye in response. Now, we grow tired. Our anger is spent, and it is time for us to return to our children and our old ones. We want nothing more than to continue *the journey* and move on with our lives. We will agree to abandon the land of our birth and leave this *empire*.'

"Orlin spat the word as if he had a mouthful of bitterroot and then continued. 'We will join our loved ones in the bitter north and leave this all behind if you will but let us go.'

"I considered his words and ruminated into my cup of tea before responding. After years in the Hala Atu I too had grown tired of killing when there wasn't a need. But the orders of the emperor were clear, and Emperor Chen never changed his mind. He saw indecision as a sign of weakness. More than that, Chen was unwavering in his belief that he was a god, and that his word was divine will that must be followed without question.

"I tried to frame my response with care. 'Master Malamay...'

"Orlin stopped me with a raised hand. 'Please, Orlin, we speak as brothers.'

"I nodded and continued. 'Orlin. You have more than blacked the eye of the emperor. You have committed treason, in his eyes, and have spat in his face. There is no greater crime, in his mind, than treason. He has ordered your death and that of all who follow you. It is very unlikely that he will change his mind.'

"Orlin smiled, but his tone was that which one would use with a child. 'You misunderstand me, my friend. I do not seek parley with the Tyrant King. He is mad and beyond salvation. He victimizes his people and abuses his power. No peoples in this empire have failed to escape his injustice. I brought you here to speak to you, as a man, as a brother. Your reputation precedes you, Nasu Rabi --"

"Whoa, whoa, wait. Nasu Rabi? I thought you said your nickname was Old Bear?" There was excitement in Darius's voice.

"Yes, Nasu Rabi means Old Bear in the old tongue," Arthengal replied.

"So, did they give you the nickname after the hero from the stories?" Darius asked.

Arthengal coughed. "I don't know what stories you've heard, but I'm the only one I know of that has ever had that nickname."

"You!" Darius gasped. "The stories are about you?"

"Don't believe everything you hear in stories. My life wasn't that exciting, and in my experience, *stories* tend to be gross exaggerations of the truth."

"B-but you..." Darius stuttered. "The Battle of the Broken Forge. The Rescue of the Ten Maidens. The Calamity of Kasha Haaki."

"I wasn't at Kasha Haaki. That was my friend Dumazi Cherian," Arthengal interrupted.

"But still, *the* Nasu Rabi." Darius shook his head in wonder. "I'm being trained by *Nasu Rabi,* and he is going to help me rescue my mother. There is no way we can fail."

Arthengal looked uncomfortable. "Can I finish my story?"

"Please," Darius said.

"Where was I?"

"He didn't want to negotiate with the emperor. He wanted to negotiate with *the* Nasu Rabi." Darius smiled.

Arthengal cleared his throat and went on with Orlin's speech. "'I brought you here to speak to you, as a man, as a brother. Your reputation precedes you, Nasu Rabi. You are an unstoppable force, but you are fair and are devoted to justice above all else. I do not ask you to abandon your emperor or to forsake your orders. I only ask for two days. In two days we will have evaporated like mist in the desert. I will lead our people north and we will trouble you no more.'

"Indecision must have been clear in my expression because he interrupted before I could consider his offer. 'Do not give me your answer yet.' Orlin stood. 'Come, we will eat and sing and dance.'

"Orlin led me out of the tent and toward the cook fires. His people were already gathering around the fires and my men were with them. Someone handed Orlin a lute as he passed and he started playing before he even reached the fires.

"I remember the song still even after all of these years. It was a song of hope and the journey of life."

Arthengal started to sing. His deep singing voice echoed through the trees. He sang the tune reverently and held out the final notes on the second and fourth lines of each verse. Listening to the song made Darius feel an odd combination of sadness and joy.

I give my life to love the land
I give my life to follow
The Journey takes us all in hand
And forsakes all sorrow

I give my heart to brothers mine
I give my heart to all now
The Journey's path is but divine
In pain I shall not wallow

I give my soul in act and deed
I give my soul not fallow
The Journey gives us all we need
Revenge but makes us hollow

"After the song was done, other musicians started up, and the camp became a carnival of music, laughter, and dance. The women's skirts twirled as they danced, and it was more fascinating than the most intricate display of fireworks that the emperor's 'lightning bringers' had ever imagined during festivals at the capital.

"Even though Orlin and his people did not know my decision, they sang and they danced well into the night. They acted as if the world was glorious even with death on their very doorstep. Their hope and zest for life made my decision for me. I just had to figure out how to deliver on the promise I had not yet made. I would have to lie and deceive the officers and men who trusted me every day with their very lives. It went against all of my training and all expectations of the emperor, but I could not order the death and massacre of a people that no longer posed a threat and would soon be gone from the empire forever.

"I didn't talk to Orlin again that evening. As we mounted to return to our garrison, he approached. He held out the bow in outstretched arms. 'Colonel Alamay,' he said formally. 'Allow me the honor of presenting you with my bow as a sign of thanks for agreeing to this conference. You have done me a great honor by your attendance.' I gave him but the barest of nods as I accepted the gift. The nod was not only meant for thanks, but also an agreement to his terms. I could tell in his eyes that he understood.

"So, you were going to let him go?" Darius asked.

"That was my plan. Now I just needed to convince my men. My officers insisted on a meeting as soon as I got back to camp. They wanted to know what we had discussed. I told them that Orlin was not asking us to go against the orders of our emperor, but that he had sued for a two-day cease of hostilities to celebrate midsummer's eve and that I had agreed. We would use the time to refresh our own troops and to position ourselves to strike once the armistice was ended.

"It was not to be, however," Arthengal said. The pain was clear in his voice.

"One of the guards that I had taken with me had whispered in Captain Sharav's ear. It turns out that one of the Sisuma had been too open during the celebration and had let slip that they intended to escape to the north. Whether they believed my explanation and thought me a victim of deceit, or thought me complacent, I don't know. In the end, it didn't matter. Captain Sharav raised a vote of no confidence amongst the officers, and they relieved me of my command. I was sent back to the capital under guard. He led the troops north to set traps along the most probable routes to The Wastes. They caught the Sisuma near the border when they had grown too confident that they were being allowed to escape. With their guard down, it was a massacre.

"Emperor Chen shared Sharav's disappointment and lack of confidence in my ability. There was no direct proof of treason, and I had led an exemplary career up to that point, so I was allowed to retire to Magora Province. I returned home, not quite in shame, but certainly not the celebrated hero. I was still young then, only thirty, and had no idea what I was going to do now that I had been dismissed from the only life I had known. It had been a quiet word from Prince Lao Cang Yu into the ear of Baroness Magora that decided my fate. The Baroness appointed me as captain of the guard in Kasha Marka and to her advisory council. By the following summer, I was commander general leading her vanguard across the Meddian Plains."

Arthengal shrugged. "The Journey does give us all we need, I guess."

By the time Arthengal had finished his story, they had stopped for the night. A fire was blazing and two fat pheasants roasted on spits above the flames.

Darius was waiting for more, but once it was clear that the tale was finished, he spoke.

"Your stories have horrible endings."

Arthengal looked taken aback.

"All of the heroes in your stories either die or are exiled in the end. In the stories my mother told, the heroes always came back from overwhelming odds to triumph over evil."

"Your mother's..." Arthengal stuttered. "I will have you know..."

Arthengal took a deep breath.

"These stories are from my past. I keep this bow and the fishing pole to remind me of heroes who were willing to stand up against tyranny. To fight for what they believed in. To remind me that justice is worth fighting for, no matter what the cost."

"Uh huh, and when you do that, everybody dies. Is that the life lesson?"

"What? No. It's supposed to teach you that standing up for what is right is worth dying for. The fight for justice is its own reward." Arthengal's face looked pained.

"Okay," Darius took pity on the man and lightened his tone. "I understand."

Arthengal nodded.

"But you really should work on a better ending," Darius said with a grin.

A thought occurred to Darius, and he doubled over laughing.

"You're not that funny," Arthengal said, unamused.

"No, it's just that I have two old bears watching over me," the boy explained. "You and Antu. I think perhaps The Journey has brought us all together. Maybe the Sky Father put you both in my path to help me set things right. I'm not sure what role Antu will play yet, but I just know that it is true."

Arthengal shook his head. "You and that bear of yours, boy. You better take more care."

Darius shrugged and as if in answer, they heard a familiar cough and growl somewhere in the darkness of the woods beyond their campsite.

Darius smiled and Arthengal shivered.

Chapter Sixteen
The Emperor

Lao Jun Qiu strode steadily across the dirt road between fields. He wore long silk robes, red and elaborately decorated with intertwining dragons. The hem and cuffs, each more than a palm's width, were purple and brocaded with lotus flowers. The hem hung past his feet and gave the impression that he glided across the earth. Lao Jun Qiu was a short man of thirty-six years. His hair was growing thin, despite his youth, and he kept his head covered with a tall black hat embroidered with golden dragons. His pointed beard was neatly trimmed and came only to the base of his throat. A long, thin mustache trailed to either side of his beard. Beard and mustache were the same dark color as his hair.

He studied the men and women who were tending the crops. They were filthy. Most had no shoes and their feet were black from the dark soil, or frostbite, he couldn't really tell. Their clothes were all ill-fitting and hung on them like rags. They were crouched over the carpet of green leafy plants, their grubby hands working feverishly to pick something off the small plants and deposit it in wooden boxes that they dragged along after them.

"General Sharav," he addressed the man behind him without turning his head, "What is it that we are growing this season?"

"Soybeans, Your Majesty," Sharav answered with a slight bow of his head.

Sengiin Sharav, Commander General of the Imperial Army, trailed Jun by a few steps. Beyond him, twenty soldiers from the Imperial Guard swept vigilant gazes across the workers.

"I don't really care for soybeans, General. Do you?"

"No, Your Majesty, of course not. The crop will be used to feed the peasants and the pigs. Once the harvest is complete, they will plant corn or wheat."

"Ah, very good. Much better for feeding the troops, don't you think?"

"As you say, Majesty."

A gust of wind blew north off the plain. The emperor suppressed a shiver. The winter had been long in its recession, and the warmer winds of summer had not yet reached this far north. It would be much better to spend the day inside playing Weiqi. He could inspect the rest of the fields another day once the weather warmed. General Sharav's men had things in hand anyway. There was little need for him to be out here other than to rally the spirits of his subjects.

"I think I will head back in now, General," Jun tried to keep the boredom from his tone. Letting his people see him was important, to inspire them, but he really would rather be reading a book in front of a warm fire. "It's quite cold out here."

"You are doing very well," Jun shouted in the direction of the laborers. "You should be proud of your work. Your diligence serves the empire."

He turned toward a path that led up a tall hill atop which sat a large timber home. The pathway led through a large stone archway and entered into the luxurious garden in front of the house. A waist-high granite wall trailed away from the archway, meandering over the hill surrounding both garden and home. Long banners streamed from posts mounted atop either side of the archway. As the cool summer wind picked up, the banners flapped in the breeze. Jun's eyes were drawn to the black dragons, the sigil of his father's house. Their serpentine bodies seemed alive on the banners as they twisted in the wind.

He paused at the base of the hill. A movement in the field had caught his attention.

"Who is that? And what is she doing here?" he asked and pointed to a small girl picking beans next to a middle-aged woman with dirty red hair. Both were as filthy as the rest, but the child should not be here.

"She is too young to be working the fields. She should have been left behind. I told you, Sharav, we only want strong conscripts. We can't afford to waste the food on anyone who can't earn their own keep."

"I will take care of her, Majesty."

The general signaled to two guards who trotted out toward the pair. The red-haired woman noticed their approach and shoved the child behind her.

"No, please," she pleaded. "Lianna is a good worker. She is a good girl."

One of the men pulled a cudgel from his belt and raised it. He struck the woman's arm as she tried to back away.

"No, please!" She held an arm protectively over her face and used the other to shield the girl.

Jun resumed his walk to the house, the woman and child already forgotten.

"Majesty, please!" the woman screamed. "Mercy, please, Your Majesty. Lianna is a good girl and a hard worker."

"How dare you address the emperor?" the soldier yelled and struck the woman several times in succession.

"Hold." Jun's voice was low and calm but carried the distance to the sobbing woman.

The soldier's arm froze in mid-strike.

"This is your daughter, I assume." He didn't wait for an answer. "Very well, it is important for a mother to care for her daughter. Don't you think so, General?"

He continued without waiting for a response.

"We cannot afford to feed a child, you understand, though," Jun addressed the woman. "The beans must be used to their fullest to feed the hogs which will feed our army. I'm sure you understand. Of course you do."

"And the laborers, of course," he added as an afterthought.

He paused, considering. "I will grant you mercy. I will allow you to feed the child from your ration, but she will not receive one of her own until she reaches the age of majority. That is fair, I think, yes? A mother should be allowed to care for her daughter."

"Thank you, Majesty, thank you." The woman prostrated herself, pressing her face into the dark brown soil. She pulled the girl down beside her.

Satisfied, Jun started to walk again.

"You must understand as well," he paused again to call to the woman, "that resources are precious. We cannot afford to feed women who do not work their share either. Make sure that your own productivity does not suffer for the sake of the girl."

"We are obliged to show mercy on occasion, General," Jun said confidentially to Sharav. "How else are the people to love their emperor if he does not show mercy? On occasion."

"The people should love the emperor because it is their divine duty, Majesty. If you don't mind me saying so."

"You are quite right, General. However, my father taught me that mercy for the people will reinforce that love. A lesson that my blessed uncle, The Divine Emperor Chen Bai Jian, never learned, and you see where we are now."

Jun saw Sharav cringe and half expected the other man to correct him. Sharav believed very deeply that to speak ill of the emperor, any emperor, was a sin. But then again, the emperor, being a god himself, was immune from sin, at least in Sharav's eyes. Jun could read the conflict on the general's face and restrained a grin.

"Tell me, General," Jun changed the subject as he reached the steps to the house, "when will the next party of troops leave for the south to conscript more peasants?"

A servant clad in simple yellow robes slid the paneled door aside to allow him and the general to enter the house and then closed it quietly after they passed. It was much warmer inside. The hearths were well tended and the sudden change in temperature brought a flush to Jun's cheeks.

"Another month, Majesty," Sharav replied. "The orders are still coming in from the other camp commanders. We will focus on villages most able to fill the greatest needs."

Jun sat in a chair before a tall, round table. A lined board and two porcelain bowls rested on the table. Each bowl held polished game pieces. The first was filled with white, ivory pieces and the second held black stones of smooth onyx.

"Can you take time away from your duties for a quick game?" Jun waved a hand to the other chair.

"Of course." The general gave a slight bow and took his seat. He waited for Jun to place the first stone.

"Who will be leading the foray south?" Jun placed a white stone near the center of the board.

"Colonel Petrov." Sharav's hand hovered over the board as he decided where to place the next stone. "If I may ask, Majesty, why the need to dress the men like savages when they go on their conscription tours? It seems...undignified."

"We do not want to alert the barons to our recruitment efforts. Any who escape our sweeps will carry word only of barbarian raiders. It is a useful myth that lets us continue to build our forces in secret."

"Secret," Sharav spat the word as if it left a bad taste in his mouth. "The people will surely rally to our cause if they know that the Holy Emperor still lives."

"Some would," Jun agreed. "But there are still many radical elements in the empire, and some hold the current reins of power. Patience and care is the best course of action for now, General. We will bide our time. When we move to reclaim the empire, there must be absolute certainty of success.

"What of our efforts in the east?" Jun changed the subject.

"Our agents have infiltrated the merchant's guilds in Kasha Haaki and Kasha Nisir. They work to bend the will of merchants as you ordered. To sow discontent with the new trade laws. This *open market* that the barons have instituted has cut deeply into the pockets of many tradesmen who previously dominated certain markets. They will be easy to manipulate once we are ready."

"Tell me about the incident in Kantibar," Jun said casually as he placed another white stone to block the general's advance.

Sharav winced.

"An isolated incident, I'm sure, Majesty. One of the ivory traders we had converted to our cause was found dead in his home. Poisoned, by all accounts."

Jun studied the other man's eyes as he asked the next question.

"And the disk that our agents found tucked into his robes?"

Shock was clear in the general's eyes. *Good*, Jun thought. *Now he knows that I have my own eyes and ears and do not depend on his reports for all of my information. He will be less likely to hold things back in future reports.*

"A black disk with a crown painted on one side and a winged lion on the other."

"What does it mean?"

"We don't know yet," Sharav replied.

"How has this impacted our control of the ivory trade in Magora Province?"

"It has been a setback." Sharav's eyes were strained with tension. "But we will recover."

"And the perfume trade out of Ito?" Jun rested his elbows on the table and pressed his fingers together in a steeple as he studied Sharav over the game board.

"Another unfortunate incident," the general sighed.

"And another black disc." Jun raised his eyebrows.

General Sharav nodded reluctantly.

"So, not so isolated after all." He drew his lips together in a frown. "General, every effort should be taken to prevent any future *unfortunate incidents*. The flow of gold is critical. More so than our efforts here. Food for our army is important, to be certain, but we must also pay them. And there are certain resources which the north just does not provide. Moreover, if we are going to continue to win the *affections* of the merchants' guilds, it will be costly."

"Yes, Your Majesty."

Jun returned his attention to the board.

"You are getting better, General. But I think you will agree the game is over."

Jun waited patiently as General Sharav studied the pieces. Sharav had focused too much attention securing the north-western quadrant and had allowed Jun to gain control of the rest of the board. Any 'uprisings' within his own territories could be quickly contained.

The general finally nodded and stood. "By your leave, Majesty."

Jun nodded and waited for the general to leave before standing. He strode to a dark ebony bookshelf on the far side of the room and retrieved an ancient tome from the upper shelf.

"Golden crown and winged lion," he muttered to himself. It tickled something in the back of his mind. An ancient order of some kind. Something one of his tutors had mentioned when he was still a boy at his father's palace.

"There," he said out loud, stabbing a finger at the crinkled parchment. The top of the page showed two symbols above a scripted subheading. Sillu Aga, the Shadow Crown. He carried the book back to his chair to read.

Chapter Seventeen
New Friends

The next morning, after he finished his sword practice, Darius found a broad, flat leaf and began filling it with berries from several bushes while Arthengal readied the donkeys and checked the load on the wagon. The constant rocking tended to loosen the ties binding the heap of ropes and nets.

"Are you gathering that for breakfast?" Arthengal asked.

"Yes, but not for us. For Antu, in thanks for standing guard last night," he said determinedly.

Arthengal sighed. "You really shouldn't encourage that bear. It's going to lead to trouble."

Darius gave a dismissive wave and then placed the leaf full of berries in the center of their camp, or at least what he thought was the center. Looking around, he couldn't tell that anyone had even slept there that night.

He slid his sword and belt onto the floor below the bench seat. Arthengal smiled slightly but didn't say anything. Darius scanned the woods as they started to move, hoping to catch a glimpse of Antu, but there wasn't any sign of him.

Over the next several days, Arthengal continued his education of plants and their various uses. When they would stop to feed and rest the donkeys, he would point out new specimens.

"What's this?" Arthengal asked, holding up a sprig topped with closely bunched white flowers.

"Yarrow," Darius recited. "You can make a poultice for cuts, burns, or bites. It also makes a palatable tea when mixed with mint that will help with some illnesses."

"And that?" Arthengal pointed to patch of brilliant orange flowers.

"Marigold," Darius sighed. "A marigold salve will help treat skin funguses. The tea will help with digestive problems."

On and on it continued. Each new plant with a variety of uses. Even the poisonous ones had some beneficial applications.

Arthengal used a stick to hold up a branch with black berries and violet flowers.

"Nightshade," Darius said. "It makes a strong pain reliever and muscle relaxer, but must be used carefully and in small amounts. You can also boil it down to make a potent poison to tip your arrows."

Every day on the trip to Eridu was the same: sword practice before breakfast, an offering left to Antu, Arthengal's inevitable grumblings about how dangerous the bear was, and lessons and drills while they rode. The forest and hills changed as they moved south. The foliage grew more familiar as they came closer to the area where Darius grew up. He glanced around where they had stopped for their midday meal.

"I think my village must not be more than a day or so that way." He pointed west. "This looks very much like our hunting grounds."

"Probably so," Arthengal agreed. "The road turns toward the coast up ahead. There it will meet up with other trade routes, and we are likely to see other traders. Two more days will see us in Eridu. Now, what's this?"

Darius barely glanced at the thin-stemmed blue flower. "Hepatica. You can use the leaves and petals to create a salve that will help blood clot on a wound. It also treats gout and yellow skin.

"Where did you learn all of this?" Darius asked. "I know you've lived in the wilderness forever, but you don't just pick up that Hepatica treats yellow skin."

"My wife was an herbalist. She was of the mind that everyone should kn--"

"Your wife!" Darius exclaimed, stopping dead in his tracks. "You have never mentioned that you were married."

"She died," Arthengal said simply. He scratched his gray beard uncomfortably. "I don't want to talk about it. Come on. The donkeys have rested long enough. We need to get back on the road."

Darius stared for another minute before following Arthengal onto the wagon.

His mind was a torrent. So many questions. He barely

noticed as the forest thinned and was replaced by low coastal hills. A wife. He had lived with the man for more than half a year, and he had never mentioned any sort of family. And she was dead. What had happened? Did they have children? He couldn't believe that they had or else they would be in the valley. Wouldn't they?

The sun hung low in the sky when they reached the crossroads. It was close enough to the shore that Darius could see the ocean stretching out at the horizon. The yellow ball reflected in shimmering waves on the water. He sighed as he smelled the salt air and was reminded of home.

The road that they joined made the one they were leaving look like a goat trail. It was broad enough for two wagons to pass abreast with space remaining so travelers on foot or horseback would not have to leave the road to let them pass. There was also a way station, of sorts, at the crossroad. Darius spotted a well and a paddock stocked with hay. Several fire pits were scattered throughout the area, but they were all cold and showed no signs of recent use. There was no sign of other traders.

"Usually there are several people camped at the crossroads when I come through here. Maybe we are later in the season than I thought. Surely we will see someone tomorrow," Arthengal said with a frown.

"How long were you married?" Darius could contain his questions no longer.

"Why don't you draw some water for the donkeys?"

Arthengal deflected.

"Did you have any children?" That earned a grimace but no response.

"Stake down that tent more securely. If a wind picked up off the sea, it would rip that right out of the ground."

"What was your wife's name? Can you tell me that, at least?"

"Sharaea."

Sharaea. What a beautiful name. Darius considered asking another question but decided not to press his luck. There would be plenty of time for more questions tomorrow.

For two days, Darius tried to pry more answers about Sharaea out of Arthengal, but he was a stone fortress. The name was all he got and no mention of children. Arthengal never angered at the questions, he just ignored them and redirected Darius to whatever lesson they were on or to some chore that needed to be done.

The sun was an orange and yellow mass on the horizon the second day as they crested a low hill in the road. Any view of the ocean had long since been blocked by the pastureland that sloped up and away from the highway. Sheep and cows had dotted the landscape as they traveled, but there was no sign of their owners.

Darius gave a start at the top of the hill as they came into sight of an expansive farm. After so much time in the wilderness, it seemed odd to see evidence of other people. But more than that the ranch was immense. His entire village could have fit inside the confines of the low rock wall that encircled the farmyard, house, and a half dozen cherry trees beside it. Not to mention the crop fields themselves.

The dwelling was the largest Darius had ever seen. It had two floors and was constructed from stone and brick. Wide slats of wood, mounted on hinges, covered each window. A wooden door set into the center of the wall opened onto a cobblestone patio that extended the entire length of the building. Matching wooden rocking chairs rested beside a cinderblock fire pit off to one side of the deck. The chairs faced away from the house, providing a clear view of the property and the approaching road. The building was at least twice the size of the town hall back home. *How many people live here?*

"Five," Arthengal answered before Darius realized he had voiced the question out loud.

"Five!" Darius was dumbfounded. "Those fields could feed my entire village for a year."

Fields of corn stretched out behind the farmhouse on one side and a pear orchard on the other. The stable yard held several horses and cows next to another flat-roofed stone structure. There was a stone well in the center of the main courtyard, and a plump woman was drawing up a bucket of water as they approached. She was about the same age as Darius's mother and wore a light blue dress lined with yellow stripes that covered her ankles. On her head she wore a white bonnet. She glanced up the road at the sound of the wagon and shouted toward the house.

A little girl, about ten or eleven, played with a doll on the steps of the porch. She looked up at her mother's shout. She clutched the doll to her lap and watched as they approached.

"We'll stop here for the night," Arthengal stated.

"Five," Darius muttered again under his breath still taking in the estate. Then in a louder voice, he asked, "Are these people wealthy?"

"What? No, I wouldn't say they're wealthy." Arthengal seemed surprised by the question. "Why do you ask?"

"I've never seen a house so big. It must have four or five rooms inside."

Arthengal laughed. "Seven, actually. If you count the root cellar and the laundry room, that is."

"There is a whole room full of laundry?" Darius was amazed.

That brought another laugh.

"I forget that you grew up on the edge of nowhere. You haven't seen anything yet," he said, still chuckling.

A tall, lean man in dark blue wool pants and a loose red shirt exited onto the front porch wiping his hands on a linen cloth. He was clean-shaven and had a full head of blond hair, the same color as Darius's. Two tall boys, a little older than Darius, tumbled out the door on his heels. The man's face wore a grim look of disapproval as he watched the wagon pull into the lane.

Arthengal pulled on the reins and brought the donkeys to a stop a few paces from the well.

"And here I thought that mountain of yours had finally

swallowed you up," the man shouted as Arthengal climbed down. The severe countenance broke, as if he couldn't hold the facade any longer, and his face broke into a wide grin.

"Not yet," Arthengal laughed and strode across the yard to the group.

Recognition dawned on the little girl's face and she bounded from the steps. The doll fell from her lap into the dirt, forgotten.

"Uncle Arthengal!" She sprinted from the patio and leapt into his arms.

Arthengal stooped to embrace the girl and gave her a tight squeeze. She clung to his neck, a look of admiration in her eyes. After a moment, she released him, and he stood, draping an arm over her shoulder as she leaned against him.

"That's quite a haul you've got," the man said, eyeing the cargo.

The girl's head suddenly jerked up when her father brought attention to the wagon.

"Who's that *boy*?" She said the last word as if she were describing the pile of leavings after cleaning fish.

"Darius," Arthengal chuckled.

Arthengal turned as he introduced him only to realize that Darius was still sitting on the bench watching the exchange. "Well, don't just sit there, boy. Hop down and get over here so I can introduce you."

Darius leaped from the wagon and scurried across the yard.

"Darius, this is Hanish Cherian," Arthengal said. "I served with his father in the Great War."

"Darius," Hanish extended his hand and Darius grasped it. The man's hand was firm and callused.

"This is my wife Elsie and my sons Kal and Nasha, but we just call him Nash," Hanish introduced each in turn.

Nash was nearly as tall as his father and had a mop of dark brown hair. He had broad shoulders and a kind smile. He reminded Darius of Micah, probably because they would have been about the same age. Kal was closer to Darius in age and height and had blond hair, like his father.

"And this is Anna," Arthengal said, ruffling the girl's hair.

She batted his hands away, and her face turned grumpy. "Don't muss my hair," she complained.

"It's a pleasure to meet you, sir," Darius said. "A pleasure to meet you all."

"Sir," Hanish laughed. "I ain't no sir. My father, maybe, back when I was in nappies, but I'm just a farmer."

"How is the old man?" Arthengal asked, clasping Hanish on the shoulder.

Hanish bowed his head. "He passed away this last winter. He got fluid in his lungs and there weren't anything we could do to help him. The doctor came twice with tinctures and leeches but it didn't do no good. He passed in his sleep, though, so there's some comfort in that."

"I'm sorry to hear that," Arthengal said solemnly. "Your father was a good man. We had many a hard road together and many happy times. He will be missed."

"Thank you. Well, come on in, we were just getting cleaned up for dinner. You can wash for dinner in the basin, but by the looks of you, you'll need baths after that or Elsie will have you sleeping in the barn with the horses."

"Let me unharness the donkeys first and put them in with your livestock. Darius, you go on in and clean up," Arthengal said.

"Darius," Hanish said as he stretched out an arm to the house.

"You have a beautiful home," Darius blurted as he climbed the steps to the porch. "You have known Arthengal a while then."

"Thank you. My father built the house, after the war, in the Kasha Marka style. The neighbors had to copy him, of course. 'Adding a bit of culture to this backwater salt burg,' he used to say.

"I've known Arthengal my whole life and every summer for the past twenty he has stopped here on the way to sell that rot-weed he calls rope." He raised his voice at the last.

"I heard that," shouted Arthengal from the wagon. "Best damn rope you will ever find, you mean."

"So you say," Hanish shouted back.

Hanish continued. "My father and him would keep the entire house awake until the wee hours of the morning on every visit reliving tales from what they call the 'good old days' but what was good about it I can't see. Living under the shadow of a tyrant and wondering if stepping on the wrong stone in court was going to get them sent to the stocks. No, sir, give me the simple life. A strong back, a good farm, a plump wife, and a pint of ale and I'll be a happy man."

Hanish seemed a good-natured man, and he spoke with an exuberance that made Arthengal's hearty tone seem mild, but Darius was only half listening. He stared in wonder at the inside of the house. The door opened up into a spacious living area with tiled floors. To the back of the room was a brick fireplace. Arranged in front of the hearth were a pair of ornately styled armed chairs with pillow cushions on the seat on either side of a carved divan with a long flat pillow on the seat. Oil lamps, set on tables or hung on hooks, bathed the space in light. Concave reflectors of hammered tin behind each lamp added to the illumination.

"Take off your shoes by the door there, if'n you don't mind," Hanish said. "Elsie will have my hide if I let you go tracking dirt all over the floor."

Elsie and the children filed in behind them and passed through to the next room.

Darius took off his boots and then blushed as his big toe thrust itself through a huge hole in his stockings. He was suddenly very conscious of the state of his clothing.

"Better leave the socks, too," Hanish said. "They don't look to be in much better shape than the boots."

Barefoot, Darius followed Hanish through an entryway to the

rear of the house. The rear of the building was devoted to a large kitchen and dining area. A brick oven and several countertops dominated one side, and on the other sat a long table surrounded by six carved wooden chairs. Darius turned when he entered the kitchen and saw another doorway that opened to a wooden staircase that led to the second floor.

The kitchen smelled wonderful. Darius's senses were overwhelmed by the smell of baking bread, cloves, cinnamon, garlic, and baking meat.

"Who are you calling plump?" Elsie broke Darius from his reverie.

"You, my love." Hanish gave Elsie a friendly pat on her ample bottom.

"Never marry a skinny woman, Darius. Surest sign that she can't cook worth a damn."

"Hanish Cherian, you stop filling that poor boy's head with your nonsense," Elsie scolded. "Come here, Darius. There's hot water in the basin on the counter there and a cake of soap besides."

Darius peered into the copper basin and stared dumbly at the soap. Then shaking his head, he picked up the soap and scrubbed his face and hands. The water was a dull gray by the time he had finished.

Elsie gave a sidelong glance at the washbasin as she handed him a towel.

"Hanish is right about one thing. The pair of you will be

taking baths before you sleep in my beds. I'd have to scrub the bed linens for a week to get the grime out of them if you slept in them like that. By the look of you, you'll need some new clothes, too. What you're wearing isn't fit for the midden heap."

Darius blushed again.

"Kal, go up and get some of your old clothes. Those trousers I mended last week and those blue shirts that you've outgrown. I was going to give them to Dinah Merin for her boy, but Darius needs them more."

"Yes, ma'am," Kal said and sprinted up the stairs, taking them two at a time.

"Nash, get another chair and set another couple places at the table and pour two more mugs of milk."

"I'll have ale," Arthengal said as he strode into the kitchen.

"You can have all the ale you want when the boys are in bed," Elsie corrected. "We drink milk for dinner in this house."

Arthengal grinned. "Yes, ma'am. I had forgotten."

While Arthengal cleaned up, Elsie produced a fat loaf of bread from the oven and placed it on a flat square of slate in the center of the table. Then she carried an earthenware crock that smelled of sausage and garlic and onions to the table and handed Nash a long wooden spoon. Finally, she took a golden pie out of the oven and set it on the windowsill. She threw open the wooden shutters so the breeze would help the pie cool. A gust of wind from the window assailed Darius's nose anew with the smell of cinnamon and baked pears.

The meal was amazing. Darius loved his mother's cooking but it did not compare to what Elsie was serving. He savored each bite, and the combination of spices was something he had never before enjoyed. The bread seemed to melt in his mouth. The second piece, with butter on it, was even more delightful. He had seconds of everything and stared longingly at the empty crock at the end of the meal.

"What have you been feeding this poor boy?" Elsie reproached Arthengal.

"You know," he said over a mouthful of sausage. "Hard-tack and jerky. The usual."

He's joking, thought Darius, *but it isn't far off compared to this.*

"That sounds about right," Hanish joked. "Da' used to say 'good cooking may make you happy but field rations will make you tough.'"

Kal wrinkled his nose. "When granddad would take us camping he wouldn't let us eat anything we didn't catch and clean ourselves. Well, except for the hard-tack and jerky."

Everyone at the table laughed.

"Do you remember that time last summer?" Nash asked. "You caught that fat trout, but it had been raining so bad that we couldn't get the fire started and he made us eat the fish raw."

"Ew...," Anna said. "That's gross."

Kal made a gagging motion.

After dinner, the children helped Elsie clear the table, and she served up slices of pear pie topped with crumbled nuts and a drizzle of honey.

Darius actually moaned in delight at the first taste of the pie, and when it was finished, he leaned back in the chair with a sleepy, satisfied grin.

The culinary pleasures were not the end of Darius's surprises for the evening. He discovered that the laundry room wasn't actually filled with laundry. Instead, it was a small galley off the side of the kitchen. Small only when compared to the rest of the house. The entire space shared by Darius, Micah, and their mother would have fit in the room and then some. An iron wash basin and a scrub board for washing the laundry was set to one side. A window opened into the backyard, and a rope had been attached to some sort of wheel just outside the window. Arthengal explained that Elsie could attach the clean clothes with wooden pegs to the line and then pull it across the wheel to carry it outside and make space for the next piece.

The room also held a spacious copper tub. Nash and Kal helped carry hot water from the kitchen and cold from the well to fill the bath. The water lapped at Darius's chin, and the warm liquid soothed away the aches and pains of more than a week of travel. He nearly fell asleep resting his head against the back of the tub.

"Mama told me to bring these in to you."

Darius jumped at the sound of Anna's voice and then sunk

lower in the tub to hide himself. He peeked over the edge of the tub. She held a folded pile of clothes and a linen towel.

"Thank you," Darius said. He felt heat in his cheeks. "You can set it down by the door there."

She dropped the bundle, not noticing his embarrassment, and left as abruptly as she had entered.

After Arthengal and he had each bathed, Hanish led them up to his father's old bedroom and the second floor. Darius barely noticed the other furnishings in the flickering lamplight. His attention was focused entirely on the large box bed with a thick feather mattress covered with bed linens and a thick wool blanket.

Darius changed quickly into the bedclothes that Kal had loaned him and lay down on the mattress. He sank nearly two inches and still could not feel the wood of the box below. He had been sleeping on the floor, albeit a mat padded with extra blankets, or the ground since leaving his home nearly a year before. This bed was like lying on a cloud. He gave a deep, satisfied sigh and was asleep before Arthengal extinguished the light.

Chapter Eighteen
Eridu

The next morning, he woke early, well rested. Arthengal was still snoring when he changed into the spare set of Kal's clothes. He found his sword with the rest of their belongings, minus his clothes, piled in a corner of the room. Maybe Elsie really had carried out on the threat to toss them in the midden heap, or maybe she had them down in the laundry room. He snuck down the stairs and into the front yard for a bit of sword practice before breakfast.

As he was running through Swallow Skims Across Water, he saw Hanish emerge from the stone outbuilding carrying a pail in either hand. He set the pails down and leaned against the stone well to watch. Darius finished the final motion and moved immediately into Lion Shakes His Mane.

"You remind me of my father," Hanish said wistfully. "He used to come out every morning and practice as well. Every day up until he got sick."

"I have to learn. Arthengal is teaching me so we can go rescue my mother," he responded as he made a twisting motion with the blade.

"My dad tried to teach me, but I never had the knack. He said my hands were built for the plow rather than the sword, and that was a good thing." Hanish examined his hands, fingering the calluses.

There was an awkward silence for a moment. Darius glanced out of the corner of his eye at the farmer as he finished a sweep and a lunge.

"What happened to your mom?" Hanish finally asked. "Everything was so busy last night I never got the chance to hear your story."

"She was taken by raiders," Darius answered as he transitioned to Scooping the Moon. "Arthengal calls them the Daku Rabi. They kidnapped my whole village before autumn solstice last year. I met Arthengal while I was following them toward the Northern Wastes. He agreed to take me in, train me, and help me mount a rescue."

"Is she your only family?'

"Yes, they killed my brother in the raid, and my father had died years before."

Darius paused at the end of the form and turned to Hanish.

"You've known Arthengal your whole life?"

Hanish nodded.

"Do you know what happened to his wife?"

A dark look crossed Hanish's face.

"He hasn't told you?"

"No, he says he doesn't want to talk about it and changes the subject every time I ask."

"I can understand why." Hanish was silent for a minute, trying to decide whether to continue. "When the great rebellion first started, the emperor was still strong and had agents all over the continent. They identified the leaders of the rebellion. The barons, their generals, and other key leaders were all marked for death. He put a bounty on them and their families. Arthengal's wife and infant son were killed by the Daku Mitu."

"That's horrible," Darius was shocked. "You said Daku Mitu, not Daku Rabi. What's the difference?"

"The Daku Rabi was the elite army of the empire. Inside that army were several regiments. The Imperial Guard, the Mortikai warriors, the Zamani or *Lightning Bringers*, and the Daku Mitu or *Night Guard*. That was the official translation anyway, but everyone just called them the *Death Bringers*. They were the royal assassins. They came in the night and disappeared without a trace. Sometimes they left their victims' bodies as a warning to others, and sometimes their victims just disappeared and were never seen again."

Darius shivered, remembering the sensation of walking through his village after everyone had been taken.

"Arthengal's wife and child were found in their beds. I won't go into details, but the state of their bodies was said to have driven the poor serving girl that found them mad. My ma was also killed by them but not quite so brutally. Sengiin Sharav was the general of the Daku Mitu at that time. I think he had a vendetta against Arthengal, and wanted to make their deaths particularly memorable. I was only spared because my mom had spirited me away in the night to my aunt's house as soon as word began arriving of other deaths."

"Arthengal has told some pretty bad stories about the old emperor, but this is worse than all of them," Darius said. "Killing innocent people in their beds, that's monstrous."

Hanish nodded in agreement. "Emperor Chen was evil, to be sure. He had given the order, but Sengiin Sharav was the true monster behind those killings. Most of the barons and their generals escaped, but very few of their families did. General Dagon of Shalanum province and his entire family were killed at the docks of Kasha Amur while he was trying to help them escape on a merchant vessel."

"You talk too much, Hanish."

Both Darius and Hanish jumped.

Arthengal was leaning against the doorjamb sipping from a large earthenware cup.

"I believe Elsie is asking after that milk." He nodded to the two buckets.

Hanish looked abashed. He picked up the pails and hurried toward the house. He whispered a quick apology to Arthengal as he passed him.

Hanish turned just inside the door. "He seems to do very well. Not that I know much, but he moves like Papa used to when he practices."

"Most natural swordsman I've ever trained," Arthengal grunted without turning to the other man.

Darius blushed furiously.

"Oh, don't let that go to your head," Arthengal said with the hint of a smile. "You still have a lot to learn. Now, let's see Comet Chases the Moon. I haven't seen you run that one in a while."

Darius raised his sword and began the movements of the form. Darius considered what Hanish had told him as he flowed from one stance to the next. It was no wonder Arthengal didn't want to talk about his wife and son considering how horrific their deaths had been. He must also blame himself. It reminded Darius of how he had felt right after Micah had died. He hadn't wanted to talk about Micah at all. He had just wanted to wallow in his grief. It wasn't until...

Darius stopped moving and sheathed his blade. He looked at Arthengal, who leaned against the side of the house with his arms crossed over his chest. His face bore a dark look, and he appeared to be lost in thought. He hadn't even noticed that Darius had stopped practicing.

"Do you remember what you told me that first night we met?" Darius asked.

Arthengal's brown eyes shifted to meet Darius's.

"What are you talking about?" Arthengal asked, his voice tinged with anger.

"The first night we met. You forced me to talk about Micah

and my father. I didn't want to, but you drew it out of me. Do you remember what you said?"

Arthengal's eyes narrowed and his face grew darker. Then suddenly, the tension around his eyes seemed to relax. "I told you that it's important to talk about the dead because it keeps their memory alive and it honors their life."

Darius nodded and smiled. "Come on, let's get some breakfast. I would love to hear more about Sharaea and..."

"Wilem," Arthengal's voice was a whisper. Tears glistened in his eyes as he followed Darius into the house.

After a long breakfast filled with laughter and tears, Arthengal and Darius hitched the donkeys to the wagon. Beyond the farm, the road was lined with towering oak trees. They passed a few more farms similar to the one they had just left only different in the details. Some grew potatoes instead of corn, and others raised sheep instead of cows. Almost all had pear orchards.

Other roads joined the one they were on, and for the first time they saw other travelers. They were passed by a man and boy leading a donkey laden down with bushels of winter wheat, a woman and her three teenage daughters, and a lone man on horseback dressed in clothing finer than anything Darius had seen before. Soon they were part of a column of twenty to thirty people all moving toward Eridu. Several more bends in the road brought them within view of the city. Arthengal slowed the donkeys when the walls first came into view.

"There she is, Eridu, the last port of the north."

Darius's jaw dropped. The road ended at a hulking gate constructed of thick beams, two spans thick, bound in iron. The massive doors stood open, guarded by half a dozen men in polished breastplates over blue uniforms. A towering palisade built from thick oak trunks spread away from the gate to surround the city. The fence was at least six paces high and must have stretched a thousand paces on either side of the gate. Wooden towers had been erected at the corners and on either side of the entrance. The towers rose another three or four paces above the wall. Darius could see three archers in each gate tower and more armed men patrolling the top of the fortification.

Even over the barricade, Darius could see the top floors of stone houses and shops, each as tall as Hanish's house or taller. There were hundreds of buildings filling a city larger than any Darius had ever imagined. The road continued through the gateway and led straight through the metropolis. At the far end, Darius could just make out a broad grassy hill atop which an enormous four-story building had been erected. It looked like a palace built from stone and rough-hewn logs. He couldn't see the ocean beyond the wall, but the wheeling gulls to the west betrayed its existence.

"It's like a dream," Darius said with wonder. "Or something out of mother's stories."

Arthengal laughed.

"If you are comparing Eridu to stories of Kasha Marka or Kasha Esharra, then your mother's tales must have been sorely lacking in detail. Kasha Marka is a hundred times the size of this small port town. And at its peak, under Emperor Chen Bao Mu, Kasha Esharra was twenty times larger than that. Even Kasha Amur, the capital of Shalanum province, has close to fifty-thousand residents."

Numbers spun in Darius's head. They had practiced their sums, but the comparisons baffled him. He couldn't even picture a city on the scale that Arthengal was talking about.

"What is the palace up ahead? Does the Baron live here? I thought he lived in Kasha Amur."

"Palace?" Arthengal roared with laughter. "Boy, you really need to travel more. That's the town hall and the magistrates' court. Kasha Amur doesn't really have a palace, per se, but the entire town of Eridu would fit inside the palace grounds at Kasha Marka."

"How many people live here? It must be hundreds," Darius guessed.

"Hmmm...I'm not sure. A thousand or so, I'd guess. And there'll be half that again in traders and merchants with their crews and guards in port to trade."

"Almost two thousand people. All in one place?" Darius's voice was soft with awe. "Our village had seventy. Imbros, a mining settlement to the northwest, was twice as large, and I thought it was a city. They even had an inn. I never imagined a city this large before. The cities that mother described in her stories always sounded like fantasies out of legend. Micah and I never imagined that they might be real."

Arthengal continued to chuckle while they waited for their turn to pass through the gates. Four guards holding spears stood by the gate while two others stood at the center of the road to question those who sought entry.

"State your business," the younger of the two said curtly as Arthengal guided the wagon up to them.

"In town to sell rope and nets," Arthengal answered with a grin and then nodded to the oldest of the sentries, maybe thirty years old, standing at ease to the left of the gate. "Hey there, Teman. How's your father?"

"Very good, sir," the guard said brightly. He was clearly happy to have been recognized. "It's good to see you again, sir. Will you be staying long? I'm sure my father would love to see you. He's manning the store today."

"Just visiting long enough to trade and pick up a few supplies. I'll be staying at the Cherian farm while I'm here. I'll make sure to stop by the store to visit your Da. Any word from the capital?"

"No sir, it's been a long winter everywhere, and trade is picking up slowly. Very few traders from up north, so far, and no merchants from as far south as Kasha Amur yet."

"And here I thought we'd be late to the game. Thank you,

Teman. Good day to you, then." Arthengal gave a nod and slapped the reins to move the wagon forward.

The guards in their path gave a startled jump and hurried out of the way. They closed the gap again after the wagon passed, ready to question the next in line.

"Who was that?" Darius heard the young guard whisper after they had passed.

"That," Teman replied, "was Nasu Rabi."

Darius heard the younger guard gasp.

As the cart rolled through the city, Darius examined the various buildings. The first buildings they passed all seemed to be inns. The Golden Stag was a blue building with a red door and a picture showing a painted image of its namesake. The Nags Head was a red and green building with a horse head decorating its sign. They passed the Knights Inn, the Blue Anchor, and the Baron's Retreat before entering a quarter filled with merchants.

The two- and three-story mercantile buildings had a shop at the ground level and apartments for the owner on the second floor. The buildings were painted in many colors and signage hung from iron rods mounted above the door. Tailor, cobbler, and seamstress shops gave way to silversmiths, gilders, and lace makers. Tables covered with colorful canopies displayed merchandise in front of each shop and hawkers cried their wares to passersby.

Dozens of people walked the streets around them. Some stopped at shops while others hurried off on business elsewhere.

Darius's head whipped from left to right, trying to take it all in. The variety of people and clothing was unlike anything he had experienced. The sheer throng of people soon had him overwhelmed.

"I can't believe how dead it is today," Arthengal commented. "As late as we are in the spring, I expected there to be three or four times as many people here buying or trading goods. Teman must have been right. The winter hit everyone hard."

Darius shook his head, baffled by the comment.

They turned off the main thoroughfare as Arthengal guided the wagon toward the harbor and Darius's eyes grew wide again as he saw three piers stretching into the sea. At the longest, six large three-masted ships were secured to either side. Banners flapped at the top of each of the tallest masts. Most bore the image of a golden lion on a field of blue, but one showed a red eagle on a yellow background. A third banner pictured two fish, one light blue and one white, forming a circle atop a field of black. Several smaller, single-masted vessels occupied spaces on the smallest dock.

"Hmmm," Arthengal grumbled lowly. "We might have trouble selling everything. I was hoping there would be more merchantmen in port by now. Maybe I can make a deal with the dockmaster if we cut the price."

Darius was only half listening. After his initial inspection of the piers, his eyes had been drawn to the businesses that they were passing. The respectable shops were replaced with public houses and more creatively named inns as they drew nearer to the wharf. The

Stagger Inn, the Insatiable Badger, and the Witch's Brew made Darius laugh at the names and artistic decoration while the Busty Barmaid, the Nymph's Nodes, and the Swordhole made him blush furiously, if not for the names then for the pictures displayed on the signs.

Arthengal pulled to a halt a few paces down from the innocuously named Deckhand's Booty with an open chest of treasure pictured on the sign. He shouted at one of the passing sailors.

"You there, where's your bosun?"

"There," the crewman pointed, eyeing the wagon. "Overseeing the loading on Winter's Spray."

Arthengal strode down the landing toward the indicated ship with Darius trailing quickly behind. A lion banner flapped in the wind atop the mainmast.

The man was standing on the dock, directing others as they carried supplies up the gangplank.

"Beautiful vessel," Arthengal commented when the man glanced his way. "I'm not familiar with the Winter's Spray. From where do you hail?"

"Linwall Reach out on the Morbush Peninsula. We don't normally trade this side of the Sea of Tears, but there is a good market for fur and musk this year and we heard Eridu was the best place for both. It's been a bit of a disappointment so far. Trade is picking up slow this year, especially here in the north."

"I heard you are the bosun?" Arthengal asked.

"Aye, sir. Allister Corwin. And who might you be?" He extended his hand.

"Arthengal Alamay." He gripped the offered hand. "I have a load of first-rate rope that I'm hoping to sell. Are you in the market?"

"Aye, we could use some reserves. Let me see what you've got."

The bosun searched the docks for another officer on his ship, "Mister Merin, take over here while I look at this man's stock."

The other man stepped in to start giving direction, and Allister followed the pair back to the wagon. Darius helped unfasten the netting so the bosun could get a better look at the coils of rope.

"Aye, it's good quality. Are the coils cable length?"

"Of course." Arthengal nodded. "We have about forty coils and twenty fishing nets."

"I don't need no nets, but I could use about five coils and could give you two marks each."

"You won't find a better weave. Three marks each," Arthengal countered.

"Twelve marks for the five. That's the best I can do."

"Done." Arthengal shook the man's hand.

Allister slung one of the large loops over his shoulder.

"I'll send a couple of my men down with payment and to collect the other four."

"The price has gone up since last year, which works in our favor. There must be a shortage of strong rope, not that the bosun would ever admit that outright," Arthengal considered thoughtfully once the sailor was out of earshot.

"What's a mark?" Darius asked.

"Coins minted in the capital. They replaced the imperial crowns after the rebellion. Each barony mints its own coins now. They are all about the same in weight and made from gold. Gold marks can be broken into silver drachs or copper pennies. There are about five drachs or fifty pennies to a mark, depending on where you change them. Money changers always take their cut, and there aren't many shopkeepers that will change a mark, the spice merchants maybe, and a few of the importers that bring in more exotic trade goods like silk and jade."

A pair of well-muscled sailors returned shortly and gave a handful of gold and silver coins to Arthengal before hoisting a coil over each shoulder. Arthengal let Darius examine the coins.

The gold coins were heavier than the silver. Most had a lion's head imprinted on them, but a few had an eagle. The back of each bore a stylized symbol which Arthengal said represented the houses of Shalanum and Magora, respectively. The coins were all of similar size, about twice as wide as Darius's thumbnail.

Darius watched in fascination as the pattern of transaction repeated itself a dozen more times. Not only did he learn something about trading, but also a lot about the ships themselves. The taller vessels, merchantmen, almost always had a bosun who was in charge of outfitting the ship and buying supplies. They also usually had more need and more money. With the smaller craft, sloops and cutters, Arthengal had to deal directly with the captains. Most of these were local fishermen who trolled the bay. They tended to be more interested in the nets than the ropes.

The sun was sinking low on the horizon when they finished unloading the last net from the wagon. They had managed to sell all of the nets and all but five of their coils. The dockmaster didn't know of any other ships coming in during the next few days, so Arthengal sold the remaining stock to him for a mark each. His purse was fat with sixty marks and three times that in drachs by the end.

"Let's head back to the farm. We can come in tomorrow to buy our supplies."

Darius nodded sleepily.

Chapter Nineteen
Free Horses

"Come on, then. You can't sleep all day." Arthengal woke Darius by tossing a stack of folded clothes on his head.

Darius looked groggily out the window.

"It's not even light yet. What are you talking about?"

"We have another busy day, and I mean to be at it early. First stop is the tailor. You can wear Kal's hand-me-downs, but I also mean to get you a few proper sets of clothes and burn those rags of yours. Come on, then, practice in the yard while I hitch the wagon. We'll leave the second Elsie's biscuits are out of the oven."

Darius was munching on his third biscuit when Arthengal turned the wagon off the main boulevard. The side streets were narrower, but still wide enough for the wagon to navigate between the awning-covered tables in front of the shops. There were fewer people here, but it seemed even more crowded than the broader thoroughfare.

Arthengal reined the donkeys to a stop in front of an ornate storefront. A carefully lettered sign read, "Sew Elegant."

"Are you sure this is the place for us?" Darius asked.

Arthengal glanced briefly at the sign.

"Yep."

The mistress of the store was arranging clothes on shelves when they entered. Several elegant dresses with lace and glass beads clung to dress forms. Metal hoops mounted below flared out the skirts of the dresses. The early morning light through the open windows reflected off the beads and made the dresses shimmer. The woman inside was not old, but neither was she young. Darius estimated her somewhere between Elsie Cherian and Arthengal in age. Even so, she was quite beautiful with just a touch of silver in her long blonde hair. She was tall and thin and had a large bosom that was accentuated by the cut of her yellow dress. The dress was trimmed with lace and decorated with tiny blue flowers along the hem and down her arms.

"Can I help you?" the mistress asked, all business, before she recognized the visitor. Then her demeanor changed completely.

"Arthengal!" she shouted and then wrapped him in a hug. The bosom pressed tightly against Arthengal and threatened to burst out of the top of the dress.

"You are late this year. We were taking bets on whether or not the mountain or the wolves swallowed you up," she said as she let him go and held him at arm's length.

"It's good to see you, Gabby. How's Amon?" Arthengal asked.

"Bah!" the woman said with a dismissive wave of her hand.

"He spends more time in the pub than he does on the boat anymore. But the shop does well, so I say let him have his fun. He certainly earned it all those years following your lot around. How can I help you?"

"Gabby, this is Darius. Darius, this is Gabriella Porter, the wife of a very dear friend of mine." Arthengal gave introductions before returning his attention to the woman. "We need new clothes for the boy. A couple pair of wool pants and half a dozen shirts, loose in the shoulders and chest so he can grow into them a bit."

"Very nice to meet you, ma'am," Darius said a bit too loud, trying very hard to look her in the eyes.

"The pleasure is mine," she said with a warm smile. "How did you get mixed up with this good-for-nothing scoundrel?"

"I, uh..." Darius started to stutter, but before could finish his answer, Gabriella was shuffling him to the rear of the shop where she poked and prodded and measured him.

"We have a good stock that should work for him. I keep a variety on hand for the sailors that come in off the ships. They don't have time to wait for custom work and are none too picky about the fit."

She rummaged through stacks of pants on a table and returned with various sizes and shades of blue, black, and tan. She searched several other shelves and produced a pile of shirts in every color of the rainbow. She showed Darius to a curtain where he could change and insisted on inspecting each outfit to make sure it fit adequately. His cheeks turned crimson every time she inspected the lines of the pants or ran her hands down his back or chest to smooth a shirt.

Two very uncomfortable hours later, they settled on two pairs of the black pants and three pairs of brown and a stout leather belt. Darius was happy that he wouldn't have to use the knotted rope anymore.

"I'll have to take in the hem on the britches. That way if he sprouts too much this year you can always take the hem out," she explained.

The shirts were all a heavy linen, two forest green, a dark blue collared shirt, a pair in beige with longer sleeves for winter, and a purple shirt with yellow flowers embroidered on the short sleeves. The last was Darius's favorite.

"We don't have feast day in the valley, but you never know when a nice shirt like that might come in handy," Arthengal noted. "Maybe we can time our summer trip with the Festival of Yaz. I'm sure plenty of the local girls would love to dance with you."

Darius blushed to his ears.

"I'll only need to make some minor adjustments to the shirts. You can pick up everything this afternoon," Gabby said as Arthengal paid her four drachs for the lot.

The next stop was the shoemaker for a couple pairs of boots. The cobbler happened to be the father of the guard Arthengal had spoken to the previous day. He was an older man, closer to

Arthengal's age. While he measured Darius and brought out several pairs of boots to try, the men prattled about current events and retold humorous stories from the time of the war that Darius could tell had been recounted a hundred times before.

"A pair for now and a size larger for when he outgrows these," Arthengal finally agreed.

Darius wore the pair that fit out of the store. His feet thanked Arthengal more profusely than he did. He was not one to complain, but his toes had been cramped inside his old boots.

They stopped at a third shop to buy Darius a collection of light tunics. They were all serviceable, but Darius's favorites were a brown leather tunic with a high collar that laced up the front and a red one, open at the chest, with just a bit of lace, but not too frilly. Darius was astounded when the tunic with the lace cost more than the rest combined. Darius found a wide cloth belt to bind them at the waist. Arthengal also picked up a new cloak the color of pine boughs.

The shopping spree continued until the wagon was half filled with packages. A thick wool cloak for Darius, cooking pots from the blacksmith, several new handles for the axes and scythes, trenching tools, and shovels to build Darius's 'stairway to Anbar Ur,' as Arthengal called it. They stopped at a dozen more shops for cooking spices, lamp oil, tanning lime, several pounds of salt, and finally, a narrow cot from a furniture maker.

"We can't have you sleeping on the floor forever, can we?"

Arthengal said about the last.

They bought a few light provisions to round out the wagon, and Arthengal announced that they could call it a day. By the end, Darius had a greater appreciation for the value of the coin. The only time Arthengal had drawn out the gold marks was for the joiner and at the spice shop. They had spent less than half their drachs on all the rest and in return had a handful of copper pennies to add to the pouch.

"What about the potatoes and onions and garlic that you were going on and on about?" Darius asked.

"We'll have to come back at harvest time for all of that. Anything the farmers have to sell now would be from last year's crop and wouldn't last us the summer, let alone the winter."

It was after midday when they finished.

"I think I'd like to get a good way up the road before it gets dark," Arthengal said.

"We aren't staying the night again at the farm?"

"No, we don't have any more business here and it would waste half a day of travel. I do love Hanish, Elsie, Anna, and the boys, but I don't want to overstay my welcome, either. You know what they say, 'Guests are like fish, they begin to smell after three days.'"

"I do have another stop, but I won't be long," Arthengal added.

They pulled up beside the dockmaster's shack.

"You can wait here," Arthengal said.

"What did you do?" Darius asked a few minutes later when Arthengal returned.

"I wrote a quick note to Shalanum and asked the dockmaster to have it delivered on the first vessel bound for the capital. I wanted to tell him about the raider activities in the north and that scouts should be sent to investigate the Daku Rabi activities. I also wrote a similar note for Magora and instructed the dockmaster to send it if any caravans happen to travel to Kasha Marka. That seems unlikely, though. The Talai Mountains mark the border between Shalanum and Magora provinces, and there aren't any well-established trade routes."

"Are the Talai Mountains big?" Darius asked.

"We really need to buy you a map. Maybe I'll commission one when we are back in the fall and we can pick it up next spring. You need to learn more about the world you live in. In fact, maybe I will swing by the farm on the way out of town. Hanish's father had a book, written in the old tongue, that gave a pretty fair account of imperial history. It would be good reading practice for you, and you might learn a little something, too."

Their stop at the farm was short, just long enough to thank them for their hospitality and ask about the book. Hanish agreed to loan it to them. He couldn't bear to sell it, but it was gathering dust in his father's trunk of belongings.

"Someone may as well get some use out of it," he said as he

handed over the palm-thick tome.

Darius hefted the leather-bound book; it was twice as thick as any of Arthengal's books and as heavy as any three of them combined. He carefully stored it in the saddlebags strapped to the side of the wagon.

With that, they said their goodbyes. Elsie had hugs for them both. Hanish, Kal, and Nash bid them good health with firm handshakes. Anna stuck out her tongue.

When they reached the crossroads again, there was a group of men on horseback camped at the fire pit nearest the well. Arthengal pulled the wagon up at the north side of the way station, closer to the mining road, and started to unhitch the donkeys.

"Go fetch some water, will you?" he asked Darius.

Darius was drawing water from the well when a short man from the other camp approached carrying a bucket. He had narrow eyes and a pointed, waxed mustache over thin lips. He wore dark riding pants and a yellowed shirt that spoke of days on the road without a thought to clean it.

"Hallo there, youngster. The name's Danel Bline." The man extended a hand with a friendly smile.

"Darius." He gave Danel's hand a brief shake.

"Up from Eridu, are ye?"

"Yes, we are on our way home from trading there."

"Traders, are ye? What were ye selling?"

Danel's accent was strange. He didn't sound like he was from the villages to the north and he didn't sound like anyone from Eridu. The closest Darius could think was the bosun of the *Mermaid's Wolf,* although he couldn't remember where he had said he was from.

"Rope and nets," Darius answered simply.

"Good port town, Eridu. I betcha did all right selling rope and nets."

"We did great," Darius said, excited. "Enough to buy me some new clothes and a bed and enough for food stuffs come harvest."

"Well, fortune favor you, then. That's a right fine shirt yer wearing. Is that one of the new ones, then?"

Darius fingered the dark blue fabric.

"Yes, I just picked it up this afternoon."

"Well, you look quite the gentleman in it, if I don't say. Mighty fine, mighty fine."

"Thank you."

"Are you headed back Imbros way then?"

"Huh, no, we go that way." He jerked a thumb toward the old road.

"The old mining road, is it?" Danel gave a curious look. "Not many travel that direction anymore. Not in quite some time. Nothing but sticks and wolves that way."

"Uh, yeah, I guess. Where are you all going?"

"Oh, we're on to Eridu ourselves."

Darius looked over Danel's shoulder at the group. There were no wagons or trade goods. He was trying to work out why they would be going to Eridu.

"We're headed to get our horses shod, you see," Danel said as if reading Darius's mind. "Our blacksmith took ill last winter, you see, and we don't have another. They got a decent blacksmith in Eridu, they do."

"Uh huh. Where are you coming from?"

"Oh," Danel drawled, "it's just a tiny little village, by name of Koza, up the coast there. One such as yourself probably never heard of it. We don't get many visitors that way."

The skin on Darius's arms crawled, and a shiver went up his spine.

"Best of luck to you," he croaked. He hoisted the bucket. "I've got to water the horses."

"Nice to meet you," he called behind him as he hurried toward his campsite.

Danel stared after him for a moment then slowly rejoined his group.

"Arthengal," Darius hissed as he rounded the wagon. He dropped the waterskins and the bucket on the ground. "Those men."

Arthengal looked up from hobbling the donkeys.

Darius was fumbling with his sword belt trying to strap it around his waist while keeping the wagon between him and the other men.

"What about them?" Arthengal glanced at the group.

They were all walking in their direction. Darius counted thirteen of them. He saw that they all had knives strapped to their belts and two of them wore sword belts. None of them had weapons drawn as they approached. They strode casually but with a confidence born from superior numbers.

They stopped about five paces away. Danel was in front and the others were spread out on either side. Arthengal watched the group evenly. How can he be so calm? Darius thought. His own heart hammered in his chest.

"It were the name of the town, weren't it?" Danel asked. "You said you were headed that way so I figured a tiny nothing of a town up the coast would be safe to use."

"I'm from Koza, and there isn't anyone who lives there anymore," Darius's voice quavered.

Arthengal glanced at Darius curiously, and then realization dawned on his face.

"Ah," Danel said. "So you know about that then, too. We discovered that last winter ourselves. The whole town up and vanished. No trace whatsoever. Made a nice place to spend the winter, though, it did. Nice fishing there."

Darius stepped out from behind the wagon and drew his sword.

"You stay back," he shouted.

Danel's face looked truly shocked for a half second, then his casual demeanor returned.

"Now, no need for none of that, ye hear," he said with mock indignation. "There ain't no need for weapons to be drawn. We don't want to hurt no one. Just hand over that coin from the sale of yer, rope was it, and we'll be on our way."

Arthengal flashed Darius a dark look.

"I said stay back," Darius shouted. His cheeks colored under Arthengal's accusing glare.

Danel sighed and gave a nod to the men on his right. Two of them stepped forward and acted as if they were just going to take the sword from Darius's grasp.

Darius set his stance, and when they were within range, began the motions for Striking Adder. The first ruffian jerked with a yelp as the blade opened up a gash on his reaching hand. His partner drew his belt knife and approached with more caution. Darius moved into Dancing Lights, and with a few quick flicks of the blade, knocked the other man's knife away and scored a nick on his cheek.

"I said stay back," Darius shouted again.

"Vicious little whelp, aren't ye," Danel said and signaled the men with swords to advance. "We didn't want to have to hurt ye, but it looks like ye are determined to leave us no choice."

Darius risked a quick glance at Arthengal as the two thugs advanced and he was leaning against the wagon. Is he going to help? Darius thought indignantly.

The bandits advanced from opposite sides. Darius began moving through Wary Badger. The attackers circled him, searching for an opening, but the defensive form didn't leave many openings on the sides. Both thieves feinted, and Darius batted their attacks away with ease before picking up the form again.

The first brigand struck with more force a couple of times. He didn't appear to be actually trying to hit Darius, and he absorbed Darius's defensive strikes in kind.

"Too long..." he heard Arthengal murmur. "Switch it up."

Darius wasn't sure what he meant and kept repeating Wary Badger. It seemed to be holding the swordsmen at bay. The rest of the group were watching them with arms crossed as if they were watching events at a spring fair. He even heard one of them mutter what sounded like a wager on the outcome to the others.

The second thief attacked next, striking against his left side. Darius knocked these blows away, too. Each assailant feinted several more times to no effect, and Darius's confidence grew. Maybe he could try an attack.

Suddenly, both men attacked at once. The first struck from the left, batting Darius's sword into that of his partner. Both blows were deflected, but before Darius could recover, the first attacker's sword jerked up catching Darius's blade from below while the second thug struck from above, nearer the hilt. The sword was jerked from his hand and he stumbled forward. By chance or bad luck, he stumbled directly in the path of the second man's reverse slash, and he felt cold steel and then warm blood on his left eye. He jerked his hand to his face and stumbled backward. He tripped and sat down hard, still clutching the wound.

"Okay, that's enough. Fun's over." It was Arthengal's voice.

Darius glanced up. Tears were forming in his good eye, but he could see that Arthengal had his bow raised. He had an arrow nocked but held four more in his hand like porcupine quills sprouting at odd angles.

"You too then, now," the leader said. "You two really do insist on making this difficult."

Without waiting for Danel to give a signal, Arthengal's arm moved like a blur. One after the other, all five arrows were drawn and released. The first struck the brigand to the left of Danel, and he went down with a strangled gurgle, the shaft protruding from his throat. The bandit to the leader's right clutched at the fletching protruding from his chest before the first man hit the ground. Both swordsmen screamed as their arms were pinned to their sides. The fifth shot caught an unlucky thief in the wrist as he was trying to throw a dagger drawn from his belt.

"Whoa, whoa, whoa. Let's think this through. You can't stop us all, and if you make this hard, we'll have to kill ye." Danel was holding his hands out before him as if they would stop the arrows.

Arthengal reached behind him and produced another handful of arrows. Before he could draw, the leader's eyes grew wide and the other thieves' faces became aghast.

The roar behind Arthengal was deafening.

Darius peered past Arthengal. Standing at the edge of the

trees, stretched to his full height, was Antu.

Antu roared again and then dropped to all fours and charged. He bowled over the first thug he passed without slowing down and launched himself at Danel.

Danel turned and started to run, but with two great bounds, Antu had him on the ground. The crunch of bone in Antu's jaws made Darius wince.

A bandit wearing a black shirt and a vicious grin drew his belt knife, and with a yell charged the bear, trying to come to his leader's rescue. Antu gave his assailant a mystified look, and then swept a casual paw backward. He struck the man in the chest like he was brushing a branch out of his way. The attacker flew at least three paces through the air and landed with a thump.

What was he thinking? Darius thought.

The man gaped in shock as the realization of what he had just done struck him, and then relief filled his eyes that he had survived the insane ploy. Shaking himself, he scrambled to his feet and ran. The others scattered, sprinting to their horses. Leaving saddles and gear behind, they leapt bareback onto their mounts and galloped south.

Antu gave a final roar for good measure and then turned toward Darius. Darius began to sweat as the bear approached. Antu leaned forward and sniffed Darius's wounded eye. Blood was trickling between Darius's fingers and down his wrist. The bear tilted his head slightly and Darius could swear that he smiled. A horrifying, toothy smile, but a smile nonetheless.

"Grmpf," was the only sound the bear made, and then it turned and loped toward the trees.

That sounded like a laugh, Darius thought.

Moments later, Arthengal was at his side, pressing a linen cloth to the wound. He dragged the boy to the wagon and leaned him against the wheel.

"Hold this," he said as he pressed Darius's hand onto the rag. Darius did as he was told and leaned his head back, closing his other eye.

Darius heard Arthengal getting supplies from his saddlebags. After several minutes, Arthengal pulled the cloth away. He poured water over the gash and then pressed a finger full of goop against the cut.

"Ahhh. That stings," Darius complained.

"Aye, it will," was all Arthengal said, and then repeated the process on his cheek.

Once he was done, he poured more water into Darius's eye directly. He pulled apart the lids and examined the eye.

"The point missed the eye. You were lucky. You will have quite a scar, but you won't lose your sight. Let it serve as a lesson. You stayed too long in the same form. You let them test your defenses, and then you allowed them to coordinate an attack. Always leave your opponent off balance. Don't allow them the time they need or this is what will happen. Always press the attack against multiple opponents and use them against each other." He placed a clean bandage over the wound.

"How did you do that with the arrows?" Darius asked.

"Ah, a trick I picked up from the Sisuma. They were brilliant bowmen. I once saw a man do that with ten shots. I've never been able to manage more than five."

Darius surveyed at the bandit's camp while Arthengal wrapped a long strip of linen around his head to hold the bandage in place. Two of their horses nickered and danced nervously. Their lead lines were still tied to a makeshift hitching post at the camp.

"Hey," Darius smiled, despite the pain.

"What?" Arthengal asked.

"I got us two horses."

Arthengal glanced over his shoulder and then said with a smile, "So you did, boy. So you did. And quite a bit of gear, as well. It looks like we'll have more to sell when we return to Eridu later in the summer. Maybe we can even get a crate of those fat, prickly fruit that come from the Paradaisu Islands. I think they call them painappuru or some such. The fruit inside is like you've never tasted, but they're normally too expensive to bother. A dozen saddles with tack ought to cover the cost and then some. You rest. I'll load the wagon."

PART II

Spring - 34 A.E.

Chapter Twenty
Death of a Baron

Darius circled slowly, the practice sword held before him. Arthengal struck and struck again. Darius countered both strikes easily and answered with three quick strikes of his own, all batted away harmlessly. He flowed smoothly from one form to the next, adjusting at the merest sight of transition from Arthengal. He saw an opening and attacked with Wild Horse Leaps. Arthengal retreated.

"We've been at this for an hour. Aren't you ready to stop yet?" Arthengal asked.

"Not until I land first strike," Darius responded with a sweep, a lunge, a quick riposte, and a strong overhead strike. "This will be the day."

Darius used his slight advantage in height and reach to try Lion Shakes His Mane against Arthengal's Lazy Viper. Darius was driven back by the other man's quick transition into Striking Adder. The two forms did work well together.

Arthengal grinned. Over the past four years, the two had become very evenly matched. Darius had filled out and his reflexes had improved while Arthengal, almost seventy, had slowed a step. However, whatever advantage Darius held in speed and strength, Arthengal still made up for in skill. Barely.

While the two men sparred, Antu wandered into camp, sniffed the pile of nuts and berries waiting by the campfire, and lay down to enjoy his breakfast. The bear had started doing that a couple years ago during the spring trip to Eridu. Rather than waiting for the men to leave to claim his morning snack, the bear had just ambled into camp, sat down, and started eating.

Arthengal had been beside himself that first time and Darius had gotten an earful that entire day's trip. Darius had smiled through the entire tirade. Antu hadn't harassed them at all. He had eaten, and when he was done, had licked his muzzle and shambled back into the woods. The donkeys had taken an hour to calm down enough to hook up to the wagon.

When Antu had returned and done the same thing the next morning, Arthengal, and the donkeys, had watched the bear warily, but neither had been as upset. Antu had extended the time he spent in camp after his meal with each subsequent visit until the last morning of that trip the bear had lain down by the embers and taken a nap while Darius and Arthengal packed up the camp. Antu had followed along behind the wagon on that last day and cut off into the woods only when they reached the gates of Anbar Ur.

Darius was snapped out of the memory by a barrage of thrusts and slashes that drove him back against the wagon bed. He recovered quickly and countered with a sweeping strike at Arthengal's blade followed by a quick thrust at the throat. Arthengal had to dance away to avoid the strike, and Darius reset his stance.

Antu had surprised the pair again in the winter of that first year. The bear had climbed down the winding path into the valley, without triggering any of Arthengal's traps. After a quick sniff around the cabin, Antu had wandered the rest of the valley inspecting the abandoned mines. He had staked a claim to one of the caves and had spent the winter in the valley enjoying the free food that Darius provided rather than braving the winter storms and deep snows of the surrounding mountains. Darius and Arthengal had needed to go hunting twice that winter to supplement the needs of the valley's new resident.

Darius dodged another strike from Arthengal. The blade was moving more slowly now. Arthengal was beginning to tire, but then again, so was Darius. He had been using every bit of strength and speed to best the old man. Sweat soaked his white shirt. But beads of sweat were starting to form on Arthengal's brow. That almost never happened unless he was very fatigued. The old man settled into a defensive stance to catch his breath.

Darius saw an opening and charged with The Dragon Whips

His Tail. Too late, he saw his mistake. What he thought was a retreat and an open posture was only the first sequence of Fashionably Late. The final thrust caught him square in the ribs.

"Rat spit," Darius cursed and bowed to Arthengal. "You always get me with that."

"I keep telling you, spend a few years at court and you'll never fall victim to it again." Arthengal laughed and returned the bow.

"I was so close."

"You were," Arthengal admitted. "There were several times when I thought you had me."

"Let's go again." Darius raised the practice sword.

"No, enough is enough. We have to get on the road."

Darius stripped off his sodden shirt and snatched a linen cloth off the side of the wagon. It was hot. Spring had come early this year, and it felt like it was already approaching summer. He clasped his hands behind his back and stretched his chest. Relief spread through the rippling muscles of his shoulders and chest and sweat trickled down his forehead, making the scar across his eye itch. He released the stretch to scratch the scar and then pulled his long blond hair free from the thong that tied it. He bent forward and shook the sweat from his hair.

"Here, I have something for you," Arthengal said. He held a small package wrapped in cloth in his outstretched hand. The cloth was tied closed with a bit of string.

Darius gathered his hair and pulled it into a tight ponytail. He tied it tightly again before reaching for the proffered gift.

"What is it?" Darius asked and took the package.

He carefully untied the string and folded back the cloth. Inside was a small wooden box made from mahogany. The lid of the dark box was carved with the same emblem as their scabbards. Darius had come to learn that it was the crest of Nasu Rabi, awarded to Arthengal by Baroness Magora. He lifted the lid and smiled. A flat ivory disk banded with silver lay in the box. Etched into the ivory and stained with ink was the likeness of a roaring bear with a white muzzle. He lifted the disk out of the box from the leather cord that was strung through a loop on the silver banding.

"I love it. It looks like Antu. But I don't understand, what is this for?"

"Your eighteenth name day. You said it was the first full moon after the spring equinox. That is today."

"I had forgotten," Darius laughed and pulled the leather loop over his neck.

He lifted the ivory disk and studied the picture. "It looks just like him. How did you get him to sit still for that long?

"Antu!" Darius turned and shouted.

The grizzled bear lifted his head from where he lay a few paces away under the shade of a tree.

"Did you see this?" He extended the necklace. "It looks just like you."

The bear gave a disinterested grunt and lay his head back down.

"Let's go," Arthengal urged, "I would like to be to the Hanish's farm by nightfall."

Darius tucked the practice swords beneath the seat and pulled on a fresh shirt. He tucked the necklace into his shirt. The ivory felt cool against his chest.

"Thank you for the gift," Darius said as he climbed into the driver's seat. "I really do love it."

"You are welcome," Arthengal said. "Wear it well and always remember that your two *Nasu Rabi* will always have your back."

Darius smiled and snapped the reins.

Antu grunted as he rose to his feet and shambled after the wagon.

Darius held the reins loosely in his hands. The rhythmic rocking and the repetitive creaking of the wheels lulled him into a light drowse. Arthengal rocked side to side next to him with his arms crossed over his chest. The older man's gray beard brushed softly against the linen of his tunic. Every time they hit a bump or slipped out of a rut in the road, Arthengal teetered precariously on the edge of the bench so he always seemed on the verge of falling out. Antu had long since faded into the wooded hills to the east. They were coming too near to Eridu for his taste.

The donkeys crested the hill to the north of Hanish Cherian's farm and rolled easily down the other side. A loud crack startled Darius fully awake.

He nudged Arthengal with an elbow and the man grunted.

"There may be trouble," Darius said.

Arthengal raised his head and inspected the scene below them.

The farmyard was a beehive of activity. Nash was carrying large crates of pears toward Hanish who was hurriedly loading them into his wagon. Kal was staring blankly at a shattered cask watching the cider spread across the dusty ground.

"Forget it, boy," Hanish shouted. "Go grab another."

Kal sprinted toward the barn and passed his brother carrying another crate.

"What do think that's all about?" Darius asked.

Elsie trotted out of the house, holding her skirts with one hand and carrying a basket of oatcakes in the other. Anna was at her heels, carrying a sealed ceramic jar in each arm. Elsie deposited the basket at Hanish's feet and hurried back toward the house.

Darius turned the donkeys toward the farm.

"You late for something?" Arthengal called across the yard.

Hanish barely paused in his work to wave toward the two men.

Concern furrowed Arthengal's brow. He leapt from the wagon and strode toward Hanish.

"Hanish," he called more loudly. "What's going on?"

Hanish finally stopped and crossed toward Arthengal. Darius wasn't sure how to interpret what he saw on the man's face. It looked like part fear and part anger.

"They've killed him, Arthengal."

"What? Who? What are you talking about?"

"They murdered him in his sleep. Him and his whole family. The palace guard didn't see or hear a thing."

"Hanish," Arthengal said slowly. His voice was edged with a dangerous tone that Darius had never heard before. "What are you talking about?"

"The baron, Arthengal. They've murdered the baron. Shalanum is without a leader. The capital is a mess, what with ministers and the generals fighting each other. General Aydin wants to raise an army and there's talk of war. The ministers, in their blasted tall hats, want to raise a new baron but can't two of 'em agree on who it should be. There's been talk of skirmishes in the streets as different factions try to seize control."

"When did this happen?" Arthengal asked.

"Almost two weeks ago. A troop ship just arrived this morning to secure the town. Eridu is the first major port of the North, and they mean to establish an outpost here. They've already started conscripting the local boys into a militia."

"What are you doing?" Arthengal asked.

"We're leaving. I don't want my boys getting caught up in the middle of this. We're headed east. Elsie's brother's got a farm out on the Taspin Plains near to Isan. We'll wait the trouble out there. Once things get back to normal we'll return."

"If there is to be war you have a duty..."

"Don't talk to me about duty," Hanish said fiercely. "You don't have sons."

Hanish gave a quick glance to Darius and his cheeks colored.

"Sorry," he said quietly.

"Hanish, your father..." Arthengal started.

"Arthengal, don't," Elsie said, having returned from the house. "We've seen firsthand what war does to men. Three nights out of five Hanish's father would wake this house screaming from the terrors that haunted his dreams. You can speak all you like of honor and duty, but we don't want that life for our boys."

"We don't even know who we're fighting," Hanish complained. "No one has claimed responsibility."

"The Daku Rabi?" Arthengal asked.

Hanish laughed bitterly. "Maybe, maybe not. You hear the same rumors I hear. Shalanum sends scouts north every year, and sure, the passes are guarded. But there aren't any reports that have a settlement larger than a couple hundred people. There is no evidence of a large army. All the rumors say that the Daku Rabi are a broken people scattered across The Wastes, just like we always thought."

"Maybe the scouts aren't going far enough north," Arthengal said more to himself than Hanish.

"Even if'n that's true. Sure, it could be the Daku Rabi that done this, or it could be some coup from a faction in the ministers. It's just as likely that we'll end up fighting a civil war while men in tall hats struggle for power in the capital, and my sons would end up dying for no good cause."

Kal and Nash had returned with fresh loads and were listening to the exchange.

"But father..." Kal started.

"Quiet, boy." Hanish cut his son off resolutely. "We're leaving. If'n it becomes clear that there is an enemy we can see and a threat that can be managed, we can have this conversation again. You've made your mind clear, but I won't be having you getting mixed up in some squabble between tall hats."

"You are welcome to use the house, but we will be gone as soon as the wagon is loaded," Hanish said to Arthengal.

"What if it is the Daku Rabi?" Darius asked. "It would mean they are getting ready to move, wouldn't it?"

"It would be a bold opening move. It would throw Shalanum into disarray and give them an opening," Arthengal admitted.

"Then we have to ride north, now," Darius said excitedly. "We have to rescue my mother before the war starts."

"Calm down, let's think this through," Arthengal said in a quiet tone.

"No. I've waited long enough. We have to go now. It was your bargain. We have the horses from the men that gave me this."

Darius fingered the scar. "Antu will follow us wherever we go, and I am as good as you with the blade, on most days, even if I haven't mastered your tricks with the bow."

Darius felt heat rising in his chest. He hoped Arthengal didn't press the point that Darius hadn't actually disarmed him. But in his current mood it didn't matter. He *had* waited long enough, more than long enough.

Arthengal studied him as if inspecting a beehive and trying to figure out how to get the honey without getting stung.

"We can leave the rope and nets in the barn and take the wagon back today." Darius didn't feel like giving him the time to figure his way out of this. "We'll travel faster without the load. As soon as we get back to Anbar Ur, we load the horses and travel to The Wastes to rescue my mother. If you won't help me then Antu and I will go by ourselves."

Arthengal sighed, "We're not even sure it was them."

"I don't care. I can't take that chance." Darius said hotly. "You've said it yourself. Once they start moving, they aren't going to drag a bunch of slaves around behind them. They might take the blacksmiths, farriers, cartwrights, and the like, but my mother doesn't have a skill trade like that. They'll abandon them all in The Wastes to starve, if they don't just kill them outright."

Seconds passed like hours while Arthengal quietly considered.

"Fine," he said quietly. "Hanish, do you mind if we stash our goods in your barn?"

"Not at all, we won't be using it. I can't guarantee that it will be here when you return, but you are welcome to it."

Darius and Arthengal helped the Cherians finish loading their cargo, and in return, the Cherians helped them to unload theirs. Within an hour both wagons were ready for their respective journeys.

"Darius?" Anna's voice was quiet.

She stood meekly beside her mother, holding something behind her back. Her brown hair spilled over her shoulders, resting on the gentle rise of her chest. She wore a yellow dress embroidered with blue lace blossoms on the sleeves and bodice. He hadn't really noticed her during the frenzied activity, but now, suddenly, he did. What had happened to her? Last summer she was still a gangly girl that only wanted to bat the sheep's bladder around the yard with Darius and her brothers. Now, at fourteen, she was suddenly a woman, or nearly so. Darius felt his cheeks color, and his palms started to sweat.

He stared dumbly at her before he realized she was waiting for him to answer. "What is it, Anna?"

"I made this for you for your name day." She drew out her hands and held out a small green cushion.

He took the pillow and examined it. It was square and the perfect size to rest his head on. The stitch work on the face was not as clean as Elsie's work or as elaborately beautiful as Gabriella

Porter's work, but it still held him dumbstruck. It showed a man, a boy really, with blond hair standing with his arms to his side wearing a white shirt and a blue cloak. A sword was strapped to his waist and a quiver of arrows extended over his shoulder. Behind the boy was an old man with a gray beard and long gray hair wearing a green tunic. In the background rose a great brown bear with fierce-looking teeth and claws. The likenesses were not exact, but Darius could easily tell who they were meant to be.

"I thought maybe you could use a pillow for your bed," Anna said shyly.

"Thank you, Anna," Darius said with quiet sincerity. "It's beautiful. I will treasure it."

Anna's cheeks turned crimson. She smiled nervously and ducked behind her mother. Elsie put an arm around the girl and squeezed her shoulder gently. Kal and Nash were covering their mouths on the other side of the yard trying to hide the fact that they were clearly chuckling and were on the verge of bursting into all-out laughter. Hanish narrowed his eyes and gave Darius an appraising glare.

Darius climbed into the wagon and set the cushion on the seat beside him. Arthengal clasped Hanish's right hand and grabbed his shoulder with his left.

"You take care of your family, Hanish," he said. "If we find out what's really going on, I'll send word to Elsie's brother."

The farmer nodded. "Her brother's name is Eban Malik. They

live about a league southeast of Isan."

As soon as Arthengal had settled onto the bench beside him, Darius flipped the reins.

"Darius," Anna called.

Darius turned to see the pretty girl standing by her mother. It bewildered him how much she had changed in a year. He still remembered the little girl he had met, just a few years before, who had stuck her tongue out at him.

"Be careful," she shouted after him.

He blushed and waved and then steered the donkeys onto the road north.

Chapter Twenty-One
Sillu Aga

Sengiin Sharav pounded his fist on the wide map-covered table, crumpling the rolled scroll in his hand. Small wooden figurines in the shape of castles, horses, and foot soldiers scattered from their places on the largest map in the center.

The soldier that had given him the note flinched.

"Is this all that arrived? No more details than this?" Sengiin growled.

"N-no sir, that was all," the soldier stuttered.

"Very well. You may return to your duties." He knew better than to punish the messenger, but someone must surely be punished for this news.

"Go tell Emperor Lao that I would very much like an audience," Sengiin spoke to a servant standing quietly out of the way at the far end of the room.

The man bowed and scurried from the room.

Sengiin retrieved a long black coat from a hook on the wall and pulled it on. The coat was trimmed with dark blue silk at the cuffs, collar, and hem. He fastened the buttons in such a way that the square embroidered insignia of his house and rank appeared unbroken. A crane on a field of blue standing above the clouds but below the sun. The entire badge was trimmed with four intertwined golden threads. He completed the ensemble with a red sash fastened just below the insignia.

The servant returned as Sengiin was strapping on his sword belt.

"The emperor will see you at your leisure, Lord General."

Sengiin knew that meant immediately.

He followed the servant from the long log building that was his home and his command center. The path from the command center to the imperial residence entered the garden through a side gate. The flowers in the garden were in full bloom. Bees and hummingbirds flitted from one vibrant meal to the next. The scent of honeysuckle and roses filled the air, but Sengiin noticed none of it.

His fist further crumpled the missive as he waited on the broad porch that surrounded the ornately decorated two-story building. The building was well built, but it still shamed him that he was unable to provide the emperor with residences more suited to his station. He should be in the royal palace in Kasha Esharra, not some log cabin in the wilderness.

"Commander General Sengiin Sharav to seek audience with His Divine Majesty Lao Jun Qiu," the servant announced from a prostrated position on the floor just inside the residence.

"Enter," a voice called from within.

The servant shuffled backward and did not stand until he was fully on the porch. Upon standing, he extended an arm toward the door inviting the general to enter. Sengiin entered the room, walking stiffly until he was four paces from the seated emperor. Then he bowed deeply at the waist with his arms held stiffly at his sides and held the position.

Lao Jun Qiu was sitting in a broad basket chair cushioned on all sides with pillows. He held a large book open on his lap. The emperor's tall silk hat rested on the table next to the chair. He must have set it there recently as his thinning black hair still showed the imprint from the hat's weight. The emperor continued to read until he finished the page. He picked up a long piece of blue silk ribbon from a table that rested next to the chair, placed it carefully between the pages of the book, closed the book slowly, and set it on the small table.

Sengiin could feel the emperor's gaze on him. A muscle twitched in his back but he remained still.

"You may stand."

Sengiin straightened but did not speak. He knew protocol, and he would not speak until he was given permission.

The emperor pressed his palms together and raised them. His chin barely rested on his thumb and the tips of his index fingers brushed his nose. His long mustache brushed the sides of his hands. Sengiin stood erectly under the intense eyes that studied him and refused to let his discomfort show. The emperor seemed to be taking in every detail of his appearance.

"So," Emperor Lao spoke slowly, "this is an official visit then."

His eyes flitted briefly to the crumpled parchment in Sengiin's right hand.

"What news do you have?"

"Your Majesty," Sengiin started. "A message has arrived from Shalanum Province. The baron and his family have been killed."

"Who has done this?" the emperor asked, his voice, cool and calm, betraying no emotion. "Not us, I pray."

"No, of course not, Majesty. You ordered that none of the barons were to be harmed until you were ready to announce your return."

"This is very unfortunate." The slightest twitch of an eyebrow betrayed the severity of his annoyance.

"We know who is responsible?" It was part statement, part question.

"We may, Your Majesty." Sengiin lifted a long black string from his palm. "This was used to tie the scroll. The message was delivered to one of our operatives in Eridu."

He took a few steps forward, extended the string to the emperor and then retreated to his former position once the man took the item. It was not the string that drew the emperor's attention but the flat wooden disk that dangled from it. The disk was painted black with a golden crown etched in the center of one side and a golden winged lion etched into the other.

"Sillu Aga." There was no mistaking the edge in the emperor's voice this time.

"Yes, Majesty, that is our thought."

"They betray us again, it seems. These past three years have been very trying, General." The emperor wound the string around his fingers. "First, they interfere with our efforts to build a financial base. They sabotage our efforts to build any kind of naval support in the Sea of Tears. They assassinate our allies in the courts of Rusticar and Hurasham. Not to mention that debacle with the horses we were moving out of Orlyk. And we are no closer to learning who is behind them than we were three years ago. It has been very frustrating, very frustrating indeed."

"As you say, Majesty." Sengiin shared the emperor's frustration. They had placed spies in every province and had uncovered very little. The operatives that they had captured were so far removed from anyone of real importance to the group that they had little information to give other than the details of their own mission.

"This seems different though, General. Every act until now has delayed our return. This would seem to hasten it. Before we are ready, for sure, but not by much, I think. We were prepared to move next summer, yes?"

"Yes, Majesty."

The emperor perched his fingers again, thinking.

"What do we know, General? I would know your mind."

"We have grain stores enough for the march and to fuel our supply lines through the winter. We had hoped to harvest more reserves this summer but more for emergency than necessity.

"We know that Shalanum was growing suspicious as is evidenced by the increasing number of scouts and spies that he sent north each year. They never penetrated far enough north to discover our armed camps, however, so it is likely they are unaware of our strength. It is likely Baroness Magora has been alerted as well, but we have seen no spies from her.

"The legions have been sharpened to a fine point this past five years. Fifty camps are spread across this portion of The Wastes with at least a thousand men each. Regiments of spear and horse and javelin and bow. Admiral Kasumi oversees twenty camps arrayed along the Sea of Tears awaiting ships, and General Hamazi commands the final fifty camps closer to the borders of Orlyk and Magora."

"But we lack the iron or copper for armor or sword," the emperor interjected.

"True, Your Majesty. We have workers in the mines we discovered but very little iron remains. The forges work day and night and what steel they are able to produce is used for arrowheads and lance tips," Sengiin reported. "Of armor, have no fear, though, Majesty. Hardened leather will work as well as bronze at least and if there is one thing that these lands have no shortage of it is beasts from which to harvest hides."

"How long would it take to call the men in to assemble?"

"One cycle of the moon at most, Majesty."

"And do the Shalanum armies march north?"

"Not as of this message." He held up the letter. "They were still not sure if the enemy came from within or without. They were struggling to establish order and decide on a leader. The generals were anxious to move but did not yet know which direction to move, and without stability in the capital, their supply lines would be fragile."

"How old is the news?"

"Three weeks. Our agents received this message before any other word had reached Eridu and rode north as fast as their mounts would carry them."

"If we move too soon we may march the entire length of Shalanum, stretch our supply lines, and open our flanks to Magora."

"Yes, Majesty." Sengiin hadn't actually considered that, but it sounded right.

"If we move too late, we may not have time to assemble before they are on top of us."

"Yes, Majesty." He had thought of that and had considered dispatching more men to watch the passes before coming to see the emperor.

"I think our original plan may yet be the most sound. Send

out additional spies. We must know everything that goes on in
Shalanum and Magora provinces. And operatives to start spreading
rumor of my return. Consolidate the factions of support that we have
managed to secure in secrecy. Continue our efforts to foster
suspicion and distrust amongst those allied with the barons. Offer the
merchants riches, the peasants freedom, and anyone with a grievance
against the barons the chance for revenge. In the meantime, alert the
regiments and have them prepare. We will not move yet, but we
must be ready to do so on a moment's notice. If our luck holds we
can take the Dechora Plains, south of the Dragon's Spine, in the fall,
and establish a foothold. We might even strike as far south as Eridu
before winter."

"Yes, Majesty."

"You're not moving, General. What have I forgotten?"

"The workers, Majesty."

"Ah, yes. Them."

He paused, considering.

"For now, let them continue to work. We may as well bolster
our supplies as much as we can while we wait. Once we have word
that we must move, we will need to take the tradesmen with us.
Anyone that is needed to support the army, that is. The rest we
should no longer need. Their purpose will have been served. I leave
it to your discretion how to deal with them."

"Of course, Your Majesty." Not exactly the answer he was
looking for but good enough. The slaves would be an inconvenience

now that they were finally preparing for war. It made some sense to squeeze as much from them as they could while time remained, he supposed. Once they no longer served their purpose, however, his *discretion* would be clear. He would deal with them as one would deal with sick cattle before they could endanger the herd. Sengiin gave another long bow and then turned to leave.

"And General."

"Yes, Majesty." Sengiin turned.

"Double your efforts to find out anything you can about the Shadow Crown. We must know if Sillu Aga works toward our purpose or against it. I do not like being manipulated."

"Yes, Majesty."

Sengiin strode out of the royal residence and rather than returning to his own hut he headed south toward the stables. A three-hour ride east saw him at the hidden entrance to a small basin. The camp inside was not as large as the others, only four or five hundred men. He spotted the man he was seeking almost immediately. A tall Rus with flaming red hair trimmed short above his ears. He wore a black shirt with short sleeves and equally dark loose-fitted pants.

Captain Vasiliev was watching as fifty black-clad men completed maneuvers under the shadow of the towers that guarded the entrance to the valley. The men moved with lithe grace, and one could see the true spirit of the animals that gave the movements their names. The Lazy Vipers swayed seductively, the very essence of danger waiting to strike. The Dancing Mongoose hopped, the tips of their toes barely touching the earth before springing again. Each movement of the feet was accompanied by quick, deadly strikes. The Dragon Whipped His Tail with unparalleled strength and ferocity.

The Mortikai had once been the most feared fighters among the Daku Rabi but no longer. The Daku Mitu had been Sengiin's regiment under Emperor Chen, and after the fall he had seen to their ascension as the best of the best. Captain Vasiliev had been one of his first recruits in the new night guard almost twenty years ago. He didn't have the talent for command, but there was no one more adept at finding and training new recruits.

Vasiliev watched his approach with half an eye while keeping most of his attention on the training men. He would occasionally shout instructions or corrections to their form.

One recruit, in particular, drew Sengiin's attention. He was perhaps twenty and had cropped blond hair. His movements were like water. So young, but he moved as if he had been born with a sword in his hand. Sengiin was reminded of another that had moved like that.

Sengiin had been jealous of how easily Arthengal demonstrated battle skills from the first day they had met. He couldn't believe that this man who had come from nothing would be commanding him in battle. Sengiin came from a strong noble family. It did not matter that Arthengal had ten years on him and that he had proven himself in battle many times over before Sengiin was assigned to the Hala Atu. Peasants should not be commanding nobles.

Nasu Rabi, what a stupid name. But Arthengal had gotten his just deserts in the end. Sengiin had destroyed the man's career, and the traitor had been exiled from the capital in shame. If only Sengiin had been able to gather more proof at the time. He would have enjoyed seeing the mighty *Nasu Rabi* swinging from a rope in the traitor's square.

As his reward for finishing off the Sisuma and reporting Arthengal's treachery, Sengiin had been promoted to his rightful place as commanding general of the Daku Mitu. The youngest commanding general in the imperial army. Once the traitor had shown his true colors and joined the rebel barons, Sengiin had finally been able to repay Arthengal properly through the death of his wife and son.

"Who is that boy?" Sengiin asked Vasiliev as he came within speaking distance.

"A conscript from the plains," Vasiliev said with pride. "They had him mucking stalls at one of the cavalry camps when I found him. He had been injured during the recruitment raid, and when they were giving assignments, they weren't sure he was going to live. The stables seemed as good a place as any for him to die, I guess. Have you ever seen anything like it?"

"Only once." Sengiin kept the bitterness from his voice.

"I need you to do something for me," Sengiin said, getting to the point of his visit.

"Anything." The captain turned away from the practicing soldiers to give Sengiin his full attention.

"There has been an incident in the south. The baron of Shalanum Province has been killed."

"Aw, what a shame." Vasiliev's lip twisted in a sneer.

"The capital is unbalanced, but it won't take them long to stabilize, and they will be out for blood once they do. Some there may have suspicions of what we do here, and even though it wasn't our work, we would make a convenient scapegoat to rally against. We need them to remain *unbalanced* until autumn. I need you to pick a dozen of your best men. They must be smart and able to think on their feet and adjust to political sands that will be shifting under their feet. Make sure a new baron isn't elected until we are ready to move against them."

"It will be done," Vasiliev said with confidence.

Chapter Twenty-Two
The Northern Wastes

"Hurry up," Darius urged Arthengal who was trudging up the hill behind him. "We took a week in getting back, and now you've wasted another day getting supplies together. We can hunt on the road. We don't need all of that. I'll run ahead and saddle the horses. You catch up."

"You may be thanking me for some of these supplies a week from now," Arthengal heaved. "Besides, I may be old, but I can still keep you from landing first strike," Arthengal called after him. He leaned heavily on a thin pine tree near the top of the hill. "You go ahead," he waved. "I'll catch up."

Darius gave a long low whistle as he approached the mill. After a moment, two speckled geldings trotted in out of the woods. The first was brown with a white rump and brown spots. The second was nearly white all over with black spots. Micah, the brown, named after Darius's brother, approached Darius and sniffed his hand, hoping that it contained oats. Darius patted the horse on the nose and scratched him behind the ears.

He retrieved the saddles and tack from the mill. He was

sliding a blue and white striped blanket onto Eranen, the white, when Arthengal finally plodded up.

"What's wrong with you?" Darius looked at the man, concern replacing impatience. Arthengal was certainly not as spry as he had been on the day they had met nearly four years ago, but today he seemed particularly slow. He was sweating, which he never did, and looked flushed.

"Nothing," Arthengal sighed. "I'm just tired. It's been a long three weeks sitting on the bench of that cursed wagon and sleeping on the ground. We didn't even get a bath at Hanish's, and you wouldn't let me bathe last night. These old bones need a good soak. I'll be fine once we get on the road. I'll nap in the saddle a bit, maybe. I'll have a little willow bark and rosehip tea when we stop for lunch. That usually makes me feel better when I get winded like this."

Darius knitted his brow. "We need to travel quickly. I can't explain it, but I have a bad feeling. We don't have time to lose."

"I know you are worried," Arthengal said, nodding his head. "But we can't push the mounts too hard. We have a long way to go, and we will need to preserve their strength. The Wastes are a hard land, and it will be a rough journey on them and us. I've packed a few extra horseshoes, but if we use those up, we will be leagues from the nearest blacksmith. Don't let your impatience and worry cause you to press too hard and make bad decisions."

"Where do we go?" Darius asked, fastening the saddle on the

gelding.

"We'll start near where we met." Arthengal was transferring the supplies from his pack into saddle bags. He glanced around. "Where's that bear of yours?"

Darius shrugged as he pulled himself into the saddle.

"He'll find us. He always does." He heeled Micah and trotted up the road toward the cave and the river.

Antu did find them, a day and a half later as they were nearing the creek crossing where their journey together had begun. The bear sniffed the air and growled grumpily as they passed the fateful copse.

"You don't think he remembers, do you?"

Arthengal laughed; some of his energy had returned. "I know I would never forget."

By evening they drew to a stop atop a low, grass-covered hill. Antu was trying to catch a rabbit in a hollow a hundred paces behind them. Four more such rabbits dangled from a thong off of Darius's saddle.

Arthengal gave a long low whistle.

"Well, they've certainly turned it into a slaver's highway, haven't they?"

The broken, churned trail that Darius had followed so many years before was a hard-packed road a dozen paces wide. The scar had been carved across the plains by thousands of feet of horses and cattle and men. Darius stared curiously at a white stone at the far side of the road. He shuddered when he realized that it was a weathered skull, picked clean by scavengers and savaged by the wind and rain.

Arthengal caught him staring at it and cleared his throat.

"Maybe another hour or so before we camp?"

"Yeah," Darius nodded, pulling his eyes away from the bone.

They picked up speed on the more even terrain of the road. Antu gave up his chase and hurried to catch up. The horses whickered nervously as the bear ran up behind them. They had grown used to his scent over the past two years, like the donkeys, but still didn't fully trust the bear. For Antu's part, he ignored the horses. Sure he liked a good elk haunch, if it was offered, but Darius had rarely seen the bear hunt anything larger than a rabbit, especially since he had adopted the humans and they had started feeding him on a regular basis.

By the time they had set up camp and had a fire burning, the horizon was a long orange line that faded into blue and then black in the sky above them. Stars were beginning to wink into view.

"We have to be careful from this point on," Arthengal said as he turned the rabbits.

"See that range there?" He pointed to a black line, barely visible on the northern horizon. "It's called the Dragon's Spine and it marks the southern edge of The Wastes. They are sure to have scouts watching all of the passes. Baron Shalanum has sent men to try to see what the Daku Rabi have been up to and none that have passed the Spine have returned."

"So, what do we do?"

"I know a way in that is unknown to most. We can hope that the Daku Rabi don't have it guarded, at least not too well."

Mid-afternoon the following day, Darius studied the long black ridge in the distance that stretched as far as he could see in either direction. They had been traveling since dawn, and the finger-width line on the horizon had barely changed. "Are we getting any closer to it?" he asked.

"It does seem that way, doesn't it?" Arthengal chuckled. "Don't worry, it's only another eight to ten leagues, we should reach it by tomorrow. We'll leave the road tomorrow and bear that way." Arthengal extended his arm northwest. "Do you see the triple knuckle there?"

Darius squinted at the distance before he found the slight ripple in the horizon where Arthengal was pointing. He nodded.

"They call that the Wyvern's Break. It has a gap and what you *might* call a trail. The horses should be able to make the climb. At least I hope they can because once we start up there'll be no way to turn them around." He laughed but there was a sour tone to it. "That would be irony, wouldn't it? Get halfway up to find the trail is out, and be stuck on a two-pace-wide ledge with two horses and a bear."

Darius didn't laugh.

Arthengal had been right. The next day, Darius watched as the thin line coalesced into a shear wall. When they stopped the first time to rest, he couldn't tell the difference. By lunchtime, the wall was two fingers wide. From there, the barrier seemed to rise from the plains like a giant granite tidal wave until Darius was staring, with his mouth open, at a cliff towering above him.

The grasslands ran up to it and then stopped abruptly. Gray granite stared back at him, indomitable. At the very top, he could just make out the shapes of a few fir trees like so many short hairs atop a giant's bald forehead. The long wall was not as unbroken as it had seemed from a distance. The length was scored with crags, clefts, and landslides. It looked like a titan had used the wall for sword practice. But each cleave was as impassable as the next.

He supposed they could have made the climb with the proper ropes and gear, but that would have left them without horses and Antu. Also, they would have been easy targets for any Daku Rabi patrolling the top of the wall.

"You expect us to get over that?"

Arthengal dismounted and started to lead Eranen toward a narrow crack in the cliff wall. Darius followed suit, and as they approached the crack, he saw that it was more of a crevice that ran the height of the wall. It separated two equally impressive slabs of stone.

The ground sloped upward inside the fissure forming a

narrow, rugged trail barely wide enough for Antu to squeeze through. The gap widened a short distance from the opening, but the trail did not. It climbed steeply upward and made sharp, unexpected turns. The wall remained sheer to their right and dropped into an ever-widening serpentine canyon to their left. They led the horses carefully, cautious of each step, slowing to a crawl to get around each tight bend.

The sun was mostly hidden by the soaring heights, but every time it came into view, it had seemed to jump across the sky. Darius risked a dizzying glance into the canyon at midday. There was as much space below them as above, so he guessed they were about halfway to their destination.

Darkness was starting to spread into the ravine as they approached another harrowing turn. Arthengal held up his hand and raised a finger to his lips. He let the reins in his hands drop, and Eranen whickered nervously.

Arthengal crept up to the bend with his back pressed against the wall. He leaned forward slowly to peer around and then pulled his head back quickly. He held up three fingers, and Darius nodded.

Silently Arthengal slunk back to Eranen and with some difficulty unfastened his bow and quiver. There was no way for Darius to get around the horse in front of him, but he did retrieve his own bow, just in case. Antu grunted from several paces back as if wondering why they had stopped. Then, as if content for the break, flopped down, sitting on his haunches. Gravel spilled into the canyon below, but the bear didn't seem to notice. Instead, he started trying to pry out a stone wedged beneath one of his claws by picking at it with his teeth.

Arthengal eased the arms of the bow together and silently slipped the string into place. He pulled three arrows from his quiver and set the rest on the ground at his feet. Holding the other two arrows in his hand he nocked the first arrow.

He eased forward so his eyes could barely see around the edge. Sweat began to trickle down Darius's back as he nervously watched.

With a sudden, swift motion Arthengal swung around the corner as he drew the bow and loosed the arrow as soon as his foot was planted. His hands were a blur, and in the blink of an eye, all three arrows were away.

"By the sands of Saridon," Arthengal cursed and scrambled back around the corner to jerk another arrow from the quiver. Sliding around the corner a second time, he let the fourth shot fly.

He stood another moment, scooped up his quiver, and then returned to pick up his reins.

Darius stared at him, waiting for an explanation, and when it was clear one wasn't coming broke the silence.

"What happened?"

"The fourth one was sitting down."

He started to lead Eranen around the bend. Antu saw that they were moving again and scrambled to his feet, heedless of the precipice beside him.

Darius shook his lead and followed. The trail widened slightly as it climbed the last hundred paces to the top of the cleft. A flat, wide bench waited at the top of the trail.

Two men lay where they had fallen, shot in the heart. The third man was dragging himself across the ground toward a disorderly pile of spears. The arrow went all the way through his leg, and he was leaving a smeared trail of blood behind him. The final soldier, sitting closest to the fire, looked very drunk, and was leaning against several boulders studying the arrow jutting from his shoulder as if it were the most unusual thing he had ever seen.

Beyond the camp, a more gentle, tree-covered slope rose away from the broad hollow on three sides. Antu sniffed the dead men dismissively and then began inspecting the sentries' supplies. He tore open a large sack and a pile of limes spilled out across the rock shelf. He sampled one and quickly spit it out with a grunt of disappointment.

Arthengal walked steadily over to the man moving toward the weapons and pressed a boot onto the back of his wounded leg. The man gave a shout. He rolled over and tried to swat at Arthengal's foot. Arthengal's sword was out in the blink of an eye, and the tip was pointed toward the soldier's throat.

"You shhot me," the fourth guard slurred, pointing an accusing finger slightly left of Arthengal. He blinked his eyes and then corrected his reproachful digit to center on Arthengal.

Arthengal ignored the drunk and kneeled beside the other. The tip of his sword pressed into the soft flesh underneath the wounded man's chin.

"We are looking for a woman," Arthengal said very softly. He didn't look away from the man's face while he spoke. "This boy's mother. You are going to tell me where you think we can find her and in return, I won't let our bear eat you."

The soldier's eyes danced first to Darius and then Antu, still rummaging through the camp looking for anything interesting to eat.

"You can see he's famished," Arthengal continued in the same soft tone. "We don't feed him much, you see. We like to keep him hungry for just such occasions as this one."

"Thars mutton in the creek o'er thar," the drunk swung his arm in a wide circle to point over the hill behind them. The motion caused him to list sideways so that his face fell against one of the rocks supporting him.

"I-I-I don't kn-know this boy," the guard stuttered. "I've never s-s-seen him in my life. How am I supposed to know his mother?"

"Think hard," Arthengal's tone grew more hard.

"They s-s-send all of the women to the farms," he said quickly. "Is she pretty? Sometimes they send the pretty ones to the pig farm that Captain Andukov runs."

"Oh, he does like the pretty ones," the drunk mumbled into the rock. His shirt was growing dark as the stain spread away from his wound.

"Where are the farms?" Darius blurted.

"They're all over," the soldier whined. "The closest two are about eighty leagues northeast of here, along the river."

The drunk started snoring.

Antu gave up rummaging the supplies and wandered over to sniff the man that Arthengal was interrogating.

"Please don't let the bear eat me," the man screamed. "That's all I know, I swear."

Antu jerked back at the shout and gave a low, dissatisfied growl.

A dark stain began inching its way across the front of the man's trousers and down his right leg.

Darius and Arthengal gathered up the guards' food, adding it to their own supplies on the horses. Then they led the horses north.

"You can't just leave us here," the guard protested. "I told you what you wanted. Aren't you going to help us?"

He was still shouting as Arthengal and Darius crested the rise. From the top, Darius could see forever in both directions. The differences were astounding. To the south, golden hills rolled in all directions as far as the eye could see. To the north, a steep but passable slope opened to a land out of nightmares. Rocky, painted hills with striations of red, orange, and brown were broken only infrequently by seas of green or gold. Even amongst the fields of grass, jagged spires stabbed upward like giant knives thrust skyward from below the earth. Steep ridges and washed out canyons formed a spider web of chaos. It reminded Darius of the twisting gullies near his home but on a scale beyond reason.

"What now?" Darius asked.

"Northeast, I suppose," Arthengal said. "I know the river that he's mentioned. A few days will see us out of the broken lands. Beyond that, the wilds are not much more hospitable, but it should be easier travel. Let's try to make it to that closest valley by nightfall." He pointed to a patch of green in the distance.

They led the horses down the rocky slope, and soon the shouts faded behind them.

Progress toward the dale was painfully slow as they tried to find a clear path through the shattered landscape. They had to backtrack several times when their path ended in a box canyon or dropped off too sharply for the horses to traverse.

They finally found an entrance to the vale and made camp next to a slow-moving stream of fresh water. The surrounding peaks hid the valley in shadow even before the sun had fully set. They enjoyed a nice meal of roast mutton before bedding down.

The night was filled with the sounds of animals Darius had not heard before. A long vicious-sounding cry like when Mother Shala's cat had tried to scare away raccoons in the night but much too large to be any cat Darius had seen. Another long, mournful whooping sound and dozens of chattering cries from the hills and rocks all around them. The cacophony made Darius's skin crawl.

"The Daku Rabi aren't the only dangers in The Wastes," Arthengal noted. "But I doubt any will come close to us once they smell Antu there."

That put Darius somewhat at ease, but it was still some time before he was able to sleep with the myriad sounds echoing off the spires and walls throughout the broken lands. The symphony only grew louder as the sky passed from azure to indigo to black. The thin crescent of the moon did little to light the valley, and it seemed that a thousand killer beasts roamed just outside the light of their campfire. Antu's loud snore, strangely comforting, was the only sound that finally allowed Darius to find sleep.

Chapter Twenty-Three
Slave Camps

The patrol had caught the two by surprise. They had approached from the east while Darius and Arthengal were refilling their waterskins from the river. Only Micah's wary nicker had alerted them in time.

"Don't let that one get away," Arthengal shouted as he dodged a spear thrust from the soldier he was fighting.

Darius saw the scout fleeing to the east. He ducked under a sweeping strike from his own opponent and twisted quickly. The downward sweep of Scooping the Moon severed the man's left calf, causing him to drop to one knee. The reverse sweep ended the fight as the soldier's head rolled across the sepia-colored grass of the plains.

Darius dropped the sword and hurried to retrieve his bow from behind Micah's saddle. He strung it quickly and readied an arrow. The running man was more than a hundred paces away and running wildly.

Darius let out his breath, carefully drew back the arrow, and cleared his mind. The sounds of the nearby fight faded away, and he released.

The man stumbled and fell.

It wasn't the clean shot in the back that Darius had hoped for, but an arrow in the buttock will slow any man down.

The soldier scrambled to his feet and began limping away, dragging his right leg, while Darius nocked another arrow.

The second shot was on target, and this time the scout didn't get up.

Arthengal cleaned his blade while he assessed the shot. "Not bad."

Darius retrieved his own weapon and wiped it clean on the shirt of his former assailant.

They had been lucky enough to avoid the frequent patrols until now. Once they entered the broken lands, it had taken Darius and Arthengal three days to navigate the maze of canyons, tunnels, and hidden valleys. Cautious scouting on Arthengal's part had led them wide of three such parties.

The thick forest between the canyon lands and the plains had been too dense to make scouting very effective. Guards could have passed within a few hundred paces, and they never would have seen each other.

Stone spires had thrust above a thick canopy of elm, alder, and oak. The landscape had been disorienting, and Arthengal and Darius had nearly gotten lost several times. Several times a day Arthengal had been forced to climb one of the buttes just to keep their bearings.

Antu ambled up licking his chops. Apparently his fishing trip downstream had been successful.

"Thanks for joining us," Arthengal said.

Antu gave the dead bodies a curious glance and then shot Darius a look which seemed to say, "What did I miss?"

"The first farm should be upstream," Arthengal noted. "It must be close. My guess is that these scouts came from there. Help me dump the bodies in the river, so they float downstream farther."

They smelled the farm before they saw it. The warm afternoon sun baked the landscape, and the gentle breeze was thick with the smell of feces. Arthengal found a small stand of trees, and they tied the horses to a slanted ash tree. Antu contented himself with laying in the shade by the horses.

They walked north until they could see the tops of the buildings and then crawled on hands and knees the rest of the way. Hiding behind a misshapen shack, they were able to get a decent view of the swine farm.

Dozens of pens stretched out across the farm all the way to the southern bank of the river. Each was crowded with sows and piglets. Ashen-looking women plodded between each coral carrying buckets of water or slop. They would deposit their loads in the wide troughs to a cacophony of squeals and grunts. Then they would slog back to the makeshift barn for another load. All of the wooden structures on the farm looked about to fall down. It was obvious that whoever had constructed them lacked experience.

Most of the guards lounged on the porch of a long, single-story barracks. A few wandered among the workers, and anytime one of them drew too close, the women would flinch and drop their eyes to the ground.

Darius counted less than ten guards and more than thirty women. The women could have easily overwhelmed them, and Darius didn't understand why they didn't try to escape.

"Those poor women," Arthengal whispered. "They have been abused beyond caring. Do you see your mother among them?"

Darius searched the multitude of blank faces. "No, I don't think so."

"Good," Arthengal said. "I'm glad she isn't here. Four years in a place like this could destroy anyone."

Darius looked at him sharply.

"We have to help them," he said.

"They are beyond help," Arthengal said sadly. He was looking northeast, possibly trying to get a sense for where the next farm might be, when Darius crept from their hiding place.

"Blasted boy," Darius heard Arthengal hiss. Darius already had his bow strung and was scampering, in a crouch, toward the nearest building.

He waited until one of the soldiers patrolling the farm rounded the back of the barn, out of view of his companions, and let the arrow fly. It struck the man solidly in the chest. He gave a low grunt and collapsed against the side of the building.

Darius was already moving before the man finished falling. He pressed his back against the wall of the barn and was sidling up to the corner when Arthengal finally caught up to him.

"What are you doing?" Arthengal hissed.

"We can't leave them here like this," Darius responded.

Darius watched as another guard harassed one of the women. Darius couldn't hear what he was saying, but the fear in the woman's eyes was enough. The soldier grabbed her arm, and she dropped one of her empty buckets.

Darius scanned the rest of the yard. The sties hid the pair from view of the others. Darius drew the arrow and allowed his mind to clear. He released.

The woman didn't even scream as the arrow pierced the man's neck and jutted out the other side. She scooped up her bucket and hurried toward the stone well to refill it.

"Curse you, boy," Arthengal muttered as he strung his own bow.

Darius saw another guard approaching the pen where his most recent victim had fallen. He fired again, but too quickly this time and his shot was off. It struck the soldier in the shoulder and he cried out in alarm.

"To arms!" The guard had time to shout before Darius's next shot dropped him to the ground.

It was enough, though. Darius heard a clatter of spears and boots as the soldiers on the veranda were suddenly on alert.

Arthengal sprinted to the other end of the barn as Darius stepped into view, bow drawn. He saw six men running across the farmyard in their direction. He fired, hitting another man in the chest, and then drew his sword.

Arthengal felled three more and the remaining guards separated, one coming toward Darius and the other attacking Arthengal.

As the soldier approached Darius, he dropped into a slide and thrust the spear upward. Darius had been prepared for a frontal assault and the maneuver caught him off guard. He leapt to the left, but the tip of the spear glanced off his right thigh and opened a cut in his leg.

The man completed his slide and was suddenly on his feet again, thrusting the spear at Darius's chest. Darius blocked the attack and countered. The two traded blows several more times. Darius could feel his leg beginning to throb and could feel blood trickling into his boot.

The soldier attacked again and nicked Darius's left shoulder. Darius moved in close to take away the advantage of the longer weapon. Instead of attacking with the spear, the guard switched to a one-handed grip and punched Darius in the chin with a vicious uppercut.

Darius stumbled back and saw stars. He struggled to keep his sword raised and clear his head. The soldier crouched low, spear extended upwards at an angle. As Darius started to advance again, the man scooped a handful of dirt and dried pig manure and threw it right in Darius's face.

Blinded, Darius stumbled back again, swinging his sword wildly. He felt a sharp pain as the spear glanced off his side. Then he heard a grunt and a thump as the man fell. Darius wiped the debris from his eyes and saw that his opponent had been shot in the back.

Arthengal was striding toward him, bow in hand.

"He threw dirt at me," Darius complained.

"You have to be prepared for anything," Arthengal said. "Not everyone you face is going to fight fair. In fact, the less trained they are, the dirtier they are likely to fight. Come on, let's see to those wounds and then check the rest of the farm."

Throughout the fight and after, the women had continued to work. They didn't seem to notice that their captors were dead. They didn't respond when Darius tried to talk to them, other than to shrink away or run to the company of the other women.

Arthengal cleaned and bound Darius's wounds, and the women kept working. Arthengal stuffed the corpses of the guards in the back of the barn, and the women kept working. They inspected the rest of the outbuildings, and the women kept working. The sun sank low on the horizon. The women stowed the buckets and lumbered to the collection of rough shacks near the edge of the camp. They began preparing the evening meal as Darius and Arthengal watched in wonder.

"They are broken," Arthengal said. "I don't think we could force them to leave if we tried."

Darius shook his head in sadness, trying not to imagine his mother living in similar circumstances.

They returned to the horses and made their own camp for the night in the grove of ash and elm.

"We should cross here," Arthengal commented, about a league northeast of the pig farm. "The water looks shallower than what we've seen so far. We can lead the horses across."

They dismounted, and Darius followed Arthengal into the swift-moving waters of the river. The water was over his knees, and the current pulled at his feet, making the footing on the smooth river stones that much more treacherous.

Once across, they turned toward a tall butte in the distance.

"We can get a better view of the surroundings from up there," Arthengal explained.

They approached the tree-covered butte from the west.

It was an easy climb for the two men. They had left Antu and the horses in a thicket near the base.

"What do you see?" Darius asked as he crept up beside Arthengal at the edge of the cliff.

Arthengal turned his head. "You tell me. What do you see?"

Darius studied the terrain. The Wastes were less wasted here. Gentle, grass-covered hills spilled away from the butte and then opened up to a sheltered expanse.

In the distance, he could see a valley, alive with the color of spring planting. A surrounding arc of tall cliffs formed the northern boundary, and a broad tumultuous river raged from out of the hills, creating the border for the eastern edge of the valley and curving to block most of the southern advance as well. The banks widened further toward the southern end, and the water was more blue-black than white. It still looked fast and the banks were swollen. Only the west was clear, and clear it was. The land was unbroken by tree or boulder. The rolling hills alone provided any kind of shelter. Several buildings were visible as well as tall guard towers blocking entrance to the farm.

"There," Darius pointed. "They have four -- no, five -- towers securing the approach from the west. They are spaced so they can easily view each other and cover the entire area from the ridge to the river."

"Good," Arthengal nodded. "What else?"

"Well, it's definitely a farm. And it's big; it occupies the entire valley. I can't make out people from this far out, but there must be a lot of slaves to work that much land." He squinted. "It looks like there is a house toward the back. It looks like it's several stories. Maybe a command center or something?"

"I agree," Arthengal said. "How would you sneak in?"

"Well," Darius considered. "The towers would be tough to sneak by. Maybe it could be done in the dark. Those cliffs over there might be scalable; it's hard to tell from here. We couldn't get back out that way, though, not unless the captives all happen to be expert climbers."

"Not all," Arthengal corrected. "Just your mother. If she's there."

Darius glanced at the man sharply but didn't press the point. In either case, it didn't matter. His mother couldn't climb a lick. She hated heights.

"We need a better view from closer up. Let's circle around and come at that ridge from the north."

They inched back from the edge and descended the back side of the spire out of view from the towers. Darius retrieved a few apples and the leftover pheasant from the prior night's meal. He gave the animals all a scratch behind the ears which earned him an appreciative whinny from the horses and a disinterested grunt from Antu. He handed Arthengal, who had a faraway expression on his face, an apple.

"What are you thinking?" Darius asked.

Arthengal took a bite of the apple, still lost in thought. "One of the things that they were feeding the pigs was grain. That must come from here. That means either boats or wagons. I'm betting on boats since the river is so convenient. If they have any here, we might be able to steal one to escape downriver to the farm. Come on, we need to get on top of that ridge." He swung his feet into Eranen's saddle.

Darius stowed their supplies and mounted Micah. Excitement was building in him again. He couldn't explain the feeling, but he felt certain his mother was here.

A two-day circuitous route found them atop the cliffs, once more staring down at the farm. It did provide a better view than the butte, if not the detail they would need to identify any one person. The valley was broken into three main areas.

The house and surrounding buildings formed a sort of compound. Several outbuildings had been hidden by the hill, including one large building with a flat roof. Men were like marching ants around the compound, but they could make out the orderly, repetitive movement as they marched.

The central building rested on a tall hill buttressed by the river and northern precipice. The building was an immense three-story timber structure. Each floor was slightly smaller than the one below it. Curved and slanted roofs could be seen on each level, the top-level roof overlapping only slightly with the level below which then overlapped the roof of the bottom floor. The roof appeared to extend a distance beyond the actual building, judging by the tall wooden pillars that supported it.

"Is that a palace?" Darius asked.

"It's smaller than a palace, but it certainly has the look. See all the color in the grounds surrounding it? That has to be gardens. They would serve no practical purpose here, and I've only seen gardens like that at the houses of noblemen. This is much more than just another work camp.

"The house also has a regular patrol around it," Arthengal said. "It's hard to make out at this distance, but there seem to be about twenty guards patrolling the hill and garden at all times. The ones that don't follow a pattern are probably house servants or couriers.

"Those are definitely docks over there." Arthengal pointed. "I was right. They must use boats to transport whatever is grown here to other work sites. And it looks like a couple of grain barges are docked there. Not as maneuverable as I would like, but we can use them. The buildings near the manor house are probably for officers. The ones below us here must be barracks for the regular troops."

Directly below them were four squat wooden buildings that they could make out more clearly. Soldiers dressed in either black leather armor or in dirty white linen shirts and black pants went in and out of the buildings regularly. Several men in armor drilled with practice staves and spears in a yard in front of the buildings, while others shot at targets north of the barracks.

"Each billet will hold twenty to thirty men-at-arms," Arthengal instructed. "It's not a large garrison but more than we could handle. There must be a larger stronghold somewhere nearby. Close enough to form defensive positions ahead of any approaching enemies but probably not close enough to respond to an immediate alarm, or else we would have observed them scouting the area."

"What makes you say that?" Darius asked.

"If that is a noble's house they wouldn't leave the compound guarded by a single company. There must be a full regiment nearby. The basin isn't big enough to hold that many and still farm the land." He pointed toward the farmland.

In the center of the vale, the earth had been plowed and divided into fields. Two wide east to west and four north to south. Each field was roughly square and four hundred paces on a side. Some of the fields were alive with dark green plants while others were a deep brown. In two of the fields, workers walked behind oxen pulling plows, preparing it for the next planting. Wardens wandered among the other captives. They held black rods from which dangled long leather straps. Occasionally they would whip the slaves with the straps.

Scattered across the plain between the fields and the barracks were forty to fifty hovels made of mud and straw.

"Those have to be the laborers' houses." Arthengal pointed. "I only see a few horses and oxen in the valley, so there isn't a mounted company here. That doesn't mean there isn't one close at hand, but it should give us a head start, at least. The nearest ford was about a day's hard ride south so if we can make it across the river that would buy us more time."

"Assuming there isn't a mounted garrison on the other side,"

Darius commented.

"Yes, assuming that."

They observed for several hours. The prisoners were clearly docile but didn't have the same broken appearance of the swine farm.

"They still move with purpose," Arthengal observed, "and they appear to be better fed, if not by much. With a nobleman here, maybe the guards do not take as much liberty with the workers."

"So, how do we find out if my mother is here?"

"Only by going down. Unless you can make out her features from here."

Darius shook his head. The slaves were filthy. If they had bathed any time recently it wasn't apparent. Their skin was stained black with mud and sweat, and their hair was matted and nearly as dark as their skin. Their clothing, at least, was in better shape than that of the women at the last camp.

"What is your plan?" Darius asked.

Arthengal examined the cliffs. "They are too steep to climb, especially in the dark. We'll have to find a way past those towers. Once we get inside, we see if we can find your mother and lead her to the barges. We cut one of them loose and guide it downstream and cross to the other side. Then we run. We hope we can lose ourselves in the broken lands and forestall pursuit. We fight our way through the pass and escape onto the plains and then back home."

"As simple as that then," Darius mocked.

"It's not going to be easy, but if we can at least get away from here I think I can hide our tracks well enough so they will have a hard time following the three of us."

"What about the rest of them? Can't we free them all?"

Arthengal shook his head.

"If we tried to lead a band of three hundred ragged prisoners south, they would catch us within a day or two. It would be impossible to hide our tracks. The worst tracker could find us with ease."

"What about our horses? And Antu?" Darius asked.

"We will have to leave them on the other side of the river. There was a thicket near the piggery with fresh water. We can leave them there for a few days and hope a random patrol doesn't find them."

"So a couple of days back downriver, then three or four back here. You are talking almost another week. Then what if she's not even held here?" Darius's voice started to rise, but then he hushed it again.

"Then we figure out where the other farms are and check them."

Darius grunted with frustration. "This is taking too long," he barked.

"It will take as long as it takes," Arthengal said patiently. "But I won't be foolhardy. That will only get us all killed."

"You do know," Arthengal continued in an even gentler tone, "your mother may not be alive. The conditions in these camps are worse than I would have thought. Four years is a long time to survive like this."

"She's alive," Darius growled. "I would know it if she wasn't."

"Then that is our plan, unless you have a better," Arthengal said. "That won't get us killed," he added, seeing the expression on Darius's face.

Darius sighed and shook his head.

Chapter Twenty-Four
Into the Dragon's Lair

Darius munched on a bit of leftover rabbit from breakfast as he stared across the open plain at the archers' towers.

"We can go in tonight," Arthengal said, wiping his greasy hands clean on the grass. "Let's camp and get some sleep."

Darius glanced up at the sun, just past its zenith. "Now?"

"I want to be fresh. We don't have the luxury of mistakes tonight."

They rolled out their blankets in the shadow of the butte, hidden from the archers' view.

Darius tried to sleep but only managed a few short naps throughout the day. When sleep was impossible, he let Arthengal rest and kept watch. The sun crept agonizingly slow across the sky. By midafternoon clouds began rolling in, and the yellow sphere was masked by a sea of grey. His heart hammered harder and harder in his chest as the sun neared the horizon. By the time it was full dark, his hands were practically shaking with anticipation.

They ate a quick meal while they stowed the rest of their supplies and strung their bows. Quivers were secured on their right and swords on their left, strapped down to prevent them from making noise in the dark. With bows and light packs on their backs, they crept across the grasslands in the dark. The gibbous moon was shrouded by clouds and shed little light on the open fields.

"Smells like rain," Arthengal whispered.

Darius nodded agreement. The air was thick with humidity and danger.

They dropped to a crouch as they neared the towers and finally to their bellies. They crawled slowly past the tower, staying as close to the hillside and the cliffs as they could. Arthengal froze suddenly as a line of torches approached the towers. They were so close that they could hear the soldiers in the closest tower talking.

"You're late," a deep voice from the top of the tower called. "I'm hungry."

"Yeah, well, you're not missing much. Venison stew again. There's plenty left in the pot by the main barracks," the lead torchbearer called back.

"Any news?"

"Nah, is there ever?"

The man in the tower laughed.

Four men climbed down from the tower as the torches arrived. Darius and Arthengal lay still, just out of the torchlight, trying to breathe softly. As is always the case in such situations, Darius's nose began to itch furiously.

The four new guards handed off the torches and climbed to

their positions in the tower.

Once Arthengal was sure the retreating soldiers were far enough away, he signaled them forward again.

They rounded the bend, out of view of the towers, and rose to a crouch. The farm was dark. Few torches were lit near the slave huts, but there was enough light to see the occasional shadow of a guard patrolling the grounds.

Arthengal hugged the cliff as he crept across the farmland toward the adobe shacks. They reached the outer edge, and he dropped to one knee listening. The crunch of boots on gravel a few paces away made Darius's breath catch. The guard passed and Arthengal inched forward to crouch next to one of the huts.

"Do you want to start in the front or the back?" he whispered.

"Might as well start here," Darius said.

They ducked into the first squat shack. They paused just inside the door to let their eyes adjust to the deeper darkness. The inside of the building reeked of sweat and untanned hides.

There was a mass of shapes in the center of the building. The slaves were huddled together and covered with a few hides. Arthengal watched by the door, checking the position of the guards, while Darius stole as close to the sleeping forms as he could, careful to step around outstretched arms or legs. He examined each face as well as he could in the dim light. There were no women among the huddled mass, and he returned to the door.

The second hut was the same. When he signaled Arthengal,

the woodsman exited the hut and almost ran into a guard who had been circling around the other side of the shack. Arthengal closed quickly, knife in hand. The guard must have mistaken Arthengal for another guard or one of the slaves because he was slow to react. By the time he did, it was too late. Arthengal thrust his hunting knife straight up under the man's chin and into his brain. The guard died with a quiet gurgle.

Arthengal lowered the body quietly to the ground and glanced around. He didn't see or hear anyone, so he hooked the guard under the armpits and dragged him back into the small building. He laid the guard along the back wall and was careful not to disturb any of the sleeping men.

Darius's breath was still ragged when he entered the third hut. His eyes adjusted to the dim interior and his heart leapt as he examined the woman who lay closest to the door. Her arms were wrapped protectively around a girl of about twelve or thirteen. Her cheeks were hollow, and her red hair was matted and stained brown with filth, but there was no mistaking her.

He reached out and gently touched her shoulder.

"Mother."

The woman startled awake.

"Shhhh," he hissed.

She sat up in a sleepy daze and a woman behind her whimpered in her sleep. She peered blankly at Darius, then recognition and doubt filled her eyes.

"Darius?" she whispered in disbelief.

Tears filled his eyes, and his heart felt like it would burst. She leaned over the sleeping girl and embraced him tightly.

"Oh, Darius," she wept.

"We have to move," Arthengal whispered from the door.

"What are you doing here, Darius?"

"We're here to rescue you."

The impossibility of what he was saying was clear in her eyes.

"How?"

"We have a plan. Come on, we need to go."

"I can't leave without Lianna." She started to shake the girl awake.

The girl woke, confused. She peered first at Darius and then at his mother. Fear crept into her eyes as if she expected a nefarious outcome. She started to whimper.

"Shhh," the woman calmed her. "It's okay. This is my son, Darius."

The girl tilted her head and examined him.

Arthengal ducked fully inside the hut and pressed his back against the mud wall. He signaled for silence. A few moments later, the plodding boots of a guard approached. They passed outside without pausing and faded into the darkness.

Other women were starting to stir around them.

"What's going on?" one woman asked too loudly and was

hushed by Darius.

"My son is here to rescue us," his mother whispered.

Whispers of shock passed between the five women. Arthengal cursed under his breath. Darius thought he heard *sheep dung* and *foolish* out of the hushed stream of obscenities.

"All of us?" one woman asked. She would have been a stout woman if properly fed. Her shoulders were broader than the rest, and she had a solid jaw.

"I'm sorry. We can't rescue everyone," Darius explained. "We have to be quiet and keep the group small. Only those here."

He gave Arthengal a speculative glance, and the woodsman nodded.

The woman started to protest but was quickly quieted by the others.

Arthengal signaled from the door.

"Let's go."

Crouching low he led the small group across the yard behind another shack where they crouched and waited again before darting to the next. The stout woman ducked inside here, and a rustling could be heard from within. Arthengal cursed again as six men emerged behind her. He tried to lead the growing group to the next shack, but several of the captives didn't follow and instead spread out to other huts. As they neared the outer edge of the slave huts, they heard a shout behind them.

"Hey, what are you doing out of your shack, peasant? Get

back to your bed."

There was the crack of a whip then a muffled thud and the sound of a scuffle. The other two guards cried out in alarm and boots pounded toward the altercation.

"Run!" Arthengal hissed in an urgent whisper and sprinted into the darkness toward the fields.

Behind them, the camp erupted in chaos. The slaves who had been sneaking from hut to hut were no longer quiet. They were running now, waking everyone, shouting that they were rescued. Two of the guards were swinging their whips and cudgels indiscriminately at the darting prisoners. Sounds from the barracks indicated that more soldiers were waking.

Darius heard cries behind them as people were being beaten and curses from the guards as they tried to hold off the slaves who had decided to fight back. The cries stopped for a moment and all was quiet. Then Darius heard the telltale twang of a bowstring, and a different sort of cry came from the area surrounding the huts.

He ventured a quick glance behind him as he ran. His mother and the girl, Lianna, were close on his heels. Behind them, hundreds of men and women poured across the fields. Behind them, at the shacks, tall, erect shapes battled hunched ones in a fury of activity.

Darius heard three low thumps from the direction of the barracks followed by a high-pitched whistle that trailed into the sky. Suddenly, an explosion sounded above them, and the sky was lit by three bursts of light. Darius glanced up and brilliant white stars trailed away from the center of the explosions. The dark clouds above were cast in a ghostly light. They could see more clearly now as the valley was bathed in the glowing light.

"Lightning bringers," Arthengal cursed, "or at least their handiwork."

Soldiers started to emerge from the house compound in front of them. They were imperial guards, if Arthengal's guess was correct. The guards behind them would be common soldiers, but those guarding the house would be better trained. They spotted Darius and his group nearing the edge of the fields and began running to intercept them. Arthengal grabbed his bow and readied an arrow while he ran. Darius followed suit. The uneven soil of the fields was replaced by firm ground as they drew nearer to the river. Darius picked up speed, sprinting as fast as his mother could manage.

Three more thumps sounded behind them as the light from the first shower of stars began to fade and the sky was lit anew. They were two hundred paces from the docks when Arthengal started firing at the imperial guards. Arrows shot toward the closest sentries. Just as many missed as hit. Darius fared worse and only hit one out of his ten shots.

"Save your arrows," Arthengal shouted.

The house guard quickly organized. A dozen or more sheltered behind the low rock wall that surrounded the house and began providing covering fire for others that advanced in formation.

While they ordered themselves, Darius and Arthengal closed half the distance to the barges. When arrows started raining down on them, the chaos that followed made the previous disarray look like a well-ordered retreat. Slaves scattered in every direction and only a devout core managed to continue to follow Darius.

He heard a woman cry out a few steps behind him and then the sound of her falling. Another burst of light above them illuminated four banners twisting in the gentle wind above the archers. Long serpentine figures with the faces of lions and claws to match set on a field of blue. The creatures were fierce and beautiful at the same time. Dragons, Darius remembered from the pictures in the story of the yellow emperor from the completed works of Han Yu Pin.

The front line of the advancing guardsmen was twenty paces away when Arthengal slung his bow over a shoulder and drew his blade. He did not stop running. He cut the first man in the line down as he sprinted past. Darius hurdled the body and it skidded across the ground in front of him. The line of soldiers hit the mass of slaves with an audible crash that knocked many of them to the ground. Darius ignored the cries behind him, once he was sure his mother was safely past, as the soldiers began cutting into the fleeing slaves.

Then they were at the barges.

"Keep them back." Arthengal pointed toward the soldiers, reorganizing now for a charge on the boats.

Darius turned and loosed an arrow into a man not ten paces

away. A soldier behind him jumped over the body and then fell as Darius's arrow pierced his chest. Freed slaves were flooding onto the barge while Arthengal hacked at the ropes. Darius continued to fire.

"Get on," Arthengal urged once the last rope was cut.

Darius jumped on to the barge and then turned to continue firing. The archers near the house repositioned themselves and began firing on the boat. Arthengal lifted a large pole from the deck and began heaving against the dock. Two men fell behind Darius, arrows jutting from their chests. Others scooped up more poles from the deck and began helping Arthengal.

"I'm out," Darius called as he fired the last arrow.

"Then pick up a pole," Arthengal yelled back.

The barge was in the current now and was starting to spin. They labored to keep the craft steady and get it moving toward the opposite bank. More slaves were pouring onto the second boat while others wrestled with the guards. Darius spotted another group of slaves making a charge toward the western end of the valley to escape. Arrows rained down from the towers, and they fell by the dozens before any of them came within fifty paces of the fortifications.

Another burst of light illuminated the river. Darius glanced toward the compound. A tall, commanding man in black britches and a nightshirt stood on the hill holding a sword. He paid no heed to the confusion and chaos below him but stared intently at their barge. Darius glanced at Arthengal as the man paused. Arthengal locked eyes with the man.

"Sharav," he spat the name.

The nearest two towers began firing on the barge. Most of their arrows fell uselessly into the water, but two more women fell overboard when struck. The second barge was loose now but slaves and soldiers battled on its deck as it spun wildly. The current began to outpace their pursuers, and soon Darius could only see running specks.

Then the storm broke. Fat drops of rain began to splatter on the deck of the barge. Within minutes, the drops became a deluge and the river began to churn with the rising wind. The deck became slick, and two men slipped on the slick planks and were washed overboard. The dark and the rain made it impossible to find them before they were claimed by the river.

The other barge was barely visible through the torrent. Dark figures continue to struggle onboard, and more than one could be seen falling into the dark waters.

When they finally managed to ground their barge on the opposite bank, the second barge passed them twisting and bucking in the current. Ten or fifteen slaves at most remained on the deck, and they were struggling to work the oars to bring it under control.

Arthengal ushered the people off of the boat and then with the help of half a dozen of the others shoved the craft into the current. It pivoted wildly and then followed the second craft into the swift waters.

The prisoners scrambled up the muddy bank and huddled in small groups waiting to be told what to do next.

"We crossed more quickly than I had thought," Arthengal shouted over the storm. "This way." He led them away from the river, angling downstream toward the grove where they had left their horses and supplies.

Darius counted the people that followed them. Thirty in all and only ten men. He gave a start as he recognized one of them. Or rather, thought he recognized him by the tell-tale wound on his left hand.

"Marku?" he cried out in disbelief.

The blacksmith gave a tired grin. He was not the towering bulk of muscle that Darius remembered. He still stood a hand taller than Darius and had broad shoulders, but his thick muscles had been worn to lean, and his clothing hung from him like loose rags.

"It's good to see you, boy," the man grunted in his thick, quiet voice.

"What are you doing here?" Darius asked in surprise. Surely a man of Marku's size would have been sent to the mines.

"They needed strong backs to work the plows," he explained with a shrug. "And they kept me on to keep the farm tools serviceable. Better smiths than I work their forges. I don't have much of a hand for weapons. Well, hunting arrows maybe, but not the types that the imperial army is crafting."

Darius shook his head in wonder. He scanned the other faces

of the group but didn't see anyone else from their village.

"Was anyone else from Koza at the camp?"

Marku shook his head. Sorrow was clear in his eyes.

"Just your mother and I."

His mother drifted toward the pair.

"Is Micah with you?" she asked hopefully.

Years-old pain jabbed at Darius's heart.

"No, Mother," Darius replied. "Micah was killed in the raid."

"What? No," she corrected. "He was with us still when we crossed the Spine. He was in bad shape. He had taken an arrow to the chest, and no one thought he would live. But I had hoped."

Darius was dumbfounded. Then who had he prayed over in the Valley of Ravens?

"Where was he taken after you crossed the mountains?" Darius asked.

"I don't know," she answered with a sad shake of her head. "They split us into many groups. Only ten of us from Koza were taken to the farm. The others died during the first winter. It was a hard winter that year. Many didn't make it to spring. Marku and I are all that remain."

"But Micah could still be alive," Darius said hopefully.

"It's not likely," Marku cut in. "I saw his wound. It was bad. I thought they were going to leave him in that meadow where they slaughtered the sick and the old, but one of the officers with us decided to take a chance on him because he was young and strong.

He was feverish when we parted though and the wound..." He trailed off with a shudder.

Darius felt a pain deep in his chest as if an old wound had been ripped open. The brief hope that he had allowed himself was dashed with Marku's words. It was like losing his brother all over again, though he had never really had him back.

"Well, at least you are here," Darius's mother wrapped an arm around his waist. He draped his arm over her shoulder and pulled her close while they walked. She leaned her head against his chest, and he felt her body shudder as she wept. Darius fought the tears that wanted to fall and squeezed his mother's arm. He let the joy of finally having rescued her overshadow the pain of losing his brother. He smiled despite himself.

Chapter Twenty-Five
Nasu Rabi

Lao Jun Qiu stood on the porch of his house sipping tea from a porcelain cup decorated with finely painted blue sparrows in flight. He surveyed the carnage in the valley below him. The sun shown down on a cool summer morning and birds chirped in the garden. He watched while soldiers carried the bodies of his subjects and tossed them into a long trench that had been dug at the foot of the fields.

"So, it seems the Sillu Aga forces our hand again, General," he spoke without looking at the tall man standing a few paces to the side of him.

"I don't believe it was the Shadow Crown this time, your Majesty," Sharav mused.

"No?" The emperor turned to study the man's face. "What do you think it was?"

"I'm not sure, but I know who I saw, and he would have no connection to the Shadow Crown."

"And who was that?"

"Arthengal Alamay," the general growled with disgust.

"Nasu Rabi?" The emperor raised his eyebrows. "My father

always spoke highly of him."

"He is a fool and a traitor," Sharav spat.

"And a skilled leader and impressive warrior," the emperor added, ignoring Sharav's tone.

"So you say, Majesty. I never understood why the men followed him. He was a simple commoner raised above his station. He should have been hoisting a spear in the foot. He lacked discipline and blatantly disobeyed orders. I was finally able to convince The Honorable Emperor Chen Bai Jian of that after the debacle with the Sisuma."

Jun rolled his eyes. Why did the man always insist on using his cousin's full name and title when speaking about him? General Sharav must be the only man in the empire who didn't recognize his cousin's insanity for what it was. Blind devotion and obedience to the emperor did have its uses, he had to admit.

"Sometimes an emperor needs a leader who can assess the situation as it is and respond as the situation changes," Jun replied in a mild tone.

"Bah." This time Sharav did spit.

"Mind yourself, General," Jun cautioned.

"Apologies, Emperor." Sharav looked abashed and quickly got his emotions under control.

"I don't say that he didn't take his freedom of judgment too far with the incident with the horsemen, based on how you've described it to me. But he was a skilled swordsman, and he had many successful campaigns up to that point. You yourself have admitted as much, if reluctantly." Jun's tone was gentle and a touch condescending. "From what I remember of my father's words, he was well respected among the men and nobles alike, a legend almost."

General Sharav frowned and shifted his gaze to the battlefield. Yes, Jun guessed it could be called a battlefield. He studied the general for a minute before continuing. There may be a fine line between his blind devotion to the emperor and his blind hate of this man, Nasu Rabi. He hoped that it would not cause problems.

"None of this answers the question at hand, though, General. What would bring Nasu Rabi here?"

Sharav cringed visibly at the use of the nickname.

"And why now?" Jun said. "For decades now the only word we have received of him is that he is living quietly in retirement in the mountains somewhere. He only ever goes to Eridu to trade and visit old companions. He hasn't gone near the capital of Shalanum and as far as we know hasn't returned to Magora since the tragic death of his family."

"Maybe he was here to assassinate you," Sharav said. Hate still edged his voice. "He has already killed one emperor. I wouldn't put it past him to try again."

Jun pursed his lips.

"Maybe," Jun's voice was skeptical. "Then why didn't he

attack the royal residence? His only purpose seemed to be to liberate the workers, which, as we've discussed before, has very little impact on our plans. It's a mystery, don't you think, General Sharav?"

"Yes, Majesty. We interrogated what few slaves..."

"You know I don't like that word," Jun interrupted.

"Apologies, Majesty. We questioned those of your *imperial subjects* who survived, and none of them knew anything. They all told the same story of others coming to wake them, saying they had been rescued. Most of them did not hear the name of their rescuers. Arthengal Alamay was foreign to them, and Nasu Rabi was just a story from tales they told their children."

"Well, we must find him and ask him ourselves then. Or at least seek recompense for what we have lost today. Good soldiers are hard to replace."

"Yes, Majesty. I have already sent word for trackers and soldiers to pick up their trail."

"Maybe the Daku Mitu should be sent," the emperor said calmly. "They seem better suited to get answers than a foot soldier. Or recompense," he added as he turned back to the scene below.

Sharav nodded.

"I will send word to Colonel Saranov at once, Majesty. I'm sure he and Captain Vasiliev can put together a detachment to track them down and extract *justice*."

"What were our losses here today, General?" Jun changed the subject.

"Thirty men killed, mostly by Arthengal and that archer of his and twenty more wounded, mostly cuts and bruises from the uprising. Sixty workers escaped, and the rest are dead."

"I thought you said some survived to interrogate?" Jun questioned.

"They didn't survive the interrogation."

"Mmm, shame. It is they who should be cleaning up this mess rather than good soldiers." He took another sip of tea.

"Should we bring back the slav...uh, workers that we track down?" Sharav asked.

"No," he said after considering a moment. "I think we are done here. By the time any are returned, this will be cleaned up, and I don't think we will get much of a harvest out of what we could return."

"Don't let them escape to the south, though," he said, giving Sharav a sidelong glance. "We don't want details of what we do here to reach Shalanum or Magora Provinces until we are ready."

"As you say, Majesty."

"I think I will relocate to the camp of the Isten Erman though and await further word there."

"The First Order will welcome your company, Majesty. I will have an escort assembled at once."

"Bring the banners, too," Jun nodded towards the flags flapping in the wind. "The capital of the New Empire is to be relocated, I think. For now. Have what men remain recover the barges and load what fodder we have for the farms downstream. We may as well try to increase the harvest as much as we can at the other camps."

"As you say, Majesty. By your leave." He gave a curt bow and when Jun waved his hand strode off the porch.

Sengiin saw to the organization of an imperial escort out of what was left of the Imperial Guard and thirty additional archers. Then he had one of the stable boys saddle his horse. At least they had been isolated from the slave uprising. None of the five boys had even woken from their beds in the hayloft until the activity was all but over.

Colonel Saranov smiled despite himself when Sengiin gave him the news. Not for the debacle, Sengiin was sure, but for the opportunity to finally do something. Years of training with no enemies to fight started to wear on a man. Especially a professional soldier like Saranov. He called for Captain Vasiliev, and they explained the situation again.

"Nasu Rabi." Vasiliev cut a whistle short at Sengiin's glare.

"I respectfully ask permission to lead the detachment, Colonel," Vasiliev addressed Saranov. "It would be a great honor to bring a man like Nas...Alamay to justice."

"Granted," Saranov nodded. "Do you have any ideas for the rest of the unit? They must be good trackers as well as proficient fighters. The slaves may not be much of a threat, but I would prefer to contain Alamay and this archer of his with minimal losses on our side."

"I have a few ideas. Lieutenant Popov, of course, and his platoon of Night Birds, but I would like to take a few of the newer recruits as well to give them a taste of battle and test their skills."

"Very good, see to it," the Colonel instructed.

"General. Colonel." Vasiliev gave a quick bow to each man and practically trotted from the room.

"If the emperor is relocating to The First, does that imply we will be getting ready to move earlier than planned?" Saranov asked once the captain had left.

"That is yet to be determined," Sengiin said. "I can't imagine that the emperor will want to remain idle in the tents for long when he can be living in comfort at the imperial residence. But he has surprised me more than once with his patience. I think he will wait until our agents in the south indicate that the opportunity is right."

"Well, I hope that day is soon, Sengiin," Saranov said. "We have spent too long in exile. It is beyond time to reclaim our rightful place and restore the empire to His Holy Emperor."

"I agree and will do what I can to sway him," Sengiin replied. "The traitors in the south have much to answer for, and it is near time that the bill be paid."

Chapter Twenty-Six
Gone but Not Forgotten

Arthengal sighed when the thicket came into sight just before dawn. An exhausted, soaked, huddled mass trailed behind him. Thirty. How in the Sands of Saridon was he going to sneak thirty captives, himself, Darius, a pair of horses, and a bear past the soldiers that guarded the pass? More to the point, how was he going to keep them all fed during the time it would take to even reach the pass?

The storm from the prior night should give them some respite. The rain had stopped an hour ago, but it would have washed out most of their tracks closer to the river making it harder for trackers to find.

The freed captives were jolted into a panic when Antu strolled up from behind the horses. It had taken some effort to calm the people again and convince them to enter the glade. One woman collapsed and began crying hysterically at the edge of the wood. Two men had to pick her up and carry her into the cover of the trees, but she cried for an hour more with two women comforting her, rubbing her back and trying to convince her to eat something.

"She's in shock, Antu," Arthengal addressed the bear. "Don't take offense."

The bear grunted, sniffed the air in disgust, and loped out of the copse for fresher air. The captives did emit a distinctly pungent odor. Arthengal couldn't blame the bear, whose nose was more sensitive, for wanting to distance himself. He scanned the refugees. They were a bedraggled lot. All wore ill-fitted clothing stained with sweat and dirt. Most only wore simple leather slippers, fine for protecting their feet in the fields, but it would make for a rough hike out of The Wastes.

Arthengal grasped the arm of one of the men as he passed. "Why don't you and the others take advantage of our brief stop and bathe in the stream? I'm sure getting clean will help you feel more human again. I'll ask Darius to start distributing supplies. We don't have much but what we have is yours."

The man nodded his thanks and hurried off to speak to the others.

He glanced around for Darius. The boy hadn't left his mother's side since they had come off the barge. He spotted the two of them seated on a log near Micah, the horse, gnawing on dried meat and talking. She was a handsome woman, even in her current state. The years of captivity had not been kind, but she projected an inner strength that enhanced her natural beauty.

"Cordelia, I presume." Arthengal gave a deep bow. "I am Arthengal. It is a pleasure to finally meet you."

She was taken aback but recovered quickly. She extended her hand in greeting. "The pleasure is mine. I can't begin to thank you. Not only for the rescue but for taking care of my boy all these years."

"It has been my pleasure," Arthengal replied. "Darius was a fine boy and is a fine man. I think he has you to thank for that more than me."

Darius blushed at the compliment.

Cordelia smiled and glanced at Darius.

"He is a good boy, isn't he?" She reached up to ruffle his hair. "And tall. How did you get so tall? You were always a slight boy. And handsome. You look just like your father did at your age."

"All right, enough of this." Darius brushed his mother's hand away. His cheeks were bright red now. "How long before we need to move?"

"Let the others rest for a few hours. Can you pass out whatever food we have left? I'll see what I can do about catching some fish."

Darius nodded.

"We can't stay here long," Arthengal continued. "We took their boats, which will slow them down. They will have to cross downstream, but they will have trackers here by this time tomorrow. I would like to have a good distance between us and them by then."

"Where did you meet him?" Arthengal heard Cordelia ask as he moved to find his saddlebags. He wished he had brought his fishing pole, but he should be able to fashion something suitable out of the supplies they had.

What had Sengiin Sharav been doing at that camp? It was surprising enough that the man still survived but that he was attached to that outpost and whatever noble lived there was more so. He would need to question the survivors about that. Any information that he could find to relay back to the garrison at Eridu would be helpful. The operations that they had seen in their search pointed to a support system for an army that must number in the thousands. It should be stamped out in force. If this clear threat didn't cause the ministers in Kasha Amur to set aside their petty bickering, he didn't know what would. They could resolve their political disputes after the Daku Rabi were dealt with. He knew the generals would agree with him at least. Maybe that would be enough.

And if Sharav was involved, it increased the threat. He wished the man had not been wearing a nightshirt. Arthengal hadn't been able to see any insignia of rank. At the very least he was probably commanding that garrison, maybe more. Sharav had never been a brilliant tactician, but he made up for it with brutality and blind obedience to orders, even to the point of death.

Darius watched Arthengal hoist his saddlebags over a shoulder and march upstream. He hoped that Arthengal wasn't too upset at the extra people. He had expressed his concern over and over again that evading pursuit would be difficult enough on horseback with just the three of them. With thirty captives, they would have to travel on foot, and it would be almost impossible to hide their passage. Their best hope was to make the best use of their head start as they could and try to beat their pursuers to the badlands. Once there they should be able to lose any trackers in the twisting canyons.

"I'm sorry," he said to his mother. "What did you ask?"

"I said, where did you meet him?"

"After the raid, I tried to follow you north. I followed the trail for almost two weeks until I ran out of food. I had stopped to fish in a stream, and there he was, offering me advice on how to catch fish. Arthengal fed me and took me in. He promised to train me and help me rescue you. I'm sorry it took so long." At the last, his voice was filled with shame.

"That's okay, dear," she smiled and patted his arm. "You came, and that's all that matters now."

Darius put his hand over hers and gave it a squeeze.

"You said he trained you. Trained you how?" Her eyes flickered to the sword at his waist.

"He taught me all sorts of things. Sword and bow, of course, but he also educated me on herbs and medicines. He trained me to move quietly through the woods, how to hunt, and how to cover your tracks and hide your scent. He taught me how to read better and how to do numbers. I have learned so much about the rest of the world and our history; I don't even know where to begin. Did you know that this all used to be one big empire and thirty years ago there was a rebellion and the old emperor was killed?"

"I'd heard something about that when I was a girl," she winked. "Your grandfather fought in the war with Dagan Almwood and the other men of that generation. Even Marku served, young as he was at the time. I think he was a squire or something like that."

"How come you never told us anything about it?"

"When the men returned from the war they didn't really want to talk about it. All but Dagan that is, and him only when he drank. They wanted to return to simple lives of fishing and hunting and tending sheep. I guess by the time you and your brother were born most of us had just gotten used to *not* talking about it, and it never occurred to us. I told you stories, though, don't you remember?"

"Yeah, but those were only stories. Legends of heroes of old."

"Some were. Some were tales about the lands and cities and strange people that my father had met during the war. He would tell me of the happy times when I was a girl, and the interesting adventures. He just wouldn't talk about the war itself. Those were some of the stories I told you and your brother, although I might have added to them a little bit." She smiled.

Darius had missed that smile.

"Hadn't you better do as Arthengal asked and get everyone some food? Half of them look like they are half asleep on their feet. They should eat before they rest. I think I'll go clean my clothes and wash my hair." She fingered her red locks, stained brown with filth, and stood. She glanced upstream to where Arthengal was tying some string to a stout length of fir and turned downstream.

Darius watched as she disappeared behind some bushes near a bend in the brook then turned to the rest of the group. Their remaining supplies were meager, but he was able to supply each with a biscuit and a handful of dried meat. He had been forced to quarter the apples to make sure everyone got a share.

Darius was lifting the saddle onto Micah's back when his mother returned.

"Much better," she said, wringing her hair as she approached. Her clothing was cleaner, too, although most of the stains would never wash out. The simple woolen blouse clung to her, and the baggy trousers would have fallen off of her if not for the cord cinched at the waist.

Darius frowned as he watched her. She looked more like the woman he remembered, to be sure, but also less somehow. She was thinner, and lines etched her once smooth face. Long days in the sun would do that, he supposed. He red hair lacked the luster that he remembered from his youth. He saw her arms more clearly now that they were clean too. Wicked-looking scars crisscrossed her forearms. Darius could only guess that they were from those horrible switches that the guards had carried.

He pulled her into his arms without warning. Sadness and relief mixed as tears welled in his eyes.

She clung to him for several minutes and then stepped back, patting him on the chest. Her eyes shone as well. She studied him.

"You've grown so much." Her voice broke slightly as she spoke. "I'm so proud of you."

Darius felt like his heart was going to explode. He wanted to laugh and cry all at the same time.

Cordelia cleared her throat and wiped her eyes as she turned to survey the group. About half of them, mostly the women, had followed her example to clean up. The others had dropped off to sleep as soon as they had eaten.

"Come on." She reached for his hand. "Let's get something to eat."

Darius and Arthengal led the horses while the child Lianna rode double with one of the women on Micah and another woman rode Eranen. The women rotated, but Lianna rode except when they took breaks.

Cordelia had laughed when Darius told her the name of the horse. "I'm sure Micah would be happy that you honor him that way. It's a fine gelding."

The men all walked. Most had carved roughshod staves from the trees at the thicket, and they spread out on either side of the women and horses. Antu remained aloof, not wanting to get too close to the unfamiliar humans. He would range ahead, hunting rabbits or mice, and would return to check on them periodically.

"You must tell me the story of that bear," Cordelia said to Darius. "He is the most unusual animal I've ever seen."

"That's Antu. Whether in the flesh or sent by the Sky Father, he is here to protect me and test me," Darius said with all seriousness.

Cordelia coughed, which drew a reproachful glance from Darius and a smile from Arthengal.

"Uh huh," she said condescendingly. "And where did you meet Antu?"

"When I shot him in the eye," Darius said simply.

This time she choked. "When you what?"

"It was when I first met Arthengal. We were walking down this stream toward the valley where Arthengal lives when we saw this giant bear across the creek. The bear charged us. I was so scared, but I remembered what Micah had taught me, and I shot him. Right in the eye. It scared him away and we were able to make it to a cave to hide and rest. But then Antu tracked us down, and we were forced to jump in the river. The stream had grown to a river by then. Anyway, we had to jump in the river to get away. Enki tossed me around so much I thought I would drown, and then he spat us out over this waterfall and into a pool, right in Arthengal's valley."

Cordelia stared.

"So you got away again?" Cordelia asked once she had recovered from her shock.

"Well, yeah, but then Antu tracked us back to the valley

another way, and he got all tangled in Arthengal's traps. We went up to investigate what had set off the alarms, and there was Antu all wrapped up in nets and ropes, dangling from the ground." Darius laughed which earned him a sidelong glance from the bear. "Arthengal wanted me to kill him, but I couldn't do it. I walked up to the trap and used my sword to cut the ropes free."

"You did what?" Cordelia gasped.

"He leaned in real close to me and roared right in my face. I almost pissed myself," he laughed and then blushed. "Oh, sorry. Anyway, Antu must have been thankful for the rescue, and I guess he forgave me for shooting him in the eye. After scaring me half to death, he turned and ran away. We've had other adventures since then too. He saved Arthengal and me from some wolves when we were out hunting one winter. He saved us from some bandits that next spring. That's when I got this from a thief's sword." He fingered the scar across his eye. "After that, we became fast friends and have had great adventures together. We share our fish and our hunts with him, and he watches our backs."

"That's quite a story," Cordelia stuttered.

"All true," Arthengal interjected. "Strangest pair I've ever seen, those two. Antu has saved our hides more times than I can count. I'm not ready to admit he is the Sky Father in the flesh, mind you, but I've given up arguing against it."

"Huh," Cordelia said and studied the loping bear with fresh eyes.

"He seems to have adopted Darius as his 'cub' and protects him furiously," Arthengal added. "He's still wild, mind you. I wouldn't recommend any of you trying to cuddle with him at night, but he seems to recognize that you are part of Darius's pack and shouldn't bother you unless antagonized. After four years he is tolerant of me and only growls in my direction occasionally. I've given up trying to warn Darius off. He never listened to me anyway when I tried."

Darius shook his head. "That's because he is Antu. He is firm but fair. He tests me but wouldn't do anything to outright hurt me. Just like you, Arthengal. My two old bears." He smiled affectionately.

The first day's travel saw them to the edge of the river plain and into thickly wooded forest that bordered the badlands. Broad oak and maple trunks rose around them interspersed with smaller birch, aspen, and lime trees. Dappled sunlight poured in through the leafy ceiling. The stone towers that seemed to be everywhere in The Wastes thrust out of the ground with greater frequency than they had in the flatter land closer to the river. Moss and ivy hung from the spires like green shawls. Travel was slower than planned. The former slaves were not used to the dense underbrush that choked the area, and the terrain became rougher the further south they travelled. The lime trees, at least, provided a steady supply of nourishment even if it failed to quench their thirst.

The humidity increased as well the deeper they traveled into the forest. The thick, dangling mosses began to drip water on them as they passed beneath slanting stone obelisks. And with the humidity came the bugs. Gnats, mosquitoes, and biting flies harassed the party with every step. Fresh water was scarce. Most of the pools they encountered were stagnant or covered with the thick film of mosquito eggs.

They camped their second night in the woods in a deep alcove formed by two crossing rock spires where an artesian spring bubbled up from beneath the rocks. Arthengal backtracked their trail to try to cover their tracks and set a few false trails while the others rested. He forbade fires at night, saying that the light could be seen for miles. They ate a cold dinner of berries, nuts, and mushrooms that they had foraged along the way.

Marku and Darius shared the first watch. They sat on a wide ledge halfway up one of the spires where they could see clearly over the tops of the thick leafy canopy.

"That's a fine sword you wear, Darius," Marku commented. "Where did you get it?"

"Arthengal gave it to me," he answered as he scanned the darkness and absently slapped a mosquito on his neck. "Do you want to see it?"

"No, no." Marku waved his hands as Darius started to release the straps. "That's okay."

Darius shrugged and returned his hands to his lap.

"He was a soldier then?" Marku asked.

"Uh huh, a long time ago," Darius replied. "Before the Great War and during. He fought with the barons against the emperor."

"Did he now?" Something dark crossed Marku's eyes so quickly that Darius thought he imagined it. Then he was all smiles again. "Well, he must have been an officer to carry a blade like that. I've rarely seen such a finely decorated scabbard."

"He was," Darius said warily. He must have imagined it. Marku never had a harsh word for anyone. "He was a colonel for Emperor Chen, and then later he was a general for Baroness Magora."

"A general. Impressive. For Baroness Magora, you say? Do you have any idea what the markings on the scabbard mean?" Marku probed.

"I never really thought of it, but now that you mention it I think it's probably because of his nickname, Nasu Rabi. It means Old Bear--"

"*The* Nasu Rabi?" Marku interrupted. His face showed shock that didn't extend to his eyes. There was also something odd about his tone, like he was confirming something he already suspected. Marku peered out into the darkness. He pursed his lips and drummed a finger on his chin.

"You've heard of him?"

"Everyone who served in the war has heard of Nasu Rabi," Marku said.

Darius leaned back on his hands and looked at the man.

"Mother said you fought in the war? I never knew that before. What did you do?" Darius asked.

"Well, not fought, exactly. I was too young for that. In the beginning, I was squire for a wushai."

"What's a wushai?" Darius asked.

"Sort of like a knight, I guess you'd say. They were elite warriors pledged to the noble houses. Often they are the younger sons of the house who had no right of inheritance. They served at the pleasure of the house rather than the empire.

"Later, after he died, I became a runner," Marku continued. "I was fast in those days, fast as the wind. I would carry messages from my commanders back to the capi...rather, to Kasha Haaki," he said proudly.

"Fast? No offense, Marku," Darius said. "But I never would have guessed you had been fast."

The blacksmith laughed.

"I was tall and skinny in my youth. The forge and good cooking earned me my girth." He looked down at himself and his brow furrowed. "I guess I'm tall and skinny again."

"Good cooking? You weren't married."

Marku laughed again.

"No, I wasn't. But every woman in Koza was determined to see that I was. They would ply me with pies and fresh bread and even sweets sometimes to try to win me over to their way of thinking. But back then, I was married to the forge. After the war, I wanted to make things after seeing so many things destroyed."

"And now?"

"Oh, I don't know. These past years have been..." he paused. "...hard. I'm not really sure what I want, I guess. Maybe in time I'll figure it out."

"Not me. Now that I've finally rescued my mother, I just want to live a peaceful life in the valley with her and Arthengal and Antu. Raise hemp and fish and hunt until I am old and gray like Arthengal."

Marku laughed again.

"Well, life has a way of changing your mind about things like that. You are young yet. I bet you have many adventures ahead of you still."

Something that Marku had said pulled at the back of Darius's mind. "Wait, did you say Kasha Haaki? You were from Merkar Province? I thought you were from Koza, born and raised."

"No," Marku said. "I settled there after the war. There wasn't much left for me at home, and a small town on the edge of the wilderness was just what I was looking for. Peace and quiet, you understand."

"Of course," Darius said. "The war must have been horrible."

"I saw atrocities that you wouldn't believe." His forehead creased, and his brows drew down. "Our way of life was shattered, and after it was over, we all had to find something to start over. The hammer and the forge brought me a sort of peace that I hadn't really known before."

"Shattered? An odd word," Darius said. "Most people I've talked to think their lives are better out from under imperial rule."

"Of course, of course. That part is better," Marku said hastily. "I only meant that it was war-torn. Towns and villages destroyed. People uprooted. Families lost. That's what I meant by shattered. Anyway, this is hard for me to talk about."

"I'm sorry, it must be painful," Darius said. "Arthengal doesn't like to talk about the war much either."

Marku sighed. "It was a different time, and at times you weren't really sure what you were fighting for."

Darius nodded. "I think I understand. Anytime I've had to fight, it has either been to protect myself or to help those I love. It's hard to imagine having to fight or kill someone who may have been a neighbor or a friend just because you have different views or just because they were conscripted into the wrong army."

"Or a brother," Marku said so softly that Darius wasn't sure he had heard him right.

Marku cleared his throat and wiped a hand across his eyes. "Do you mind if we talk about something more pleasant? Tell me about this bear of yours."

Darius repeated the story that he had told his mother earlier and added a few more of their adventures. Marku laughed at all the right places and showed awe at others, but Darius got the feeling his heart wasn't in it. Darius felt bad for dredging up old, painful memories, especially so soon after being rescued from another horrid circumstance.

They were setting up camp the following day when Arthengal returned, out of breath.

"Sorry folks, we have to keep moving,"

"Why?" Darius asked.

"There is a search party only a few leagues to the north. They've set up camp for the evening, but they are moving more quickly than we are. We'll have to press through the night to avoid them catching us tomorrow. I'll try to find a safe place where we can rest for at least a few hours up ahead. You keep everyone moving south."

The entire group was half asleep on their dragging feet by the time Arthengal led them to a cave carved into the side of a jagged plateau. Water dripped from the limestone stalactites inside the cave, and they managed to find several pools of fresh water. They drank greedily before finding places to huddle together for sleep.

Arthengal shook Darius awake as the first rays of light were breaking outside. Others were already starting to stir around the cave.

"I want to get into the broken lands by nightfall. We can lose ourselves more easily in the ravines and canyons there, and work our way toward the main pass into the plains."

Darius found his mother, who was helping Lianna into the saddle.

"Are you getting enough to eat?" he asked her. She still looked very tired, and her face was drawn.

"Yes, I'm fine. I'm still adjusting to eating anything other than soybeans and rice. Nuts, berries, limes, and fish have been a great treat, but my stomach is a bit sensitive. I had forgotten how good fresh fish tastes and how rich it is."

"Okay, well, eat more if you can. You need to regain your strength. I will try to find us some rabbits or birds today. Arthengal has a few arrows left, and I hope to make good use of them."

"We'll continue to stick to the less-traveled trails," Arthengal explained to everyone. "We don't want to have a chance encounter with a patrol or search party. We should be well ahead of the group I spotted yesterday, but there may be others. Stay quiet and stay close."

They plodded slowly, still moving at half the pace Arthengal and Darius could have made alone. The slow pace allowed Arthengal ample time to scout and mask their trail. By nightfall, they found a twisting canyon into a hidden glade. Darius had managed to bag half a dozen fat grouse, and Arthengal risked a low fire built into a stone alcove. It wasn't much for a group of their size, but in combination with what they had scavenged it was enough.

Arthengal and Darius climbed the rock walls of the canyon

and scanned the area to the south. A league or so to the north they could see light flickering in the trees, enough for several fires.

"They gained more ground than I thought they would," Arthengal said. "At least they aren't bothering to hide their fires so they'll be easy to spot. They will catch up to us by tomorrow. Hopefully, my false trails slow them down some, but we must try to stick to the canyons. I'll scout ahead to make sure we don't get caught in a dead end and behind to cover our trail."

"How long do you think it will take?" Darius asked.

"It's hard to say," Arthengal mused. "It took us three days on the way in, but we were moving pretty fast. I'd guess at least a week, maybe longer. It's about to get interesting."

Chapter Twenty-Seven
Foxes and Hounds

What Arthengal had guessed to be a week quickly became two. Every day they dodged and outmaneuvered their pursuers. The refugees were slowly gaining strength with regular meals of meat, even as sparse as they were. The open meadows between canyons were alive with game, and it was not uncommon for Darius to take six or eight birds or rabbits while the party passed through to the next ravine.

They had been forced to backtrack twice, losing more than a day each time, when Arthengal judged that search parties would intercept them on their current course. One night when Arthengal and Darius climbed a spire for a look, the campfires of the soldiers were only two chasms over. Arthengal scrambled down the spire quickly and kicked out their own fire to the protests of the group and forced everyone to march east through the night.

The next day Arthengal surprised them by sprinting around a bend waving his hands. Confusion overtook the survivors until he got close enough for them to hear his whispered, "Run!" They all turned and ran back down the narrow valley that they had just crossed. Arthengal grabbed Darius's arm as they exited the gulch and instructed him to place his back against the wall. He raised six fingers, and Darius nodded his understanding.

The last of the refugees were just entering a draw on the opposite side of the glade when the soldiers burst past them with bows in hand. As the last one ran by, Arthengal's sword flashed, and he hamstrung the archer who then toppled into his nearest companion. Darius and Arthengal fell upon the men, and the battle was fierce but quick. Only two of them had time to drop their bows and draw their short swords before the fight was over.

Only after it was done did they realize that the first two bowmen had been able to fire shots before turning to fight. The bodies of two women lay sprawled in the grass, arrows protruding from their backs. The only silver lining, if it could be called that, was that Darius and Arthengal were both able to refill their quivers from the supplies of the slain soldiers.

They were able to avoid further confrontations but only by taking longer, slower routes well away from the search parties. Fifteen days after entering the badlands, the sharp back slopes of the Dragon's Spine finally came into view.

Leaving the survivors in a sheltered cave, Arthengal and Darius tracked forward until they could see the pass and road more clearly.

"This is unbelievable," Arthengal commented. "I don't know how Shalanum's scouts could have failed to report this."

"Maybe none of them that came this way made it out of the pass," Darius commented, pointing to the dozen archers visible on the cliffs to either side.

The camp was immense. The forest had been cut back several hundred paces from the entrance to the pass to make room for large corrals. There were at least thirty of the pens.

"This looks like a way station, but I don't see any cattle, and there are only twenty or thirty horses," Arthengal commented.

"I don't think the pens are for livestock," Darius said, surprised that he was the one to make the connection for once. "Well, maybe some of them are."

"Oh, right," Arthengal said in a slow drawl.

"Where are all the guards?" Darius asked. "I thought there would be a lot more for a camp this large."

There were only a handful of soldiers wandering throughout the vast compound, and a few dozen tents were staked to the west of the pass.

"They probably only leave a skeleton crew here when they aren't processing captives," Arthengal said.

The twelve archers had been easy to pick out, but otherwise it was difficult to tell exactly how many soldiers there were. Some wandered the grounds while others, probably the night watch, slept in the tents.

Darius surveyed the rest of the camp. Most of the horses were housed in corrals. A few were saddled and picketed near the tents. A narrow, winding path snaked up the steep incline to either side of the pass granting the archers access to the heights.

"Those horses would sure help our cause," Arthengal commented. "I think I have an idea. Let's go back to the others."

Arthengal laid out his plan for Cordelia and the others.

At first light, Darius made his way west. He hiked along the cliffs until he found a rock slide that he could climb easily. Once he was on top of the ridge, he turned back to the pass. He snuck through the trees and boulders like he was stalking prey. In a sense, he guessed that he was.

He reached a vantage where he could see one of the archers clearly and could see the cliffs on the other side. Arthengal had said to wait for his signal. The sun was nearly clear of the western peaks, and his mother would be moving soon.

A scream broke the still of the quiet spring morning and then ended abruptly at the foot of the cliffs.

The archer Darius was watching was instantly alert and had his bow drawn.

Darius nocked an arrow of his own and aimed it at the soldier's back. He released and was moving before the arrow even hit its target. He ducked behind a large boulder and sprinted through the hollow behind it. He slowed on the other side and crept through the trees looking for his next target.

The second archer was shifting nervously, first looking at the trees behind him and then turning to survey the opposite ridge. His bow was half drawn, but he couldn't find a target. Darius waited until he turned back to check the pass and fired. The arrow struck the man in the side, just below his raised elbow.

Shouts of alarm came from nearby, and as Darius hurried to a new spot, he heard someone crashing through the bushes where he had just been hidden. Darius risked a look back and glimpsed the soldier kneeling to inspect the ground.

"Rat spit," Darius hissed. He barely had time to load an arrow when he saw the man's eyes following Darius's trail through the woods. Their eyes met briefly over a patch of raspberry bushes. It was too late, for the soldier. Before he could cry out, Darius's arrow struck him in the chest.

An arrow struck the tree near Darius's head. He turned and dove behind a fallen log.

Darius peaked over the edge of the log and saw the archer on the rise of a small hill through the trees. He ducked down quickly again as another arrow sank into the log.

"Over here," he heard the soldier shout.

Darius couldn't stay here. He searched frantically for a better hiding spot. The rocks formed a small, protected alcove a few dozen paces beyond the log. If he could crawl to the end of the deadfall, it would be a quick sprint to safety.

Arrows peppered the ground behind him as he ran, but he made it. Now he was perfectly pinned down and had nowhere else to go. He nocked an arrow, in case someone came close enough, and waited for the soldiers in the camp to arrive and finish him off.

Cordelia waited for the sun to clear the eastern peak, as she'd been instructed, before signaling the group to move. She led one of the horses and Marku lead the other. Nobody spoke, and they traveled as quietly as they were able.

They reached the edge of the woods and the camp beyond was in chaos. There was no sign of the archers that Arthengal had said would be on the cliffs. Instead, there were eight men standing near the opening to the pass, bows drawn, surveying the hillside. More soldiers, ten to a side, were slowly climbing up the winding path to the heights. They carried spears and wore light armor. Half a dozen frantic soldiers remained in the camp and worked to calm the horses who were becoming anxious with all of the activity.

An arrow shot suddenly from the eastern ridge, and one of the archers dropped to the ground. Arrows clattered off the rocks above as the archers returned fire, but there wasn't anyone there.

Cordelia waited, watching for an opening.

Another two archers fell near the pass, and the rest moved several steps back toward the camp to get a better view. The soldiers ascending the cliffs were about halfway up the treacherous trail.

A rapid barrage from the eastern heights disabled three more men and the rest began shouting and running back toward the center of the camp, trying to get out of range.

In the corrals, a particularly large stallion bolted at the screams and broke through the gate. He and the five mares stabled with him charged out of the pen and scattered. What had been chaos quickly devolved into anarchy as the soldiers tried to round them up and keep from getting trampled in the progress.

"Now!" Cordelia shouted.

The mass of captives rushed out of the trees, dividing into small groups, each bound for a separate corral and the remaining horses. Cordelia mounted Micah and Marku struggled into Eranen's saddle. They charged the horses in the direction of the pass. One of the soldiers tried to block her escape. She leaned over Micah's neck and dug in her heels. The man's leg was crushed by the horse's hooves as he tried to dive out of the way.

Darius couldn't see what was going on in the camp below, but by the sound, his mother and the other captives had entered the fray. He scanned the woods, still waiting for the soldiers to arrive. He saw a flash of brown. One of the archers was trying to flank him. He fired, and the arrow glanced off a tree near the man, sending him diving for the bushes. A pair of arrows clattered off the rocks to his left.

The sneaky archer sprinted from cover trying to make it to a boulder to Darius's right. If he made it, Darius would be done for. Darius shot once, and the arrow glanced off the archer's right shoulder. As Darius drew another arrow and fired again, the soldier dove behind the rocks. Darius couldn't tell if he had hit the man or not.

"Okay, I can't stay here," Darius told himself. "Now or never. Two left...I hope."

He nocked an arrow, looping a finger over the shaft to hold it in place. He gripped the bow tightly, took a deep breath, and then ran. He ran for all he was worth. He dodged from one tree to the next, moving in a zigzag toward the archers. Arrows assaulted the trees behind him and beside him. Finally, he got a clear view of his assailants and slowed enough to raise his bow. He ran past two more trees and then stopped suddenly and shot. The archer on the right cried out and dropped his bow as the arrow struck his arm.

The second archer took advantage of Darius's brief pause. The arrow grazed Darius's side, and he felt a jab of pain.

"Aaaaaaaahhh!" Darius screamed and charged the man.

The man was startled by Darius's reaction, and before he could prepare another shot, Darius was on him.

Darius crashed into the soldier. Darius stumbled but managed to keep his footing as he pushed the man backward. He dropped his bow to secure his grip on the archer's jerkin and drove his legs faster, picking up speed. The man was stumbling backward, but Darius kept him upright.

Darius skidded to a stop at the precipice and released his grip. The archer's hands flailed as he tried to grab Darius's arm. Then he was falling. Darius drew his sword as he heard the crunch on the rocks below and turned back toward the injured soldier.

Cordelia wheeled Micah to a stop at the mouth of the canyon. Several of the men were struggling with one of the guards while others helped the women and Lianna mount horses. A scream to the left drew Cordelia's attention. A woman, Sarah, she thought, lay face down in the dirt with a black arrow jutting from her back.

As Cordelia watched, another arrow streaked from the tree line and struck one of the men in the thigh. He stumbled and fell.

"Marku, help him," she shouted.

She guided Micah to the dead archers and dismounted. She picked up one of the bows and snatched a handful of arrows from the quiver. She drove the arrows point first into the dirt. Selecting one, she raised the bow and scanned the far edge of the camp. Several men had emerged from the trees and were firing on the fleeing refugees.

Two more of her fellows fell as she fired at the closest sniper. The man stumbled back and fell, clutching his chest. She had drawn the attention of the others. A volley of arrows streaked through the air toward her and fell a dozen paces short.

She prepared to fire again.

A deafening roar echoed across the camp and through the hills.

Antu thundered out of the trees and engulfed one of the archers. Cordelia could hear the sickening crunch even from where she stood.

The men at the trees shouted in dismay. The closest fired at Antu and the arrow sunk into the meat of the bear's thick shoulder. Antu slowly raised his head. Blood dripped from his maw. The look he gave the man was one of rage and disgust. Then the bear roared again and charged.

Damn, he's fast, Cordelia thought.

She took advantage of the distraction to shoot another of the soldiers.

Horses began to gallop past as her companions entered the pass. Marku rode up, bareback on a black mare.

"Where's Eranen?" Cordelia asked.

Marku shrugged. "He went that way when I got down to help Johan." He waved an arm vaguely to the east and then continued into the pass.

Darius paused and watched his mother shoot. She was good. The archers were well over a hundred paces away. His fingers began to ache as he clung to the cliff wall, and he started to move again, lowering himself to the next foothold.

He hadn't wanted to chance going back into the trees, not knowing the status of the final archer. The soldiers from the camp would be there any minute. His only option had been to climb down. The wall was vertical, but it had plenty of good holds. It wasn't much different than the cliffs he had grown up climbing. Except a road of solid rock waited below rather than the ocean.

Darius heard voices above him. The other soldiers must have arrived. There were shouts as they inspected their dead. He froze, not wanting to make any noise, and glanced up. He could hear movement near the lip of the canyon.

A bearded face appeared, scanning the canyon and the cliffs. He spotted Darius and raised his spear. An arrow whistled through the air over Darius's head and struck the man in the chest. The soldier stumbled back and was gone. Darius heard frantic shouts above him. He ventured a quick glance to the opposite ridge and saw Arthengal. He fired another shot for good measure, and Darius heard running boots.

Darius let out a relieved sigh and continued to climb down. His mother saw him as he was reaching the bottom.

"Darius!" she shouted. "You're okay."

He turned to face her, brushing his hands off on his pant legs.

"You're bleeding." Her voice was concerned.

He looked down at his shirt. A dark patch had soaked his right side.

"I'll be fine. Did everyone make it out?" he asked.

"Most. There are a few coming still."

As if on command, four more captives thundered by on horseback.

"Here," Cordelia offered. "Climb up in front of me."

Darius mounted Micah and scanned the camp. Antu was

loping in their direction. Several refugees lay dead along with more than a few soldiers. The remaining soldiers were rallying and moving toward the pass.

"Time to go," he said and turned Micah south.

The riders waited for Darius at the base of the gap, uncertain where to go next.

"Head east," he instructed as he approached, and they veered in that direction.

Darius wheeled to a stop, and watched up the pass. Ten or fifteen men jogged after them shaking fists and spears. Antu trotted up to his side.

Together they waited, watching.

Suddenly, Eranen charged down the hill toward the soldiers. Startled, the men tried to raise their spears, but Arthengal charged through them, forcing them to dive to the sides.

"What are you waiting for?" Arthengal hollered as he galloped past.

Darius smiled and turned to follow.

They rode hard for an hour and then slowed to a trot.

"Which way do we ride?" Darius asked. "The valley or Eridu?"

"The valley first," Arthengal said. "There is something I need to get there. Then we will ride to Eridu and tell the captain of the garrison there what we know."

"They'll be after us," Darius said. "Besides, our stores are nearly empty. We can't feed all these people."

"I know," Arthengal said. "The stop will be brief. Only a day or two. There is enough in the garden to last that long."

Arthengal looked tired again.

"Are you all right?" Darius asked, concerned.

"Yes," Arthengal smiled. "I'm just getting old, Darius. Too old for all of this."

Shock crossed Darius's face. He had never before heard Arthengal complain about getting old. In fact, he had never heard the man complain about much of anything. Not seriously, anyway. His worry increased that much more.

"Cheer up, boy." Arthengal slapped him on the shoulder. "I'll be fine."

He heeled his horse and rode to catch up with the others. He pulled up next to Darius's mother.

"Cordelia, there is something I've been meaning to ask you."

"What's that, Arthengal?" she smiled.

"The house on the hill. Do you know who lived there?"

"The emperor," she said.

Darius and Arthengal exchanged looks of shock.

"That can't be right. The emperor is dead. I saw it with my own eyes."

"Not Emperor Chen, from before the war. He calls himself the New Emperor," she explained, "Emperor Lao Jun Qiu."

"Did you say Lao?" Arthengal's voice sounded sad and

mystified at the same time.

"Yes, Emperor Lao Jun Qiu," she repeated.

"Not Lao Cang Yu?"

"No, that was his father. The old emperor had ordered his father killed but had spared the boy. The commander general rescued the boy near the end of the war and, with the help of what few imperial servants he was able to save, raised the boy to be the heir of the empire."

"The commander general?" Arthengal's face had gone white.

"Commander General Sengiin Sharav. He is the commander over all of the emperor's armies and led the Imperial Guard that was there at the camp."

The breath went out of Arthengal. "May the gods protect us," he gasped.

"Eridu first?" Darius asked.

Arthengal shook his head. "No, now more than ever, I must retrieve what is hidden in the valley."

Chapter Twenty-Eight
Homecoming

Arthengal inspected their group as they rode through the gates of Anbar Ur just after dawn. They were a bedraggled and miserable lot. He had pressed them to ride straight through, stopping only to rest the horses and for brief meals of hurriedly roasted pheasant or rabbit. There was never enough to go around, and with very little foraging on the plains, most of them looked like they were starving.

Antu flopped down in the center of the town and refused to move. With Darius's help, Arthengal instructed the rest of the group how to unsaddle the mounts and wipe them down with straw. Most went through the motions in a daze.

"At least the horses were well fed on the plains. Their strength is what carried us here more than our own." Darius gave each animal a scoop of oats.

Arthengal and Darius led the horses to where they could graze on grass just outside the southern entrance. Marku was standing near the crumbling gate, stretching his back while he stared down at the orchards.

"Is this your valley?" he asked.

"No," Arthengal replied. "That's a bit further on."

"Are those apples?" Marku asked longingly.

"Yes, but we don't have time now," Arthengal said as he strode by. "There is plenty of food in the valley. Let's go, on your feet. We're almost there."

The disheveled group dragged their feet after him. Only Marku seemed to have any energy left at all from the group. It was like arriving at Anbar Ur had energized him. Arthengal led the group on the road until it reached the tunnel that had been caved in years before, then turned up into the terraced gardens that surrounded the city. Darius helped his mother and several more of the refugees descend the stairs that he had helped build, on the other side to rejoin the road. Arthengal waited at the head of the canyon.

"Darius, lead them down and get everyone something to eat," Arthengal said. "I'll finish up here and meet you down there."

"Do you need help?" Marku asked

Arthengal sighed wearily and finally nodded in assent. He instructed the blacksmith how to set the triggers on the pit traps first and then the nets. Both were similar to what a bear hunter might use in the forest and Marku followed directions as if he had done it before. When they reached the more mechanical traps that guarded the path to the valley, Marku was more impressed.

"These are ingenious," he said as he inspected the tripwires and metal bars. "Five or ten men could be swept off the mountain with one misstep of the person on point. I like what you've done with the trips too. Each is different, so even after the first trap is triggered, you can't look for the same thing to prevent triggering the next. And the false triggers you've set..." he trailed off, realizing Arthengal was staring at him.

"You know an awful lot about traps for a blacksmith," Arthengal said suspiciously.

"I wasn't always a blacksmith," Marku answered simply. "In the war, I was squire for a wushai with a very cautious nature. He didn't trust for men alone to guard his camp at night and insisted on snares and traps as a supplement. To be sure, on more than one occasion, it was the traps that alerted us rather than the men, so I don't know that he was wrong."

Arthengal nodded. He had known men like that during the war. Honestly, he had been a man like that more than once when leading troops deep into enemy territory.

By the time Arthengal and Marku arrived at the cabin, the others lay on the ground outside, likely where they had collapsed upon arrival. Cordelia was carrying around a bucket of water letting the others sip from a ladle while Darius distributed handfuls of dried goods and shriveled apples from the storehouse.

"Thank you," a short man with greasy black hair said as Darius handed him two soft apples and a hunk of cheese still encased in wax.

"I'm sorry we don't have any bread," Darius said. "But maybe

I can make some as soon as everyone has settled in. We should have enough cornmeal to scrape something together."

Arthengal disappeared into the cellar and came out carrying a bundle wrapped in a wool blanket and set it down in the center of the camp.

"These are some of Darius's and my old clothes. I'm sorry they may not fit well, but I have needle and thread if anyone has a hand for stitching. After you've eaten, Darius can show the women to the baths where you can clean up and change into whatever you can find that fits. I need to run an errand. Do not leave the valley while I'm gone. It may not be safe to venture out on your own."

The refugees nodded in agreement but most looked like they didn't have the energy to climb back out of the valley if they wanted to.

"Darius, there are more weapons in the cave. You know the one?"

"Yes, of course," Darius responded.

"We should arm everyone before we head south, just in case."

The women started digging through the clothing first, selecting garments that might fit. There was a shortage of pants, but both men were tall, and some of the longer shirts looked like they could be adjusted as dresses for the shorter women.

The women trailed after Darius as he led them to the baths

near the end of the lake. Exclamations of joy came from the women when they came within sight of it. His cheeks colored as several of the women began stripping off their ragged garments and entering the water without waiting for him to leave. Sighs of relief and tears of joy were shared by many when they discovered that the water was hot. One woman laughed out loud as she settled onto a submerged bench.

"I'll be at the cabin if you need anything else," he stammered, but the women had already forgotten him.

As he reached the cabin, he saw Marku coming the other way holding a large box in one arm and munching on an apple with the other. The box, too, he saw was filled to the brim with apples.

"Where did you get those?" Darius asked.

"I took a quick ride down to the orchard for some fresh apples. The fruit in your stores is all soft and brown. I haven't had a fresh apple in four years." Marku smiled as he took another bite. "I love apples," he muttered around a mouth full of fruit.

"Arthengal said not to leave the valley," Darius shouted with more anger than he had intended. The long ride had worn his patience to a fine edge. "You may have put us all in danger if anyone saw you."

Marku looked startled at the younger man's anger.

"Nobody saw me, I'm sure," the blacksmith stammered like a boy caught by his mother with his finger in a cooling pie. "I won't go out again, I promise."

"See that you don't." Darius trudged off to grab a fresh set of clothes for himself.

Darius, and most of the other men, washed in the colder water of the lake near the cabin rather than waiting for the women to return. The air in the valley was hot compared to the cooler summer air of the north.

Darius was pulling a dark blue, loose-fitting shirt over his head when he saw his mother returning up the path. She wore a purple shirt with yellow flowers embroidered on the sleeve and an older pair of black pants. She was running fingers through her long red hair to pick out the tangles. Some of the luster had returned to her hair from the soap.

The girl, Lianna, trailed after Cordelia. She wore a dark green, heavy linen shirt as a dress. It was cinched at the waist with a sash from one of Darius's old tunics.

"I have to go gather weapons for everyone," he told his mother. "Do you want to help me?"

"Sure," she replied. "Lianna can help, too."

He grabbed a lantern from the house and led them to the cave behind the waterfall. He lit the lantern and looked around. His mother gasped at first sight of the weapons cache. Crates and boxes were stacked all around the cave.

"Who is this man?" Cordelia said in wonder.

Darius laughed. "I used to ask myself the same question

almost every day."

They started with a set of long boxes that were stacked on the left side, a dozen in all. Darius found an iron bar and pried open the lid of one of the boxes. Packed in straw were two bows and forty to fifty arrows. He rummaged through the straw and pulled out a small airtight tin box. He broke the seal and looked inside to see half a dozen tightly wound bowstrings packed in wax.

"Let's start with these," Darius instructed. "As soon as everyone that can shoot has a bow we'll come back for close-quarter weapons."

All of the men claimed some ability to shoot and half a dozen of the women, including Cordelia.

"Where did you learn to shoot, mother?" Darius asked. "I don't remember you touching a bow when I was younger."

"Your father taught me," she replied. "He always said I was a natural. I even entered the contest during the summer festival the year before Micah was born and took second place. I guess after your father died, I just didn't have much taste for it anymore. It was always one of those things that the two of us did together. Besides, I had a household to run and two energetic boys to raise. I don't think I could've found the time if I'd wanted to."

"Well, you certainly looked like a natural back at the pass."

"What, that? That was nothing. They were easy targets. They just stood there and let me shoot them. Antu helped by keeping them distracted."

Darius laughed. "I remember when Micah first began to teach me fifty paces may as well have been a league. You were spot on at a hundred."

"I hit five targets out of seven at two hundred paces the year I took second," she winked.

"I'm better with the sword, I think," Darius said. "I'm a fair shot, but Arthengal can do things with a bow that I never dreamed. I try to match him but never come close. Of course, he is incredibly skilled with the sword, too, but at least there I can hold my own."

"That's impressive," Cordelia said with pride. "The stories all claim that Nasu Rabi was unmatched with the blade."

"Yeah, well, he's probably slowed down a bit. I'm sure in his prime I never would have stood a chance."

Cordelia chuckled. "I thought you were pretty amazing during the rescue and after."

Darius blushed and then busied himself unpacking the boxes.

Once the bows were distributed they passed out hand weapons. Most of the women, and Lianna, were all given long daggers with belt sheaths. A tall woman, Dacia, wearing a belted green tunic, said she preferred a quarterstaff as did twin brothers, Nicolai and Gunnar.

There were no other swords, but they had found a dozen spears packed in straw with the steel tips wrapped in oiled leather. The tips of the spears were vicious looking. They were razor sharp and three hooked teeth curved back toward the shaft on either side.

They looked like they would do much more damage coming out than they would going in.

Marku took a hatchet, like he was going to cut kindling, his hand trembling slightly as he picked it up. Darius raised an eyebrow at the choice but figured the man had the right to choose his weapon.

The light was fading by the time they were done, and they settled in for an evening meal. Arthengal reappeared while they were eating, carrying a large box wrapped in cloth. He took the box inside the house and then returned to join the group.

As the crowd prepared for sleep, Darius and Arthengal brought a collection of blankets made of either wool or tanned hides outside. The group instinctively clustered into pods of four or five people each and huddled close together to sleep.

The night was quiet. More quiet than Darius was used to. It was probably just his imagination, and the constant travel and activity from the past couple of weeks, but the peace and stillness within the valley unnerved him a bit. With a shiver, Darius returned to the cabin.

Chapter Twenty-Nine
Daku Mitu - The Night Guard

Darius awoke in the night to the sound of a woman's scream. At first, he thought it was just someone having a nightmare. Many of the former slaves had cried out in their sleep while they were escaping The Wastes. Then he heard a man shout with alarm, followed by the unmistakable roar of Antu.

Arthengal and Darius moved as one. They jerked on pants and pulled blades from sheaths without bothering to strap on the belts.

Outside was darkness. As his eyes slowly adjusted, Darius saw shapes moving through the trees. Another scream shattered the night, and he ran in that direction.

A soldier, clothed in black striated leather armor, was pulling a long-bladed spear from a woman's chest. Dacia's head lilted to the side, and dead eyes met Darius's gaze. The quarterstaff lay on the ground beside her, untouched.

The villain saw Darius, and the sword, and advanced.

Darius ducked under the spinning spear, knocked the soldier off his feet with Scooping the Moon, and left the murderer dead in his wake. He searched the darkness, trying to make sense of the chaos. Screams were all around him, and people darted through the trees. He cut another attacker down who was chasing after a half-clothed woman. The tattered remnants of one of his old shirts barely clung to her back. She was clutching the ruined garment to her chest while she ran, trying to cover her breasts.

He saw Arthengal fighting one of the dark-clad warriors near the cabin. His opponent wore a long frock, buttoned up the side, over his armor. The swords rang, and Darius could see sparks created from the ferocity of the blows.

The twin brothers battled three soldiers, mirrored quarterstaffs whirling in time to deflect thrusting spears aside. Antu loped by him in the darkness, chasing a fleeing shape. Another dark figure emerged from a tree at his side and was abandoned in a heap behind him.

Suddenly, torches began to flare. He glanced around to see his mother lighting them and passing them out to other women who thrust them into the soft earth at the edges of the garden. Five women formed a curved line inside the ring of torches and began firing as black-clad shapes emerged from the darkness.

Darius stumbled over a dead body and recognized one of the rescued captives. Aaron, he thought his name was. He had been a tall man with red hair and was dressed in one of Arthengal's old tunics. Darius had always liked that tunic.

He felt a sting on his left arm as a thrusting spear scored

along the bicep. Had he not stumbled, the blade would have been in his back.

He whirled to face the opponent and found three. He danced between them. Fox Dances with Dandelions pushed the first opponent into the second and severed the third combatant's thrusting arm. Water Crashes Over Rocks tumbled the second fighter to his back while the first warrior retreated. Darius did not give the fallen soldier the chance to stand. He faced the remaining invader alone now, but it lasted only a moment and then he was searching the darkness again.

He saw one of the other refugees go down, too late to help him.

Arthengal battled to his left. The two circled each other, swords flashing in the torchlight. Arthengal's brow glistened, and both he and his opponent bore several wounds where blood flowed freely.

Cordelia stood with three women in the garden, keeping up a steady rhythm. Pull an arrow from the ground in front of them, take aim, fire. Pull an arrow from the ground, take aim, fire. Darius could see a couple of bodies at the edge of the trees but couldn't tell beyond that how effective their barrage was.

The brothers continued to dance with the three men - no, four now - who surrounded them. Antu swatted at the spears and blades of half a dozen more. Marku...*where was Marku*? He didn't have time to consider further as another shape dropped from the trees above him.

Darius appraised his foe. He wore the same dark armor as the rest but also had a palm-sized patch sewn over his heart. Darius couldn't make out the image, smeared with dirt and blood as it was. He, too, held a sword and glared at Darius with a wicked gleam in his eyes.

Darius held his sword extended and glided to match the officer's movements as he circled. He advanced with Wild Horse Leaps but was countered easily by Rose at Sunset. Then Darius was forced into a series of defensive stances to hold off a flurry of attacks. A dozen nicks and cuts decorated his chest and arms before he recovered the advantage and was able to score a strike to the right shoulder with Dragon Emerges From the Water.

The warrior retreated and began circling again. They traded assessing blows, and when his adversary launched a second series of attacks, Darius was able to counter more effectively. Darius's arms and legs ached by the time he saw the opening and Fashionably Late caught his opponent in the chest with the delayed thrust. Surprise filled the eyes that stared back at him over the hilt of his blade. Darius put a foot on the man's stomach and jerked his blade free, letting the armored body fall.

He took in the scene again. Arthengal was staggering, but his challenger was in no better shape. Antu was sniffing the bodies of six men on the ground around him. The twins drove three men back, their staves working as one to beat the men relentlessly. Their fourth opponent leaned heavily against a tree holding a hand to his head. Cordelia stood alone in the garden, still firing into the darkness. Marku...*Damn you, Marku, where are you?*

Then his heart froze in his chest. A ghost from his nightmares entered the flickering light. Blood streaked his face. He held a pair of spears, the shafts broken short so he held them almost like swords. The figure wore the same black armor as the rest of the attackers, but that couldn't be. The face wore no expression as if the battle that raged around him were as every day an occurrence as gutting fish.

"Micah?" Darius whispered.

The ghost's face twitched at the name. His eyes went blank for a moment, as if lost in a memory.

"You're good," Micah said without passion, pointing a spear toward the dead man.

"What?" Darius was dumbfounded. This ghost wore his brother's face but something was wrong.

Micah cocked his head, considering. "You may even be better than me."

"Micah, what are you doing here? With these murderers?" Darius's voice gained strength.

"Serving His Holy Emperor Lao Jun Qiu." Micah said.

Was that pride in his voice?

"Serving...these men kidnapped your mother, enslaved your neighbors, and slaughtered our friends." Darius was shouting by the end. "Your *emperor* is a vile criminal who wants to put the world back under his thumb of tyranny."

"The emperor saved us, Darius. He saved me." Micah's voice softened. He spoke quietly, without anger. His tone was almost pleading. With each word, he took a step closer to Darius. Darius had to strain to hear his words over the clash of the battle around them.

Unconsciously Darius raised his sword. Micah stopped and looked curiously at the blade. His own spears remained pointed toward the ground.

"Saved you?" Darius hissed. "He kidnapped you. After his men shot you in the chest. I thought you were dead."

Micah's blue eyes met Darius's. Darius still saw his brother in those eyes, but something else as well. Something...

"He saved me from a meaningless life," Micah explained. "I have a purpose now beyond the mundane existence of subsistence farming and hunting. I've learned skills that I never imagined."

...fanatical. That was it. Micah's eyes glinted with a light of fanaticism. Darius had seen the same look in the eyes of the swordsman he had just killed. But Micah couldn't be that far gone. He had to see reason. Another scream echoed through the darkness.

"Purpose? Is your *purpose*..." Darius said darkly waving a hand toward the other groups still fighting. "...slaughtering innocents?"

Micah's cheek twitched again, and his eyes flickered to the

carnage around them.

"No. We were sent to apprehend a criminal who invaded the emperor's compound and murdered a dozen of the imperial guard. This," he glanced around uncertainly, "was unfortunate."

"Those *criminals* were my friend and me, Micah," Darius lowered his voice.

Micah narrowed his eyes at the words, and his spears twitched.

"We were there to rescue our mother," Darius continued. "And others that the emperor had kidnapped."

"Mother? Sh--." Micah's voice was cut off by the sound of a bugle in the darkness.

"Fall back," a voice cried. "The captain and the lieutenant are dead, and the assignment has been completed."

Micah glanced over his shoulder at the call. Armored figures rushed by them into the night toward the river.

"Come with us, Darius," Micah pleaded, extending a hand. "I saw you fight Lieutenant Popov. The emperor would have a place for a warrior of your skill. Maybe even in the Night Birds and then we could fight together."

"I will not help you enslave others," Darius said coldly.

"You don't understand," Micah said, raising his voice for the first time. "The emperor wants to liberate the nations. To free the people from the rule of the barons. To return the empire to its pinnacle of progress and raise it up to be a shining example for the rest of the world to follow."

Darius shook his head sadly.

"No, Micah. You don't understand. They've tricked you somehow. These are evil men that you follow. They don't want to help the people, they want to oppress them. Stay with us. Mother is here."

There was a moment's hesitation in his eyes, then Micah sighed.

"You will see, Darius. I'm right. When we meet again, you will see. I just hope it's not too late by then."

With that, he faded into the darkness.

Darius started to go after him and then stopped. He had to check on the others. He joined the survivors who had retreated to the light of the garden and were still surveying the night. Cordelia gathered a dozen more arrows and thrust them into the ground at her feet. She seemed not to have noticed Micah and Darius didn't tell her. Her heart would have broken from shame.

The twins, quarterstaffs chipped and dented, surveyed the woods on the left. Darius stooped and wiped his blade clean on the black jerkin of a body that had crushed several tomato plants when it fell. Antu lumbered into the light but stayed near the edge of the garden, separated from the others. Marku emerged from around the side of the cabin. There he is, Darius sighed. The hatchet was hanging from a loop at his belt...*pristine?* Arthengal was...

"Where is Arthengal?" Darius asked worriedly.

Darius ran toward where he had last seen his mentor. Arthengal was slumped against the wall of the cabin. His sword lay in the dirt by his side. He clutched his side, and his breathing was labored. A short distance away, the officer with the embroidered patch stared up blankly at the trees.

"Help me!" Darius cried over his shoulder.

The other survivors hurried from the garden and Darius heard his mother let out a sharp cry as she saw Arthengal.

Nicolai and Gunnar helped Darius carry Arthengal into the house. Lianna yelped from the corner of the room as they entered. She sat huddled in the corner with her knife extended before her.

They lowered Arthengal onto the cot and Darius pulled back the clutching hand to examine the wound. It was deep and wide, a large gash thrust between his lower ribs. Blood foamed around the wound as he labored to breathe.

"Mother, there is yarrow in a jar on the counter. Mortar and pestle as well." He began shouting instructions.

"Nicolai," he directed, "go get some water. Help my mother form some a paste from the yarrow."

"Gunnar," he jabbed a finger at the other brother. "There is needle and catgut in a box under the counter."

"Marku, get water and cloths to clean the wound."

Everyone started to move when Arthengal clutched his arms and whispered weakly. "Wait."

"No, we can't wait, there is not time," Darius shouted angrily.

"It's already too late," Arthengal gasped.

"No," Darius shouted as tears began to fill his eyes. "It can't be."

"My lung is pierced. There is no patching that with catgut and yarrow."

"No," Darius wailed.

The others stood silently around them. Arthengal glanced around the ensemble.

"Give us a moment, please," he said to the others. "I would have a moment alone with Darius."

Cordelia gently pulled Lianna to her feet and led the others out of the house.

"Darius," he started and then coughed. He wiped blood from his lips before continuing. "Darius. My son died before I ever got the chance to know him. These past four years, I feel like I have gotten a second chance. You have been as much of a son to me as I ever could have wished for. I am so proud of the man that you have become."

Tears streamed down Darius's face.

"You have been like a second father to me too." Darius's voice broke. "You have taught me more than my own father ever had the chance to."

"I need you to do something for me." Arthengal's voice was a whisper. "It's very important. The world may depend on your success."

Darius nodded, wiping his nose with the back of his hand.

"The box," he said, "under my bed. Get it."

Darius retrieved the box and unwrapped the cloth. It was large, not quite a chest but close. It formed a cube, just over two spans to a side. It was built from oak and banded with iron. The lid was held fast by an elaborate-looking pair of locks on the front.

Arthengal held out his hand. It held a thong from which two keys dangled.

"The keys must be turned at the same time or the box will not open. You keep one of the keys and give the other to someone you trust. Do not open the box. The things held within cannot fall into the hands of this New Emperor," Arthengal explained. "They are symbols of power that could rally support for him. Each is surrounded by a myth, and in part, they are what allowed the former emperors to hold onto power as long as they did. The mere possession of these things would increase his power with the people tenfold from the strength of the myths alone. After Eridu, you must take these things to Kasha Marka. There is a woman there, Saria. Give them to her. She will know what to do with them."

"Can't I just burn the box or melt the contents down?"

"You could," Arthengal agreed. "But I don't think you will. It is rumored that the one who destroys these items will invite the wrath of the old gods on the people and his house. He will curse the land to a thousand years of misery and will be cursed himself to wander the land for eternity to watch what his actions have wrought.

"Now, I don't follow the old gods, but even I was never brave enough to destroy them. You do believe in the power of the gods. By the Sands of Saridon, you believe one of them came in the flesh to guide you." Arthengal's laugh was cut short by another cough. "Would you take the risk?"

"I will take them to Saria in Kasha Marka," Darius nodded quickly. "How will I find her?"

"There is an inn, The Bard's Tale. The innkeeper there will know where to find her. Now put these away." He patted the keys. "Keep them and the box hidden and tell no one. The slightest rumor of these items will bring trouble like you never imagined."

Darius wrapped the cloth back around the box and stuffed the keys in a belt pouch beside the bed.

"Good boy, now make me some tea, won't you?"

Darius hurried to the fireplace and kindled the fire. He boiled a pot of water and made a tea of mint and nightshade to ease Arthengal's pain. He sat on the edge of the cot holding a steaming clay cup, but Arthengal was already gone. His chest was still, and his eyes stared blankly.

The clay cup fell from his fingers, but Darius didn't hear it shatter. Hot tea splashed across his boots as he leaned forward with a wail. He lifted Arthengal's limp shoulders and pulled him tightly to his chest. Years of stories and training and laughter and trials played through Darius's mind as he sobbed into the dead man's shoulder.

Light was breaking through the window when Darius finally lay the body of his mentor, his friend, his second father, back on the cot and gently pulled the lids shut over Arthengal's eyes.

Chapter Thirty
Into the Still Night

Darius held a torch to the pyre and watched as the tinder caught. The others stood around him in silence. A gentle rain fell as if the Sky Father cried at the loss of Arthengal as well. His tears mixed with Darius's on his cheeks, a mixture of warm and cool, salty and pure.

After a moment of quiet mourning, Nicolai and Gunnar took similar torches and began moving from one pyre to the next, twenty-two in all, setting them alight.

They had tossed the bodies of the black-clad men in a ditch and covered them with lime before filling the pit. Twenty bodies had been found scattered through the trees. Another thirty had fallen victim to Arthengal's traps. Darius had no doubt that none of them would have survived if the entire force had made it into the valley. Even so, the only reason the six of them still lived was because of the ordered retreat.

The fires burned late into the evening. Darius watched the sparks drift into the sky. He was oblivious as first Marku and then Nicolai and Gunnar left the clearing. His mother patted him on the shoulder before she and Lianna returned to the cabin. Only Antu remained. Darius rested his hand on the top of the bear's head. He did not know if the bear understood what was happening. He had sniffed Arthengal's body when they had laid it on a litter and let out a ferocious roar that caused everyone to take a step back. Now he sat silently with Darius, watching the fires burn.

The group was sullen and quiet as they arranged supplies on the horses. Darius watched them from the terraced gardens of Anbar Ur. They had been working for the past two days to stage foodstuffs and travelling supplies in the abandoned city in preparation for their trip...to where? Eridu, to start.

Then what? Darius thought.

He had to go to Kasha Marka. He had made a promise, but the rest of them didn't. He wasn't sure he wanted them to come, other than his mother, of course. And it seemed like Cordelia had adopted the girl, Lianna. So, he had a sister now.

That will be different.

Nicolai and Gunnar had saddled five of the geldings and hitched four to the wagon. The remaining animals were formed into trains to be managed by the riders. Marku would drive the wagon loaded with the extra saddles and tack. They had agreed that they would sell most of the mounts and gear in Eridu and split what they earned. With the garrison forming up there, it shouldn't be hard to get a decent price.

Darius left the others to their preparations and returned to the valley. He had some final preparations of his own to make.

At the cabin, Darius folded up the maps that Arthengal had bought for him and stored them in a leather satchel. He put the satchel in his pack and then stuffed in the rest of his clothes. Arthengal's books had already been taken up and added to the supplies.

I should return Hanish's book.

Darius took a final look around the cabin that had been his home for nearly four years. The others were waiting, but they could wait. He had told them he needed some time alone in the valley before they left. He adjusted one of the clay pots of herbs on the counter, scattered the ashes in the fireplace to make sure there were no embers, pulled the blankets up tightly on his cot, and pushed the two chairs tightly against the table. He ran his fingers through his long blond hair and tightened the thong that kept it tied away from his face.

He wore both sword belts, Arthengal's on his right hip and his on the left. He checked the buckles and then strapped his unstrung bow atop his pack. Several small pouches filled with the coin that he and Arthengal had saved over the years were hidden in his pack and about his person. He picked up the cloth-wrapped box off the floor and walked out the door.

The garden was a mess. The tomato plants had been smashed and everything else had been trampled in the fight.

We'll have to replant it all, he thought, only to realize how stupid the thought was. The garden wouldn't be replanted, nor would the hemp fields, not for some time.

"What's that?" Marku asked as Darius strapped the box to the back of Micah's saddle.

"It's some of Arthengal's belongings. Keepsakes and remembrances. He asked me to take it to an old friend of his in Kasha Marka."

"Kasha Marka?" Cordelia exclaimed. "That's halfway across the world."

"Not quite," Marku laughed. "But certainly a long journey. It seems you're destined to see a bit of the world after all, I see."

Darius smiled weakly at the man and nodded.

"Well, if you need company we would be happy to go with you," Nicolai said. "There is nothing for us here anymore. Imbros was burned to the ground when they took us, and I don't know what we would do in Eridu."

"Join the army, I suppose," Gunnar said. He sounded as if the idea didn't appeal to him. "We can find work in Kasha Marka more easily than we can around here."

"I can come too," Marku volunteered.

Marku, Darius thought sadly. *Are you a coward? Or something worse.*

Darius had inspected the bodies. None of them had died from

hatchet wounds. That didn't mean Marku hadn't fought, of course. The twins hadn't killed anyone either. But Darius suspected that the big man had hidden, like Lianna, through the entire battle.

"That's okay, Marku," Darius said as he climbed into the saddle. "I'm sure the garrison at Eridu will have need of a good blacksmith."

"Bah." The man waved the comment aside. "I don't have a hand for weapons, and I don't really want to get mixed up in another war. Of course I'll come."

Darius's stomach tightened as he remembered the pristine axe. He had known Marku his whole life and had never known him to be a coward. He thought, too, of Micah and the unnerving conversation they'd had. What evil had this emperor wrought to twist his friends and family so?

Cordelia let out a sigh. "I guess it's settled then. We'll all go. First to Eridu to sell the horses and buy supplies for the journey and then off to Kasha Marka. I always wondered if it was as glorious as my father had described."

"No, then to Isan," Darius said without thinking. He hadn't considered that previously, but it felt right. Hanish and the others had to know.

The others glanced at him curiously.

"I have friends there that I need to see. I also need to let them know that Arthengal is gone. He was a long-time family friend."

"To Isan, then," Gunnar said as he mounted his horse.

Darius hadn't wanted them all to come, but he didn't know how to make them stay. Gunnar was right. If they remained in Eridu, they would likely be conscripted into the army. Part of him, the part that Arthengal had trained, wanted to tell them that it was their duty, but a man had to make that decision for himself.

He heeled Micah and turned south. Antu strolled out of the trees as he exited the southern gate and the three of them, man and horse and bear, led the ragtag caravan toward Eridu.